PERSONA NON GRATA

BRIAN O'SULLIVAN

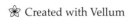 Created with Vellum

This book is dedicated to all of my readers. Every book you buy, every friend you tell; they are all so important for a self-published author like me.

From the bottom of my heart, thank you!

PART ONE: A BRUTAL DISCOVERY

CHAPTER 1

I was two hours into a thus far unsuccessful fishing excursion when my phone rang.

My face lit up when I saw who was calling.

"Well, look who it is," I said.

"Hey, Quint!"

"How the hell are you, Henry? I'm out on a boat enjoying my weekend."

"On Lake Havasu recreating your old college days? "

"Hardly. By myself, trying to catch a few fish."

"Well, that's ironic."

"Oh yeah, why is that?"

"I've caught a fish for you. In fact, it's what Vegas would call a whale."

"A big-timer?"

"No fooling you, Quint."

I laughed.

"I deserve that," I said.

"Well, to be fair, I haven't caught this whale just yet. If I'm right, though, it's someone very, very important."

"How did this happen?"

"We'll talk about it when we meet. When can you?"

"How about tomorrow?"

"That'll work."

"You want to swing by my office?" I asked.

"No, why don't you swing by my boat? I'll show you what living on the water is truly like. And I'm not talking about spending three hours on the water, unsuccessfully trying to catch a single fish."

I hadn't even told him I'd been skunked thus far. He just knew it.

"What time?" I asked.

"Anytime before noon is fine. Do you remember which boat is mine?"

"How could I forget the name?"

Henry gave me a courtesy laugh.

"I'll see you tomorrow, Quint. Now go catch that first fish."

And with that, he hung up.

∼

Henry Madsen was one of my oldest friends, but I don't mean in the sense that I'd known him the longest. I mean that he's actually old. He just recently turned seventy-five, in fact.

When I first started at *The Walnut Creek Times* a little over fifteen years ago, he was the old newspaperman getting ready to retire. I'd heard all the stories of how it was a cutthroat business and no one wanted to help each other out, especially some newbie just getting his feet wet.

That wasn't the case with Henry.

He mentored me for a good portion of my first two years and then quietly rode off into the sunset. He was still a relatively young man in his early sixties at that point, but he'd joined the *San Francisco Chronicle* at twenty-two and felt that forty years in the business was long enough. I guess you couldn't blame him.

We'd kept in touch over the years but didn't see each other in person nearly enough. Our friendship was done mostly over the phone. Henry was always great about calling when a case of mine finished up. That was partially true when I still worked for *The Walnut Creek Times,* but more so once I became a private investigator.

"*Your new job is much more exciting than sitting around and writing all day,*" he'd told me more than twice.

When he retired, Henry bought a boat and had been living on the water at the Berkeley Marina ever since. It was ironic. I rarely went fishing, and yet the guy who lives on a boat randomly contacts me on one of those days. Maybe this meeting was meant to be.

The call definitely had me intrigued. Henry had always been a no-nonsense type of guy and he wouldn't use the word "whale" if it wasn't warranted.

~

I'd become consumed by the pending meeting with Henry and was no longer interested in fishing. After ten more minutes and nary a nibble on the day, I decided to pack it in.

I'd been skunked for the day.

If you didn't count the whale I'd potentially landed.

~

I woke up at the crack of dawn the next morning and dilly-dallied for a few hours before heading to see Henry.

Berkeley was only fifteen miles from my apartment in Walnut Creek and I didn't want to arrive too early. Henry had always been a morning person, but he was seventy-five years old now. Maybe he liked getting some beauty sleep these days.

Finally, at 9:30, I left my apartment.

When I arrived, I looked out on the Berkeley Marina, memories flooding my brain. It had been less than four years since I'd hid on Charles Zane's boat, leaving from this very spot, getting my revenge at sea. I'd also managed to avenge my father's death, even though that's not how I chose to remember him. I preferred to remember how my father lived and not the way he died.

It's also what had led me to become a private investigator. After a case - really, an ordeal - like that, it's hard to go back and spend every day in your cubicle, plugging away on your computer, writing about car crashes and minor burglaries. I didn't actually get my P.I.'s license until a year later, but the Charles Zane ordeal had been the precursor.

So yes, I had a lot on my mind as I walked towards Henry's boat.

He had named his boat *The Times They Are A-Changin'*. It was both a shout-out to the song by his favorite artist, Bob Dylan, and a reflection on how newspapers were changing. In particular, how *The Walnut Creek Times* was changing. Thus, '*The Times.*'

Henry hadn't liked the way the internet was taking over newspapers (imagine what he'd think now) and *The Times They are A-Changin'* was a subtle dig at his superiors at *The Walnut Creek Times*.

As usual, Henry Madsen had a way with words.

I walked down to the marina itself and took a left turn, remembering Henry's boat was somewhere down that way. I slowly strolled by each boat.

I wasn't in a big rush. I was enjoying my time down by the water. Certainly more than the previous day, when I was on an uncomfortable rental boat proving that fish had nothing to fear from me. This was different. These boats were majestic.

I meandered further down, trying to remember what color Henry's boat was.

And then I saw it. It was a blue and white cabin cruiser, probably about twenty-five feet long. The stern was white and *The Times They Are A-Changin'* was written in blue calligraphy. It was a beautiful boat, without question.

Henry had lost his wife Helen about five years ago and had lived on the boat alone ever since. They'd had one daughter, Sophie, who Henry and Helen welcomed pretty late in life. Sophie was either thirty-six or thirty-seven at this point. We'd had a May to December romance way back when. I was twenty-seven and she was only twenty-one or twenty-two, but the age difference didn't bother Henry. He actually thought we made a nice couple.

I had no doubt that he'd bring that up at some point in our conversation. Henry wasn't against making people feel a bit awkward. If he didn't needle me, I might start to get a little worried.

"Henry," I yelled.

I didn't see him or hear him yell back.

I was half hoping Henry was going to be sitting outside waiting for me, his beloved Bud bottle in his hands, but it wasn't to be.

"Henry," I yelled again. "You must be losing your hearing in your old age."

It's a joke he'd appreciate.

After another thirty seconds with no answer, I jumped down from the dock to the boat itself.

I approached the sliding glass door on the back of the boat. It was locked, so I knocked.

It was going to be great to give Henry a big hug. It had been probably six months since I'd seen him. Maybe longer.

He's getting older, I told myself. It was time to start making my way out here more often.

I tried to look and see if he was coming to the door, but my eyes hadn't adjusted from the sun's glare. All I saw were shadows up against the glass.

I knocked again.

As my eyes started to adapt, I looked inside the boat once again. This time I was able to make something out.

My heart sank.

Henry was on the ground and the way his body was positioned didn't look natural. There was still a partial glare from the sun - and I hoped it was playing a trick on me - but I knew his head didn't look right. It was at a very odd angle. I feared the worst.

I jumped from the stern back onto the dock and ran around toward the front of the boat.

I leaped onto the bow and saw a three-step drop that led into the cabin. I shimmied myself down with one big step and walked toward the unmoving body.

By my second step, I knew that Henry Madsen was dead.

His neck had been snapped and it was almost flush against his shoulder.

It was grotesque.

I walked closer just to make sure my mind wasn't inventing something out of thin air.

It wasn't. It was more sickening the closer I got.

"Oh, Henry. Who did this to you?"

Not knowing what to do, I leaned down and patted him on his back. It was awkward, but I felt I had to do something.

"I'm so sorry, my friend."

I realized I shouldn't be touching the crime scene so I stood up and turned around. I couldn't look down at him any longer.

I tried to take in the crime scene. This was the one and only time I'd be here.

Nothing jumped out, but there was a faint smell that I was pretty sure was smoke.

I looked around one last time, knowing it was time for me to alert the authorities.

"I'm going to catch whoever did this," I said aloud.

I walked back up to the deck and sat down. I called 9-1-1 and described what I'd just seen.

And then I started crying.

"And you said this all started with a phone call yesterday?" the bespectacled homicide detective asked me.

The police had arrived a few minutes after my phone call. Local cops first and then some detectives once they confirmed this was a homicide. And there was no debating that.

I got a few looks when I said my name was Quint Adler, but no one said anything. I'd been working more and more high-profile cases and I knew my name was making its way around law enforcement. I'm not sure if that was a benefit or a drawback. I guess it depended on the cop.

"Yeah," I responded. "He told me it had been a long time and he wanted to see me."

"And you said you used to be co-workers?"

We were doing this interview out on the dock of the Berkeley Marina. Every thirty seconds or so, I'd glance over at *The Times They Are A-Changin'* and I'd feel a terrible sadness come over me. For my loss, but more importantly, for Henry himself. Strangled at the hands of another. At his age. And not just strangled. His neck broken at an obscene angle.

That's not how Henry should have gone; or anyone else for that matter.

"Yeah, we worked together at *The Walnut Creek Times* newspaper," I said. "He was my mentor for my first two years before he resigned."

"And you guys kept in touch over the years?"

I wanted to say, *"How else do you think I freaking ended up here?"* but held my tongue.

"Yeah. We'd meet up once or twice a year."

"And why did he want to see you today?"

I'd been debating whether to tell the officer that Henry had mentioned potentially landing a whale. I decided to just go with the truth. If I wanted to investigate the case, I could always do it on my own. For now, getting the police as much information as possible improved the chances of catching his killer.

"He said he was close to catching a whale."

"A whale?"

"Yeah, like a whale in the Las Vegas sense. Not a real whale."

He eyed me suspiciously, not liking my sudden sarcasm.

"I got that, Sherlock," he said and pushed his glasses up.

Detective Mixon - as he'd introduced himself - didn't look like most detectives I'd met. He more closely resembled someone punching numbers at your local CPA firm. He was small in stature as well. I'll give him some credit though. He carried himself with a certain confidence as if he was the smartest guy in the room. Or, on the docks, as it were.

"He didn't tell me what type of whale or what type of case. I assume that's what he was going to tell me this morning."

"Until someone got to him."

"Yeah."

"Does Mr. Madsen work anymore? Any freelancing?"

"Not that I know of."

"So you have no idea who this whale was?"

"I honestly don't. If I did, I'd tell you. Henry was a good friend. I'd like nothing more than for you guys to catch his killer."

"I believe you," Detective Mixon said.

I nodded. He seemed like a straight shooter.

"Hang around for another thirty minutes or so," he said. "Just in case we have any more questions."

There were more questions and I didn't get out of there until two hours after the police had arrived. I was fine with that. The most important thing to me was catching Henry's killer and if they had to ask me the same question three different times, so be it.

As I drove away from the docks, I thought about calling Henry's daughter, Sophie. Once we broke up after eight months of dating, we kind of went our separate ways. She'd headed to law school in the Midwest while I remained working at a newspaper in Northern California. It wasn't a bad breakup, there was just no reason to become pen pals, and that far of a long-distance relationship was near impossible. Last I'd heard, Sophie had recently returned to the Bay Area, but I couldn't remember what she was doing.

She was about to receive the worst news imaginable. No child should have to go through that. It didn't matter that Henry had lived a fairly long life. It would still be soul-crushing, especially when she found out the manner in which he'd left this earth.

I decided I'd call Sophie when I got home. My nerves were shattered and relaying that type of information while driving 75 m.p.h. wasn't advisable.

As I entered the freeway, I looked at my reflection in the rearview mirror.

I wasn't sure I liked what I saw. There were a few more grays than I remembered. A few more wrinkles. I was still a relatively young man of forty-three, but every year around the sun seemed to move faster. I'd be fifty before I knew it. And then seventy. And then eighty. And that's if I was lucky.

But that wasn't the reason I'd looked in the mirror.

I was trying to get a read on myself.

Am I going to investigate Henry's murder? I said aloud.

It was rhetorical.

I already knew the answer.

CHAPTER 2

"I'm so sorry," I said.

Sophie Madsen gave me a big hug and held on for a good twenty seconds.

The call to her had been brutal. With every fiber of my being, I hated having to make it, but it was the right thing to do. Sophie didn't deserve to hear the news from some random cop who didn't know her father from Adam. So I made the call.

We both shed tears several times. Finally, after twenty minutes on the phone, I told her she should probably reach out to the police themselves, but I promised to come see her.

Which I did the following morning.

I drove to her house in Pleasanton, a city of about 75,000 in Alameda County. It was only twenty minutes from me. Not that it mattered. If Sophie had lived in Lake Tahoe, I would have made the drive. She'd lost her father and she was the only child Henry ever had. Maybe I was doing this for Henry as much as I was for Sophie. He'd be happy that I was here comforting her.

"Who could have done this to him?" Sophie asked as the hug ended.

She escorted me through her house and we sat down on two

chairs in her small backyard. It was early April and the air was still a little brisk. We both had jackets on. She'd wanted to sit outside and I wasn't about to suggest otherwise, despite the chill. I noticed a few family pictures as we walked through the house. Maybe they were too tough for her to look at and that's why she wanted to talk outside. I couldn't blame her. Sophie had now lost both of her parents.

"I have no idea who could have done this," I finally answered.

"But you're going to find out, right? I mean, my Dad kept telling me what a great private investigator you've become. All in such a short time."

"Your father was prone to exaggeration."

Sophie laughed and then quickly looked at me, feeling guilty; as if she wasn't allowed to laugh after what had happened to her father. I waved it off, letting her know it was fine.

"You're right, by the way," she said. "He loved to exaggerate. Everything was the biggest fish ever caught or the best steak ever made. But about you, he wasn't lying. I'm sure of it. He really thought you were becoming an excellent P.I."

I appreciated hearing it. And I knew Sophie was telling the truth. Henry had seemed genuinely impressed with what I'd accomplished, particularly with the Bay Area Butcher case, saying I'd saved countless young lives.

"I'm certainly going to take a look at it," I conceded. "I just can't commit long term."

I regretted saying it immediately. It sounded so self-centered.

"Well, if you're as good as my father thinks, you'll solve this in no time."

I looked over and half expected a smile, but got nothing. She meant every word.

"I'll try my best," I said.

"Now that we got that out of the way, I'd prefer to remember my father in his living years."

"Me too."

"He was quite the character wasn't he?"

"He told me I was an imbecile the very first day I met him," I said.

"What? Really? How did that come about?"

"I'm sure you remember Tom and Krissy Butler, the owners of *The Walnut Creek Times*. They'd walked around and introduced me to almost everyone at the office. At one point, they told me to just walk around the office to get acquainted with it. I hadn't met your father yet, but he obviously realized I was new. Must have thought I was an intern or a secretary of some sort because he asked me to print something out for him. I didn't want to be rude on my first day so I grabbed the papers and walked up to a printer I'd bypassed earlier. I had no idea what I was doing. It was one of those huge industrial-type printers and I was at its mercy. Finally, after about five minutes he walked over, obviously in a bad mood, and said something like, 'They'll hire any old imbecile these days.'"

I looked at Sophie and she was near tears. The tears were likely half laughter-half sadness, if that's a thing.

"What did you say?" Sophie asked.

"I extended my hand and said, 'Quint Adler, imbecile-in-training. And by the way, I'm not the maintenance guy or some secretary who prints out your work. I'm the new writer.' He looked at me and laughed, put his arm around my shoulder, and then taught me how to use that enormous printer."

I looked over and saw a tear falling down Sophie's cheek.

"That's fantastic," she said.

"Thanks."

"Tell me more stories."

And so I did, spending the next thirty minutes regaling Sophie with story after story about her late father. And then we spent another half hour just catching up on old times.

When it came time for me to go, I could tell she didn't want me to leave.

Sophie hadn't mentioned a boyfriend or husband and I hadn't broached the subject. She probably wasn't looking forward to spending the night alone. I'd lost my father about five years ago and I knew those first few days were amazingly tough. I at least could find comfort by going and visiting my mother. Sophie had no one to turn to.

"So it's time for you to get back to Walnut Creek?" she asked begrudgingly.

"Probably, yeah. Unless you'd like me to stay."

"I'm a big girl. I can handle this house all by myself."

She could sense what I wanted to ask.

"I'll tell you another time," she said. "An engagement that didn't quite work out and I just kept this place for myself."

She'd already said more than I'd expected.

"We'll probably be talking a lot in the coming days," I said.

"About my broken engagement and my father's death? How fun."

"Hey, we had a few laughs as well."

"That's true. You had some great stories. I'm looking forward to more," Sophie said.

We both rose from our seats and hugged one final time.

"Just wanted to say again how truly sorry I am," I said. "Call me if you need anything."

"Thank you, Quint."

It didn't take long until I heard from Sophie again.

"I need to tell you something," she said.

The call had come at ten a.m. the following morning.

"Alright."

"And I think it's better if we do it in person."

"Do you want me to come and see you?"

"Actually, I'm going to be in Walnut Creek later tonight."

That caught me by surprise.

"Okay. We could meet at a coffee shop or something."

"I'd rather meet at your place where it's just you and me. This needs to be a private conversation."

I could tell she was on edge, but I wasn't sure why she couldn't just tell me over the phone. I'm sure she had a good reason.

"That's fine, Sophie."

"Where do you live?"

"The address is 1716 North Main Street. Text me when you're a few minutes away and I'll walk downstairs. You need a fob to get into the place. What time were you thinking?"

"How about 6:45 tonight?"

"That works fine."

Sophie showed up at 6:45 on the dot.

She was wearing jeans, a thick, off-green sweater, and a navy blue jacket.

I was in flip-flops, blue chino shorts, and a white T-shirt. I dressed casual whenever I could. I got cold as I opened the apartment building's front door for Sophie, but the warmth of my apartment was only five stories away.

"Thanks for letting me do this at your place," Sophie said as we entered the elevator.

"Of course. What were you doing out here?"

"I have an old college friend who lives a mile up the street. I decided to catch up with her before I came to see you. Two birds with one stone and all."

We arrived on the fifth floor and I led her into my place.

"My place is too big and your place is too small," she said.

I smiled. Sophie wasn't being judgmental, just trying to be funny. In fact, she probably would have preferred my place. I got the feeling her house was too much for one person.

I motioned towards the couch and she took a seat.

"You want a coffee?"

"No, thanks. I just had two cups with my friend."

"Ah. How about a water?"

"I'm good."

I took a seat on the couch next to her. I could tell she was ready to get down to it.

"So, what did you want to tell me?" I asked.

"Actually, it's something I wanted to show you."

She reached into her backpack and grabbed a single piece of paper.

"What is this?" I asked.

"A fax that my Dad sent me."

"A fax?"

"Exactly. Probably the first one I'd received from him in five years. Maybe ten. I rarely even check my fax machine anymore, but I saw this lying in its tray this morning. He'd sent it the day he died. The morning he was to meet with you."

"But why a fax?" I asked.

"Why don't you read it first," she said, a small hint of irritation in her voice.

I grabbed the piece of paper and began reading. It didn't take long. It was several short hand-written sentences.

Assuming I end up dead,
  Show this only to Quint!
  Tell him no talking to the police!
  Start by investigating a guy named Needles.
  I sent this fax because I couldn't risk texting you.
  The cops will have my phone.
  And they'd see my texts.
  I hope this isn't goodbye.
  I love you, Soph!

I was heartbroken.

Henry knew his life was coming to an end. But how? Did he see someone approaching his boat? Recognized the man and knew he was in deep trouble?

As for why he sent a fax, he'd left his answer. He was fearful of texting it. He was obviously afraid of the police and knew they'd have access to his phone if he ended up dead.

What a terrible way to spend your waning moments on Earth. Too afraid to send a text and having to send, of all things, a fax.

"Quint."

I realized I'd been deep in thought since Sophie had given me the fax.

"I'm sorry. I was thinking."

"I guess so. I thought you were in a trance or something."

"It's still me."

"So, what do you think? Do you know who this person named Needles is?"

"I have no idea."

"What do you make of the fax?"

"It makes sense. He wanted something that wouldn't be traced back to him."

"But wouldn't he have to get rid of the fax he'd sent me?"

I thought back to when I'd found Henry.

I'd noticed the faintest smell. I remembered thinking it was smoke.

"I think he burned the fax he sent and likely the cover page as well."

"What makes you think that?"

"I smelled smoke on the boat. It's the one surefire way to make sure that no one gets to see it."

"Jesus. You think he did this right before he was killed?"

"Probably. My guess is he saw someone approaching the boat. Your Dad didn't have a weapon on board did he?"

"He didn't have a gun that I know of. He cooked and ate on the boat so he probably had a few different kinds of knives on board. You'd think that would have been enough against a guy without a gun."

"You don't know that. The killer might have brought a gun on board but didn't want anyone alerted to a gunshot. If he got Henry to give up his knife, maybe he overpowered him and…"

I stopped right there, knowing I'd already gone too far.

"I'm sorry, Sophie."

"No need to apologize. It's inevitable we're going to have to discuss the way my father died."

"I know. I still hate it."

"So I assume this fax will give you a couple of things to look at."

"Yes," I said. "I'll get back to you in a couple of days."

"Thanks for doing this, Quint."

"We want the same thing."

"I hate thinking that his murderer is out there, walking around, breathing our precious air, maybe having some gourmet meal. It's not freaking fair."

I didn't have much to add, so I just gave Sophie a hug.

I said goodbye to her a few minutes later.

As I started thinking more about Henry's murder, I had a sneaking suspicion this case was going to be even grimier than I'd originally suspected. Henry's message about the police - really, it was more of a warning - weighed heavily on my mind.

I decided that going forward, I'd be as subtle as I could. It wasn't exactly my specialty, but if I was going to be asking tough questions of people connected to the case, I wanted to prevent it from getting back to the police.

It was time to adopt a non-confrontational attitude, as much as it pained me. In reality, I wanted to catch whoever killed Henry and have them hung in the village square. Or whatever the 2023 equivalent was.

CHAPTER 3

W hen I was a young adult and thought of private investigators, I imagined a guy with binoculars who was constantly ducking behind structures and running down dark alleys, being chased by seedy characters.

Maybe they'd be following evil-looking villains who smoked too much. Maybe the P.I. had a long-lens camera and took pictures of an untoward rendezvous at a run-down motel. Maybe he had conversations in dimly lit bars. Maybe buxom blondes tried to seduce him.

And maybe it really was like that back in the day.

Not now. Since becoming a P.I., I'd spent very little time running down dark alleys and even less time taking pictures at seedy motels. In fact, the time spent doing the actual investigating was often boring. It usually entailed surfing the internet. Making a few phone calls. Googling. Things of that nature.

It tended to get exciting once I identified who the bad guy/killer was. My life-or-death struggle on the Golden Gate Bridge with the Bay Area Butcher comes to mind. Or the similarly critical struggle with Leonard Rolle, the killer of Ronnie Fisk.

My point is that my binoculars and Groucho Marx disguise got way less traction than I'd hoped. It had been replaced by my trusty laptop; which I know isn't nearly as sexy.

~

I woke up the morning after Sophie's visit and was energized for the first time since Henry's death. A death - especially a murder - can zap your energy for a few days. When it's someone you know, it's even worse. I wasn't the same guy for a week after the murder of Ray Kintner. There are so many questions you want to ask. Who? Why? Sometimes, how? Sadly, in this case, I knew the how, which made it even worse.

I poured myself a cup of coffee and got down to work.

I googled "Nickname Needles," "Bay Area Nickname Needles," "Criminals named Needles" and a few other variants but nothing came up that was pertinent to my case.

There was a criminal named "Needles" Napier who poked needles into his victims in Salt Lake City. In 1841. Call me crazy, but I was pretty sure that wasn't my guy.

Facing my first dead end, it was time to call two criminals I'd come to know very well. I'd first met them while investigating my father's death and it blossomed into a friendship over the years. Their names were Dennis McCarthy and Paddy Roark. Dennis was the biggest bookie in the history of the Bay Area and Paddy was his right-hand man. They were tough guys and you wouldn't want them on your bad side, but I knew them to be good people. Bookies with a heart of gold, if you will.

"Quint, how the hell are you?" Paddy answered.

I always had to go through him first, even if I wanted to talk to the boss man.

"Things had been great until about three days ago."

"What happened? Your girl see a picture of me and decide to level up?"

"No girl at the moment and that would be a definitive step down."

I think he could tell by my tone of voice that I wasn't calling to joke around.

"So what did happen?" Paddy asked.

"An old friend of mine was murdered."

It's almost as if I could feel the wind taken out of Paddy's sails.

"I'm sorry to hear that, Quint. Who was he?"

"His name was Henry Madsen. He helped me get my feet wet when I first joined *The Walnut Creek Times*. Was a father figure of sorts."

"Sounds like a good guy."

"He was. And then some scumbag killed him on his boat. Strangled and snapped the neck of a seventy-five-year-old man."

"That's terrible, Quint. I'm so sorry."

"Thanks. Listen, let's just get down to it. I can still trust you to keep your mouth shut, correct?"

"Today and for every day going forward."

I believed him with all my heart. Loyalty meant everything to someone like Paddy.

"Just making sure. Before Henry was killed, he sent a fax to his daughter."

"A fax?"

"I know. It's weird. Once I read it to you, I think you'll know why."

"Let me hear it."

I read it to him over the phone.

Assuming I end up dead,
   Show this only to Quint!
   Tell him no talking to police!
   Start by investigating a guy named Needles.
   I sent this fax because I couldn't risk texting you.
   The cops will have my phone.
   And they'd see my texts.
   I hope this isn't goodbye.
   I love you, Soph!

• • •

"That's it. And Soph is Sophie. His daughter," I said.

"Jesus," Paddy said.

"Exactly. So, my question is, do you know a man named Needles? As you heard, Henry said no police, so it's not like I can barge into a police station and ask them to give me a list of criminals named Needles."

"How do you know he's a criminal?"

"Fair point. I just assumed he was."

"You're probably right, but you know what they say about assuming."

"I know the phrase."

"How are your spirits," he said.

"Pretty good when I'm not thinking about Henry."

"That's only going to get worse if you're out there investigating the case."

"I'll power through it."

"I'm sure you will. Look, I'll put out some feelers for this guy named Needles. And by the way, I'm asking you for the same discretion that you've asked of me."

"Of course."

"If you find out who this guy is and confront him, you aren't to mention my name."

"I would never say a word."

"I know. Just wanted to put that out there."

"Understood."

"Talk soon. I'll get back to you when I find out who this Needles guy is."

I loved Paddy's confidence. He didn't say "if I find" Needles, but "when I find" him.

"Thanks, Paddy."

"Take care, Quint."

CHAPTER 4

Needles was dead.

I found out the next morning when Paddy called back. I could immediately tell by the tone of his voice that I wasn't going to like what he had to say.

"What day was your friend Henry killed?" he asked.

"Early on the morning of the 18th."

"Needles - aka Rupert Shinn - also died on the 18th."

"Holy shit," I said.

"So you don't think this is some sort of a coincidence?"

"Unless Needles had cancer for five years, then no."

"It wasn't cancer. I heard from a friend in the police department."

I interrupted.

"Henry said not to use the cops."

"My cop friends aren't the cops you need to be worried about."

"Point taken," I said.

His point was that if he was able to find out information on Needles, they weren't cops that had any part in his downfall. Also, the cops on his payroll were trustworthy and not involved in illicit behavior. With the exception of gambling, obviously.

"Anyway, my cop friend told me that Needles took one behind the ear. He was in some parking garage out in Berkeley."

"Jeez, this can't get any worse," I said.

"Oh, it gets worse. He said he doubts this case will ever get solved. Apparently, Needles had a long list of enemies who would be happy he was dead. Also, the hit looked professional. Very little evidence was left."

"What exactly did Needles do?"

"The rumor is that he was kind of a tough guy for hire. If you need a leg broken or a message sent, Needles was your guy. Apparently, he was a pretty scary dude. My cop friend told me that himself, and if this cop was scared of him, imagine how a member of John Q. Public would feel."

A cop was scared of a citizen who went by the name of Needles. What had I got myself into?

"You never heard of him? I know there's some tough guy's in your business."

"I asked my friend that. It doesn't sound like Needles was involved at all in the bookmaking business. More likely organized crime."

I could have argued that's exactly what being a bookie was, but I resisted. I understood Paddy's point. Organized crime was more sordid than bookmaking.

"What would an old newspaperman and some random thug have in common? Why would people feel the need to eliminate both of them on the same day?"

"Sounds like a job for a private investigator. Your area of expertise, I believe. And I've got to say, I'm happy I won't be involved. Sounds like this one could get a little messy."

We both knew that messy was the least descriptive word he could have used.

"You're probably right. Alright, Paddy, I've got to run. Thanks for the info."

"Keep me posted. I'm sure there's going to be a lot to tell."

"I can't wait," I said, my voice belying what I'd said.

Paddy hung up on his end.

I was already deep in thought.

I debated keeping this information from Sophie until I learned more. Did I really want to tell her that her father's murder might have coincided with another murder? That maybe this was some sort of far-reaching conspiracy?

Then again, this was her father and I had no right to keep any information from her. That point of view won out.

I called her up.

"Hi, Quint."

"Hey, Sophie. I found out a little information."

"What is it?"

I'm not what you'd call a paranoid man, but suddenly Henry's words came to me: *Tell him no talking to police!*

If Henry was right about this and they were somehow involved or looking over our shoulder, they could be monitoring Sophie's phone. Or mine.

"I'll tell you in just a second, but I have a request."

"What is it?"

"From this point forward, let's not discuss the case over the phone or through texts."

"You're scaring me, Quint."

"I'm probably overreacting, but it's only because of what your father told you about the cops."

"He included that for a reason."

"Then I think being cautious is the right move," I said.

"Alright. How about this? Tomorrow is Friday. We'll make Tuesdays and Fridays the days I come to your place and you can update me on the case. I don't need updates every day, but twice a week might be spread out enough that you have new information each time."

"That's fine with me."

"I've got to work until 6:30 or 7:00 tomorrow. Is eight too late?"

"Eight is alright.. But don't you want to know the new info?"

"I can wait a day. Tuesdays and Fridays from here on in."

∽

After I hung up with Sophie, I went to the online version of the *San Francisco Chronicle*. Yes, Henry's death was technically in Berkeley, but the Chronicle covered the Bay Area better than any of the other newspapers. I was curious about anyone else who died suspiciously on the night of the 18th.

I scrolled through their website from the 19th and saw nothing that stood out. There were two murders, but one was a gang murder and the other was a domestic disturbance gone bad.

I switched to the April 20th version. Nothing stood out. Same for the 21st.

I called Paddy Roark back.

"You missing me already?"

"Can you ask your cop friend a question for me?"

"Of course."

"And you're positive he will keep quiet about this?"

"He owes me and Dennis fifty large, so yes, I'm sure."

Fifty large was fifty grand. Not exactly easy to pay back on a cop's salary. I wondered just how protected Paddy and Dennis were from police interfering in their business ventures. How many cops were on their "payroll?"

"Okay, just making sure. Can you ask him if there were any other suspicious murders on the 18th? Or within a few days either way."

"Sure. Do you want me to let him know about your friend Henry?"

I thought about it.

"No."

"This isn't Watergate you are investigating, Quint."

"Maybe not, but I'd still like to keep this on the down low when possible."

"Alright," Paddy said. "Talk soon."

I had two other cases I was currently working on. Neither one was all that important in the grand scheme of things.

That's not fair, I guess. They mattered very much to the people who brought me the cases, but to me, neither had the urgency of Henry's murder.

Both cases were moderately interesting, however.

A man had come to me and said he'd lost his wedding ring, hiring me to recover it. He said his wife had quite the temper and she'd kill him if she found out the truth. He'd bought one that looked as close to the original without breaking the bank. Now he was just hoping to get the original back and put it back on his finger.

The problem was that he'd lost it at a Golden State Warriors game where 20,000 people attend every game. I'd contacted the team, but no one had turned it in.

When that was a dead end, the man gave me a list of the six people who have season tickets right next to his and asked me to investigate them. I asked him to give me a few days to consider it. I found the whole thing slightly amusing, but with an overbearing wife, I guess I couldn't blame him.

The other case involved a man who hired me to check up on his wife's past. He believed she might be using a fake name and had potentially led a different life before they met and married. So far, nothing had turned up. I was starting to think the woman was exactly who she said she was. I'd continued working the case, but my intuition told me this wasn't going anywhere.

I'd continue to do my due diligence on those respective cases, but it was now Henry's case that had my full attention. I didn't care that I wasn't getting paid. In fact, if Sophie offered to pay me, I would turn it down. This case was personal. No amount of money would change that.

Now that I knew Needles' real name I could search for him on the internet. The first thing I pulled up was Rupert Shinn's rap sheet. It was long, but he'd managed to avoid murder charges or anything that would amount to a long prison sentence. He'd been in jail four or five separate times, but never for more than a year. Something told me he'd been lucky. Or had a very good attorney.

I went over each arrest with a fine-toothed comb, seeing if there was anything that I could tie to Henry Madsen. Nothing on that front, but I did find something interesting. Needles had been convicted of assault at a bar named Kincade's. As luck would have it, I happened to know the owner of the establishment.

Kincade's was owned by a man named Yancy Quizzenberry. Along with having one of the more interesting names of anyone I'd ever met, Yancy was quite the character. He had to be close to sixty years old at this point but hadn't lost anything on his fastball. The guy was still a kid at heart.

Early on in my time at *The Walnut Creek Times,* I got the assignment of spending a Friday, Saturday, and Sunday night at Kincade's, and then writing an article describing a weekend in the Bay Area bar business.

I interviewed Yancy, the bartenders, the waitresses, and the cooks. What had seemed like a very uninteresting story to begin with ended up becoming one of my favorite articles I ever wrote. I'd managed to humanize everyone who worked at the bar, telling some of their tough luck stories and how they ended up in the bar industry. This wasn't some college bar where the employees were young and just paying their way through school. The average age of the employees of Kincade's was closer to forty years old and they all had a story to tell.

The reception to the article had been met with almost universal approval. Yancy Quizzenberry enjoyed it so much that he framed it (the article was seven pages long) and put it up on the walls for all to read.

I tried to make sure to step into his bar at least once a year. It was in Oakland - and close enough to my place in Walnut Creek - to where I had no excuse to not pop in now and then.

It looked like today was going to be one of those days.

∽

I didn't show up until close to six that night.

I'd called ahead and asked if/when Yancy was coming in. They said he'd be in at five. He was a very hands-on owner and liked to look after his investment. How could you blame him?

I walked through the front door and was greeted by his voice within the first second or two.

"Quint!" he yelled and walked towards me.

We shook hands, hugged, and patted each other on the back.

"How are you, Yancy?"

"I'm the same. And don't take that as a bad thing. I'm very happy with where I am. I hope I'm the same for the rest of my life."

"Great to hear it."

"Can I get you a drink?"

"I'm starting to get the feeling you knew I was coming."

"An employee told me someone who claimed to be an 'old friend' was coming in. When I saw you walk in, I just assumed it was you."

"You assumed correctly."

He looked in the direction of a woman behind the bar.

"Paula, whatever this guy wants, it's on me. I don't care if it's ten beers and five shots of Tequila. I've got it."

While I didn't have plans on ordering ten beers and five tequilas - much less one - I still thought it would be rude not to at least order one drink.

I looked over at Paula.

"I'll take a Tito's and Tonic," I said.

"Coming right up," she responded.

We started walking toward Paula. Kincade's had one long, narrow bar that ran almost forty yards.

"So what brings you in this direction, Quint? Are you still in Walnut Creek tracking down criminals?"

"I sure am."

"I always thought it was an odd city to be based out of."

"I live there, so it was more out of convenience. You're right though, most of my cases are coming from somewhere other than Walnut Creek."

"I know you had one recent case that emanated from Walnut Creek. What was that family's name? The Keats? Was it? The one where the son killed the mother."

The murder of Gracie Keats was the last major case I'd worked on. Every single clue led back to their son. He even killed himself and left a suicide note admitting to his crimes. And yet, a few days later while having lunch with his sister, I started to think maybe she'd killed him and framed it as a suicide.

As our lunch was ending, she winked at me, all but confirming my suspicions. I didn't feel like getting into that with Yancy, though. The cops considered it a closed case and I saw no reason to open up that can of worms.

"The Keats. You got it. Yeah, that was a wild case," was all I said. "And as for your earlier question, I wanted to talk to you. That's why I ventured out this way."

"I'm intrigued," he said. "Paula, can we get two shots of Reposado?"

So much for not having any tequila shots.

Yancy would probably be considered a functioning alcoholic. I imagine it was the case with many bar owners. And the other ones usually didn't drink at all. There wasn't much middle ground.

Paula set the two shots in front of us.

"Bottoms up," Yancy yelled.

I doubted this was his first shot of the day.

We clinked glasses and threw them back and I instantly remembered why I'd never really liked TQ.

"If we have another shot, I'm making the call," I said.

Yancy laughed. "Dealer's choice."

We sat down at the bar.

"Alright, what is it you wanted to ask me?"

I could have brought up the death of Henry and the fact that he was a close friend, but I decided against it. Being a little cautious with this case seemed like the best course of action.

"I'm currently working on a case and something ancillary to it happened here."

"At my bar?" Yancy said, asking the obvious.

"Yeah. Do you know a guy named Rupert Shinn?"

"It doesn't ring a bell, no."

"He was known as Needles."

Before he spoke, his expression gave him away.

"Yeah, I know that punk."

"Punk?"

"Always looking for trouble. If it wasn't a bar fight, he'd curse out my bartenders or servers. Total jerk."

Two people came and sat at the bar, right next to Yancy. It didn't seem to bother him. He was probably used to airing his dirty laundry in front of others.

"Did he come in a lot?" I asked.

"Probably only five or six times total, but there was an incident each and every time. He got in a fight the last time, about six months back, and as the cops arrested him, I told him he was 86'd. I haven't seen him since."

Six months ago lined up with the arrest I was interested in.

"What happened that night?"

He laughed, but I wasn't sure why.

"Needles was drunk as fuck. Tried to order another shot from the lovely Paula here and she rightfully said, 'You've had enough.' He didn't take it well and started yelling at Paula. Some stand-up guy jumped in and defended her and from there, it was only a matter of time until it ended in fisticuffs. Needles was a really tough guy and even black-out drunk, he got the best of Paula's good Samaritan. Luckily, a few members of the public jumped in after two or three punches. Might have saved the guy's life."

"No bouncers?"

"This was at one in the afternoon."

Now I know why he'd laughed. I'd ask him what happened that night, but this was in broad daylight. Needles really was a piece of work.

"Jeez," I said. "Someone started early."

"That's for sure. I was in the back. Wish I'd been out on the floor. I'd have seen it coming. I always have a good eye for things like that."

"Helps having owned a bar for fifty years."

Yancy laughed.

"Ouch, Quint. Twenty-five years, but who's counting?"

"Would Needles come in alone or with others?"

"Usually alone, I think. Remember, he was only here a handful of times."

"You said usually. Was there a time he came in with someone else?"

"At least once he came in with one of our regulars."

"How did they know each other?"

"I don't know. And it was an odd friendship. Frank, the regular, was as mellow as they come. I'm surprised he'd want to deal with the volcano that was Needles."

"I'd like to talk to Frank if possible."

"No, that's not possible."

My heart sank and I remembered what Yancy had said a few seconds ago. Frank the regular WAS mellow. Not is.

"Frank is dead, isn't he?" I asked.

"Yeah. He drowned about five days ago."

I was instantly skeptical.

"In the ocean?"

"No, in his own pool."

My skepticism only increased.

"Is there a friend of Frank's I could talk to?"

"Shit, we were all friends of Frank. He was a great guy. But if you really want to learn more about him, I'd suggest talking to his wife."

"Does she come in here?"

"She used to, on occasion. Not exactly a regular per se. Why don't I reach out to her and see if she's willing to meet with you? No guarantees. She is grieving her husband's death after all."

"I understand. And thank you very much, Yancy. You're going above the call."

"I've got a request myself."

"Anything. Shoot."

"Do you still keep in touch with the owner of *The Walnut Creek Times?*"

"I sure do. His name is Tom Butler."

"Why don't you throw out this crazy idea? A follow-up to your original article about Kincade's. See how everyone's life has changed in the ten or twelve years since."

If I was still working at the newspaper, I'd love to write this article. I know their beloved, longtime chef had died and one of the bartenders had married one of the waitresses. There would be plenty to write about and I'm sure the readers would like to know what happened in the decade-plus since my first article.

"I think it's a fantastic idea, Yancy. Too bad I'm not still working there, I'd absolutely write it. I'll reach out to Tom and see if someone on his staff might be up for it."

"Thank you so much, Quint. I'd really love that."

"Why don't we talk in a day or two? I'll reach out to Tom and you can talk to Frank's wife."

"Done and done."

It was time to get out of there while I still could. I knew that look on Yancy's face. He was yearning to order another drink.

"I think it's time I got back to Walnut Creek," I said.

"No more shots?"

"If I have one more, I'd be ordering an Uber out of here. Raincheck."

"Next time, why don't you Uber out here? We'll tie one on."

"It's a deal."

We shook hands as I stood up to leave. I'd only taken a few sips of my Tito's and Tonic and I pushed it away from Yancy so he wouldn't notice. I'd already had a shot. Finishing that drink as well probably wasn't advisable. This wasn't the 80s when people could get away with it. I remember many get-togethers where my father probably had 3-4 glasses of wine and then drove us home. That's just how it was in those days. Not anymore.

"I'll call you after I talk to Frank's wife. By the way, her name is Erika."

"Great. Thanks for everything, Yancy."

"You got it, Quint. See ya."

With that, I walked towards the door. I'd accomplished more than I could have expected. I was in a good mood and it wasn't the tequila talking.

My thoughts turned to Frank the regular. Was it possible another person had been killed? Drowning in your own pool sounded suspicious.

I hit a lot of traffic on my ride home and it was almost 7:00 by the time I arrived.

Sophie texted me a few minutes before eight and I went down to let her into my complex. We'd recently got a letter from management that we could now set up a passcode and buzz people in. Originally, they didn't want DoorDash drivers and other randoms walking through the complex, but they recently caved.

Made sense to me. Having to get off your butt, walk to the elevator, and go downstairs to go collect your food kind of defeated the purpose of something like DoorDash. Or, maybe that's just my occasionally lazy ass's way of thinking.

Sophie was dressed in jeans and a lightweight, orange hoodie. Jeans and a hoodie had been her go-to the other times I'd seen her as well.

The weather report said it was about to heat up. I imagine she'd be turning in the jeans for shorts in no time.

"You ready?" I asked.

"Sure am."

We took the elevator up and walked to my apartment.

Sophie sat down on the couch. Usually, if I had a pretty woman over, I'd offer her a glass of wine, but with our history, I thought that might be a bit suggestive.

"Want some coffee or tea?" I asked instead.

"You have any red wine?

There went that idea.

"Sure. I've got a Cab or a Chianti."

"Chianti, that's a surprise."

"I bought it for this spaghetti recipe I make."

"I remember. The one with meatballs and pepperoni and you cook it for hours in Chianti and tomato sauce."

I was floored.

"I made that for you?"

"You sure did. It was excellent if memory serves."

"Damn, I didn't know that had been in my repertoire for so long."

"Yeah, you've probably made that dish for a bunch of girls over the years."

I didn't take the bait.

Sophie started laughing, taking some of the pressure off.

"I'm kidding, Quint. Just busting your balls as they say."

It felt more like flirting.

"Come to think of it, I have some leftovers. Are you hungry?"

"For that dish, yes."

It was homemade meatballs stuffed with ricotta and parmesan, andouille sausage, chopped-up pepperoni (the secret ingredient!), lots of garlic, onions, and oregano, and then you sauté it for hours with Chianti and tomato sauce. The wine really pulls the dish together and after sautéing for hours, makes your kitchen smell outstanding. I'm sure old-school Italians would say this recipe is sacrilege, but it tastes darn good and that's all that matters to me.

I took a tub of Tupperware out of the fridge and instead of nuking it in the microwave, I threw the spaghetti in a pan, added a little more Chianti and decided to heat it up that way.

"Looks like we're drinking the Cab," I said to Sophie. "The end of the Chianti is going in the spaghetti."

"Thanks. For both."

I poured her a glass and set it on the table in front of the couch. I had a dinner table, but I often ate on the couch. Tonight would be no different.

I poured myself a glass as well and drank it as I cooked.

We made small talk as I heated up the spaghetti. It didn't seem the right time to talk about her father. That could wait until after we ate.

Ten minutes later, we'd demolished the Chianti-infused spaghetti.

"That was phenomenal," Sophie said. "Even better than I remember."

"I got that dish from my Mom and have made some changes over the years."

"How is your Mom?"

"She's good. Still living in San Ramon and constantly questioning my career change."

"Wishing you were still a writer?"

"She thinks it's safer."

"She's not wrong."

I just nodded, knowing I'd come close to death a few times since becoming a PI.

"Well, tell her I said hello," Sophie said.

"I will."

"Now, can we talk about what you've learned about my father's death?"

"Of course. I've actually learned a lot in the last few days," I said and spent the next ten minutes discussing my conversation with Paddy Roark and then my talk with Yancy Quizzenberry.

Sophie was half fascinated, half disgusted.

"Are you saying that my father might have been killed as part of some larger conspiracy?"

"It's very early in the investigation obviously, but yes, I think it's a distinct possibility."

"What conspiracy could a retired, seventy-five-year-old guy living on a boat possibly be part of?"

"That's what I'm trying to find out, Sophie. And maybe he wasn't part of the conspiracy at all."

"What do you mean?"

"Maybe he discovered the conspiracy. Or maybe he heard something he wasn't supposed to. There are a hundred other possibilities."

That seemed to calm her down a little bit.

"That's good to hear. I was thinking the worst of my old man for a second."

"Don't. Henry was a great man, we both know that."

Did I really know that? I mean, he'd always seemed like it to me, but you never really know what someone else is like deep down. I sincerely hoped this case wouldn't lead to me learning of a darker side of Henry. It would kill me to have to tell Sophie.

"Thanks, Quint. That makes me feel better."

Sophie's feet were still dangling off the couch but more of her legs were now sitting on the couch, pushing slightly closer toward me. Or at least it felt that way to me. Hopefully, it was just the wine and I wasn't reading too much into this.

If it was any other woman, I would have loved this. Sophie being an ex and me investigating the murder of her father just made this all feel so awkward.

She swung her thighs back so they were now directly in front of her. It's as if she'd read my mind.

"Thanks for the excellent food and wine, Quint. I should probably be heading home soon."

"Okay. So, I'll see you Tuesday?"

"You sure will. I work all day, though. Can we meet at eight again?"

"Of course," I said. "I can always come to your place if you'd prefer."

"No, I like it here," she said. I didn't respond.

I walked Sophie downstairs and she gave me a kiss on the cheek before she left.

If she kept coming up to my apartment at night, I had no doubt we'd end up in my bed before long. Especially if we kept having a few glasses of wine.

Turned out, I didn't have to wait long.

CHAPTER 5

"He didn't deserve this," Erika Manning said.

I was sitting with Frank's widow at a coffee shop in Oakland. She'd called me the night before and decided that's where she'd like to meet. Maybe she'd spent too much time grieving at home lately, or maybe she didn't want a stranger coming to her house. Whatever the reason, I was just happy to meet with her.

She had a nice aura about her. Even in her obvious grief, there was something generous about her, as if she was someone who would lift other people up. She was wearing jeans, a Motley Crue shirt, and a jean jacket. She looked like a twenty-something in 1985, not a forty-something in 2023.

"What do you mean by deserve? Yancy told me that Frank drowned."

"If you really thought this was a drowning, we wouldn't be sitting here talking."

She had a point.

"OK, I concede that. So, what do you think happened?"

"I don't know exactly, but he wasn't drunk and he was a good swimmer. He wouldn't have drowned."

"Were you at the house when it happened?"

"No, I was out of town."

"I hate to be mean, but how are you so certain he wasn't drunk? I was told he went to Kincade's quite a bit. Maybe he decided to have a few at home."

"Sure, he probably drank too much at Kincade's, but he wasn't a home drinker. He liked the social part of drinking. Being out and about, you know."

"I get it."

"Plus, I talked to him about an hour before they think he died. He was perfectly lucid. And trust me, I would know if he was drunk."

I had no doubt. Spouses always know best.

"I believe you," I said.

She looked like she was going to get emotional.

"That's more important than you know," she said. "You know how many dirty looks I've gotten when I've said he didn't drown? No one believes me."

"I'm sorry," I said.

We both took a second and enjoyed a sip of coffee.

She paused.

"Plus…"

"Plus what?" I asked.

"He didn't always hang out with the most honest people. I think he knew some things he wasn't supposed to know."

"Any idea what those might be?"

"None at all. He would never tell me. Not because we didn't have a good marriage, but because he was trying to protect me from knowing too much."

"Do you know a guy named Needles?" I asked.

"It doesn't ring a bell."

"I don't think I asked Yancy. What did Frank do for a living?"

"You won't judge if I tell you?"

"Of course not."

"Frank was a professional poker player. That's why he spent so much time at the bar. When he wasn't playing cards, he liked to enjoy a beverage or two. As I said, he just liked the social aspect of it. It was the same with poker. Sure, he made his money at it, but he also loved sitting at the table and telling stories. A bar is not so different."

She was right. I'd played poker a few times at casinos and it was very much a communal experience. Even the people who lost money sometimes left having had a good time, enjoying the camaraderie that comes with playing cards.

"How long had Frank been playing poker?"

"Basically his whole life."

"Really?"

"Yup. He said he started playing around six and by the time he was fifteen knew that he could make a living at it. He's been on T.V. a bunch of times over the years."

"That's fascinating. I'm sure he had a million stories."

"Why do you think he liked going to the bar?" she asked rhetorically.

I imagined Frank spinning a yarn while a drink or two deep and loving every minute of it.

"Do you suspect it could have been someone he won money off of?"

"It's possible, but I highly doubt it. Poker is not really like that. Once the money is gone, it's gone. It's not like refusing to pay some bookie when you are down five grand."

I bet Erika had a few stories herself. She seemed to know this life pretty well.

"And I think Frank was killed over something bigger than a poker game," she said. "I just have no idea what that might be."

"What happened on the day he died?"

"I talked to him around noon, like I told you. He said he'd played poker till two am. and had just woken up."

"And the police think he drowned around one?"

"Between one and two, they said. And believe me, Frank wouldn't get drunk in an hour or two. That guy had a bigger tolerance than almost anyone I've ever known."

"Was it common for him to go swimming during the day?"

"Yes and no."

"Would you care to elaborate?"

"Yes, in summer. No, when it's mid-April and the water is cold."

"That makes perfect sense. Did you tell the cops that?"

"I did, but when a guy is found dead at the bottom of the pool, it's hard to convince them he hadn't gone swimming."

"So you don't even think he was swimming? You think he was forced in there and then someone drowned him?"

"Yes."

"Thanks for answering all these questions," I said.

We both took a sip of our coffees. A couple had moved about three tables away, but we still had it mostly to ourselves.

"Yancy said you're a stand-up guy and wouldn't screw me over," Erika said.

"No, of course not."

"What he didn't tell me was why you were so interested in Frank's death. It's obvious you've never met him. All he told me is that you're a private investigator."

I had to give her something, but I didn't want to get too specific.

"The guy Needles I mentioned is dead. That came to my attention as I was investigating a case peripheral to it. And then I found out that Frank died a day after Needles and they knew each other. That's when I started asking questions."

"Frank and this guy Needles knew each other?"

"That's what Yancy said. You've never heard of him? His real name is Rupert Shinn."

"It doesn't ring a bell. Honestly, Frank knew a million people and it's possible they were either just acquaintances or even met that night. Frank had ways of making people think they were fast friends"

"Frank was with him the night this guy got arrested."

"That doesn't mean they didn't meet that night."

"That's true."

"How did this guy Needles die?"

"A gunshot."

"A little less subtle than a drowning."

I just nodded.

"If more than one person died by a firearm, the police might start asking more questions," I said.

"So you obviously think these two are related?" Erika asked.

"I think it's possible."

"Interesting," she said and we both left it at that.

"And you can't think of anyone who would want Frank dead?"

"I really can't."

We both took a sip of our coffees. The place was filling up and there were now people just a table away. I had a feeling the tone of our conversation was about to change. No more discussion of poker and bars and gunshots. Erika looked to be feeling a bit uneasy with all the people around us. Quite the opposite of Yancy, who seemed to relish the opportunity to air the bar's dirty laundry in front of others.

I handed Erika my business card.

"If anything comes to mind, don't be afraid to call," I said.

"Thanks. And I appreciate you listening to me rant as well."

"No problem. It's probably healthy to get those feelings out."

It seemed like the right thing to say. Whether I truly believed it or not, I wasn't sure.

"Thanks."

"Will you keep going to the bar?" I asked, more to say something than because it really mattered.

"I don't know. It won't be the same without my Frank there."

I felt sad for Erika. A widower in her forties. It was obvious that she loved Frank.

"One last question if you don't mind."

"No, go ahead."

"Have any of Frank's friends passed away recently?"

She responded quickly.

"No, not that I can think of."

A couple took another table next to us.

"You ready to get out of here?"

She nodded.

With that, we both stood up and walked out of the coffee shop.

CHAPTER 6

The next several days went by without much advancement on the case.

Sophie came over on Friday and we spent the first thirty minutes talking about the case and the second thirty minutes flirting. Sophie was a strong-willed woman and this wasn't some case of her looking for attention because her father had passed away.

We'd had a previous relationship and she felt safe with me. That's what was driving this.

This time on her way out, she kissed me on the lips.

Over the weekend, I did some more research on Needles, but still couldn't nail down exactly who he did business with. Truthfully, I'd found nothing. I'd researched a lot of people online. Very few had no fingerprints on the internet. Rupert Shinn appeared to be one of them.

Frank the poker player didn't have much of one either, in all honesty. Guess you couldn't blame him. He probably didn't have a LinkedIn page saying he played poker and drank at bars. I even searched for Henry online but found nothing that I didn't already know.

Tom and Krissy Butler had done a great job of cataloging all of our old articles and I read a few of Henry's with a smile on my face. I was an above-average writer, but reading his articles made me think he was some sort of alien. I'd never reached the heights that he had. Maybe it was for the best that I'd switched professions.

I went back to Kincade's on Monday and interviewed a few people who knew Frank. I didn't learn any more than I had from his wife. I was starting to feel my investigation was in neutral.

On Tuesday, the inevitable happened.

Sophie and I had sex.

It happened all of a sudden. I'd just finished telling her about my interviews at Kincade's when she leaned over and kissed me. We were sitting on my couch and she inched closer as our kissing continued. It was no longer just a kiss and had become a full-on make-out session, although I'm assuming the kids call it something different these days.

After a few minutes, I moved my face back a few inches and stared at her.

"Are you sure you want to do this?"

No, it wasn't romantic at all, and my timing was off, but with our history and the ongoing investigation into her father's death, I just wanted to make sure this was what she wanted.

"Shut up and kiss me," she said.

Well, that answered that.

Five minutes later, we were on my bed ripping each other's clothes off. Everything was perfect. Were there a couple of clumsy moments? Sure, but perfect doesn't necessarily have to mean error-free. We had a darn good time.

Sophie was fantastic in bed, just as she always had been. I guess that's something that doesn't change over time. If anything, you get better. At least, women do. Men may not always be able to live up to their younger selves.

After we finished and I lay back on the sweaty bed, I felt elated. And a little guilty. I know she'd allayed my fears, but I couldn't shake that voice in the back of my head telling me this was wrong.

We'd only crossed paths again because of the death of Henry. And here I was getting naked with his daughter and thinking naughty thoughts.

I calmed down by telling myself that Henry had thought we made a good couple. Maybe he was looking down somewhere and smiling. Except during the actual act, obviously.

"That felt great," Sophie said.

I looked over at her and imagined some siren from the 1950s, smoking a long cigarette after sex. Sophie had that old-school beauty. Very little makeup, no fake boobs, no Botox. Au Naturale. She looked nothing like today's stars on Tik Tok. She looked better.

"I forgot how relaxing it can be after the fact," I said.

"Has it been that long?"

"Longer than I'd care to admit."

I tried to remember. It had been several months since I'd had sex with the attorney working the Keats trial. I couldn't place her name at the moment. Of course, that almost shouldn't count. She had used me to further her position in the case. To her, it was business. Not exactly how you'd like to describe sex.

"Well, your performance didn't suffer," Sophie said and laughed.

I smiled in her direction.

"This could get tricky," I said. "Rekindling our old flame."

"I don't think so. We're both adults and your investigation into my Dad's death is separate from this."

I leaned in and gave her a kiss.

If I'd been eighteen years old again, I might have tried to start up round two. But the forty-three-year-old me needed a little more time in between.

"I think I need a nap," I said, and Sophie started laughing.

~

There was no encore that night.

Sophie took a shower twenty minutes later, changing into the clothes she'd already been wearing. I'd offered her a T-shirt or some sweats, but she turned them down.

"So we're on for Friday?" she asked.

"Of course."

"What's next for the investigation?"

"I'm going to continue trying to find out if anyone else was murdered around the same time as your father, Needles, and Frank. Three deaths in such a short span is already suspicious. I fear this might go deeper than my imagination is already letting it go."

"Be careful. I can't lose my father and my rekindled flame so close to each other."

She smiled, meaning it as a joke. I think she just wanted to use the word *rekindled*.

It did give me pause, though.

If someone was willing to kill three people in the span of twenty-four hours, they certainly wouldn't be remiss to kill a fourth if someone (me!) got in their way.

I tried to shake that thought. I'd just had a roll in the hay with a beautiful woman. It was time to think positively.

I walked Sophie downstairs and gave her a big, long, wet kiss before she left.

~

In previous cases, I'd often worked with law enforcement. Some-times they accepted me, other times they shunned me. Ray Kintner had become a really close friend until he was killed by The Bay Area Butcher, a death I still tried to avoid thinking about. I preferred to remember Ray as he lived, not as he died. Just like Henry. I looked back on our times fondly.

With Henry Madsen's warning about the police, this case was going to be different. I'd have no friend like Ray on the inside. I wouldn't be strutting into a local police department asking if they could give me information on Henry's death. Or Needles' death. Or Frank's.

For the tenth time, I asked myself what these people had in common. I'd originally thought Frank and Needles knew each other, but Erika made me think they were just friends for the day. What about Henry? He was a retired newspaperman. How (and why) did he get mixed up with a poker player and some bully with a temper?

Maybe I was jumping to conclusions and these three deaths weren't related. After all, the police said that Frank drowned. Was it possible that Erika was just a grieving widow and couldn't admit it that maybe he did actually drown?

Maybe, but I'd believed every word Erika had said. Gun to my head, I'd guess that Frank was murdered and that his death was part of this whole conspiracy. Whatever the hell it was.

There was a question I'd been trying to avoid: Was I sure Henry had remained a good man after he quit *The Walnut Creek Times?*

Was there a chance he went down the wrong path post-retirement? I found it unlikely, but it was something I couldn't just eliminate altogether.

Despite what Sophie had said, things were going to be a little more complicated between us now and I wasn't ready to ask her pointed questions about her father.

I could always use a buffer, I told myself.

So I decided to head over and see my old bosses at *The Walnut Creek Times.* Tom and Krissy Butler. They knew Henry better than I ever had and maybe they knew some things that Sophie didn't.

"Quint Adler," Krissy Butler said.

She gave me a big hug as her husband Tom hovered behind her. They'd lived in the same house for as long as I'd known them, a beautiful home in the hills overlooking Walnut Creek. When I'd brought up swinging by the office, they wouldn't have any of it, and told me I was to come by the house.

They'd been great bosses and always fair, which is not to be confused with being pushovers. We'd butted heads just as all people in the newspaper business do. I still loved them, despite our head-butting.

I saw them every few months. There were some friendships - like Henry's - where I felt I hadn't done enough, but that wasn't the case with the Butlers. They were still very much in my life on a regular basis.

The Walnut Creek Times was still active, although Tom had told me that the online version was now much more profitable than the print version. That made me sad. Part of the fun of being in the newspaper business was seeing the paper in the flesh. It was tangible in a way that your article appearing online never would be.

After my hug with Krissy, Tom stepped forward.

"How are you, Tom?"

"Great to see you, Quint."

We shook each other's hands and realizing that was too formal, brought it in and patted each other on the backs.

"Get a room, you two," Krissy said.

We both laughed.

"Let's talk on the patio," Tom said.

I walked the familiar path from the front door, through the foyer and then the living room, and out to the patio that looked over downtown Walnut Creek.

"Do you want anything to drink?"

"I'll just take a water. Thanks, Krissy."

She returned a few minutes later with a large pitcher of water, several slices of lemon plopped on the rim. Tom started pouring each of us a glass and we all took a seat around the glass table.

"So you didn't tell me why you wanted to talk, Quint. And yet, I've got a feeling I know just why."

"Let's hear your guess," I said.

"Something to do with Henry's death?"

"You got it."

"Are you investigating it?"

"I am."

"Any theories yet?"

"No, I really don't have any."

"Who could have done something like this?" Tom said, asking his fourth straight question.

"And here I thought I was going to be the one asking the questions," I said.

"My bad. I'm just so baffled as to why someone would strangle an old man. Especially a sweetheart like Henry."

"It's such a tragedy," Krissy said. "How's Sophie taking it?"

I'd had quite a few girlfriends during my time at the *Times*. Tom and Krissy had always hoped I would settle down with one woman. Most notably with Cara, but also in the short time I was with Sophie. They had really liked us as a couple even though that felt like two lifetimes ago.

Regardless, this wasn't the proper time to tell them that we'd rekindled that romance.

"Not well. I think if it was cancer or a heart attack, Sophie at least could have lived with it. This brings too many questions along with it."

"Did she hire you?"

"I'm not sure what I'd label it. She asked me to look into his murder, but I was going to be doing that anyway. And I'm not going to charge her, that's for damn sure."

"She loses her mother and then a few years later, loses her father like this. Hope she has someone to talk to," Krissy said.

"Have you guys been spending time together?" Tom asked.

I couldn't tell if they were insinuating anything or whether I just had a guilty conscience.

"Just talking about the case," I said.

"She never got married, did she? Reminds me of someone else I know," Krissy said.

I tried to prevent myself from blushing. This wasn't a coincidence. I now knew where this was going. And it's exactly where

Tom and Krissy wanted this conversation to go. They weren't even being subtle about it.

I decided there was no point in telling them that Sophie had been engaged, but had called it off ten months ago. That's why she was still living in a medium sized house all by herself.

"You guys made a cute couple," Tom said.

"Any chance of you guys getting back together?" Krissy said, keeping it going. "I'm assuming you're single, or you'd have asked us to hold a dinner party so we could meet the new Mrs. Quint."

"Jeez, did I always do that?"

Krissy laughed.

"To be honest, it was probably us who set those things up. We were always interested in your love life, Quint."

We all had a quick laugh and took sips of our water. The weather was starting to get a little warmer each day. Spring in the Bay Area was a beautiful time.

"Where did you find this water? It is delicious," I said, insinuating I'd like to change the subject.

They both smiled. I loved Tom and Krissy, but they weren't getting any more info about Sophie and me.

"Alright Quint, we'll stop busting your balls. What do you want to know about Henry?"

"You guys kept in touch with him more than I did. What made him click these last few years? Who was he? Who did he hang out with? Did he get involved in anything that would explain this murder?"

They looked at each other and Krissy took the lead. Some people - okay, most people - thought she wore the pants in the family. I just thought they had a nice even-handed marriage.

"To answer your last question first, nothing could explain this. Sure, Henry had some interesting friends and had probably covered some less-than-savory characters when he wrote for us, but nothing would explain him being strangled."

"When you say he had some interesting friends, what do you mean exactly?"

"We had a big dinner party a few years back and told everyone to invite a few friends. Henry invited quite the characters."

"First, in which way were they characters? And second, why wasn't I invited?"

Krissy smiled.

"I think you were doing your case in Las Vegas at the time."

My mind rushed back to the case of Emmy Peters. That one had meant a lot to me and I'd been ecstatic to be able to return her to her family safely.

"And as to my first question?" I asked. "What was so interesting about these friends?"

"They were just out there. He brought a woman who talked about reincarnation all night and a guy who kept telling poker stories."

I smiled. I'd never met Frank Manning, but I could tell that he was a character. I think I would have enjoyed having a beer with the guy.

"Let me guess. His name was Frank," I said.

"Shit. That was it."

They both looked at me. There was no explaining myself out of this one.

"There were a few suspicious deaths within a twenty-four-hour period of Henry's death. A poker player named Frank was one of them."

"Wow. Are you sure it's the same guy?"

I almost said, 'I'd bet on it' and caught myself.

"It's got to be. How many poker players named Frank did Henry fraternize with?"

"Fair point."

"Did Henry say how they knew each other?" I asked.

My mind wandered to Erika….Why hadn't she told me about Henry? Maybe she didn't know him or didn't know that he'd died. Had she really not known either Henry or Needles?

"If he told us how they met, I don't remember," Tom said.

"Was this out of character for Henry? Bringing a poker player and a woman who believes in reincarnation to your dinner party?"

"You idolized Henry, Quint. He was really helpful to you those first few years."

"What is that supposed to mean?"

"I'm just saying that maybe he wasn't the perfect father figure you painted him out to be. Henry was a great guy, but he wasn't infallible."

"I never said he was perfect. You're judging him because he was friends with a poker player and a wannabe Shirley MacLaine. It's not like he was partying with Hitler and Stalin."

Tom laughed. Not at the Hitler and Stalin references obviously, but at the mention of Shirley MacLaine.

"Even when you're fired up, you always manage to drop a gem. Nice Shirley MacLaine reference."

"I'm only fired up because you are telling me I put Henry on a pedestal. Is there something I'm missing? Was he not the great guy we all thought he was?"

Krissy interjected.

"We're not saying that at all, Quint. We loved Henry and as far as we knew, he was that great guy we all remember. This case sounds a little sordid though. Three dead? We're just saying to entertain the possibility that Henry could have been involved in something unsavory."

"I'll entertain it, but I'd also bet he wasn't."

"That's fair," Tom said.

He took out his white napkin and started waving it, suggesting this part of the conversation was over.

"Did you ever meet Frank the poker player again?" I asked.

"Nope. One time thing. Luckily, never the reincarnation woman again either. She was batshit crazy!"

"That must have been something," I said. "What other bodies did she previously inhabit?"

"Cleopatra and Joan of Arc."

"It's always the famous ones, isn't it? It's never Marge the homemaker."

The Butlers both laughed at my joke. The tumultuous part of the conversation was over.

"Any suggestion where I should investigate next?" I asked.

"It sounds like you know a lot more than us," Krissy said.

Erika entered my mind again. I'd asked her if anyone close to her had died recently. She'd said no.

We all took a sip of our water. The clouds were covering up the sun and it was starting to get a little chilly. I took it as a sign that this meeting was wrapping up.

"How's the paper?" I asked.

"Doing well. Why don't you stop in later this week? Some of the old heads would like to see you."

"I miss the camaraderie. Being a P.I. is generally a darn lonely job."

"Then spend more time with Sophie," Krissy suggested.

"You guys are incorrigible," I said.

They smiled.

"Why don't we have a nice dinner here next week?" Tom asked.

"You can bring a plus one if you want," Krissy said.

"I reiterate my previous sentence."

"That's not a no," Krissy said.

"I'll think about it."

"We're just pulling your chain, Quint. I know this has to be a really tough time for Sophie. We all loved Henry very much. Maybe she would enjoy a nice dinner. And we will be on our best behaviors."

"I doubt that. I'll ask her and get back to you."

"Let's go inside. I'm getting cold," Krissy said.

We all stood up from the table.

Tom spoke next.

"If we have this dinner, what type of food do you want?"

Tom and Krissy were both great cooks.

"Surprise me," I said.

I shook their hands and turned to go.

And then I remembered my meeting with Yancy. I told them about his request.

"I think it's a great idea," Tom said. "Let me talk to a couple of our staff writers."

And with that, they led me to the door.

$\sim$

I texted Sophie when I got back to the car.

Me: *Are you sure you haven't heard of a guy named Frank? He played poker.*

Her: *I told you I've never heard of him or his wife.*

Me: *Alright. Sorry. Henry's old bosses at The Walnut Creek Times met him.*

Her: *That's odd. How?*

Me: *They hosted a dinner party.*

Her: *And my father brought him?*

Me: *Yeah, and some woman who believed in reincarnation.*

Her: *Haha. Well, I know who that is.*

Me: *Who?*

Her: *Clementine Ya.*

Me: *That's quite the name.*

Her: *She's quite the character.*

Me: *I bet. Why is your father hanging out with someone like that?*

Her: *He owed her.*

I'd grown tired of texting so I went old-school and dialed Sophie's number. Well, I really just pressed her name on the phone, but you get the drift.

"Glad you called. I was about to do the same," she said. "Rapid texting gets the best of me."

"Why did your Dad owe this woman?"

"You could probably guess. He really, really owed her."

I racked my brain. I had no idea how or why.

"I literally don't have a guess."

"Think about a very personal article my father wrote way back when."

I re-racked my brain. After a few seconds, I got it.

"Wait, is she the woman who…"

"Yup. That's her."

"Wow."

During my first year at *The Walnut Creek Times,* Henry had written one of his most beloved pieces. Probably because it was more personal than anything he'd ever written.

There was a fire at Henry's house.

A next-door neighbor risked her life and went in and woke up a still-sleeping Henry.

The paramedics said the smoke would have engulfed him and killed him within a few minutes.

"So a crazy lady who believes in reincarnation was the one who saved Henry's life?"

"Yeah, pretty odd, huh?"

"And her name is Clementine Ya?"

"Ya," Sophie said, making an obvious - and yet, still funny - joke.

"Can I meet with this Clementine?"

"I've got her number somewhere."

"Send it on over when you find it."

"I will. We still on for tomorrow?"

"Of course."

"I'm *really* looking forward to it," she said, accentuating the word really.

She was not referring to discussing her father's case.

"Me too," I said.

CHAPTER 7

"Let me guess. You were Napoleon."

I was five minutes into my conversation with Clementine Ya and she was already trying to guess who I'd been in a previous life.

"Not unless I've grown a foot in the intervening years."

Clementine patted me on the shoulder and laughed much louder than necessary.

"I'm going to keep my eye on you. You're a funny one."

I was at her house in Berkeley. It was busy. Not with people, but with paintings and statues and who knows what else? There was a Buddha that I was pretty sure was a bong and a picture of George Washington in drag. I stopped looking at the walls after that.

Clementine was dressed like I imagined gypsies would dress. Scarves were prevalent. So were odd pastel colors. She wore a long, multicolored, free-flowing skirt that reached her ankles. She was probably around fifty but had the vibe of a hippie half her age.

While Erika Manning dressed like she should have been seeing Guns N Roses on the Sunset Strip in 1987, Clementine Ya dressed like she was seeing Joan Baez at Woodstock in '69.

"So, we were talking about Henry and his poker-playing friend Frank," I said, trying to get her back to the reason for my visit.

"No, we weren't."

"We weren't?"

"We were talking about Napoleon Bonaparte."

I wanted to scream.

"Oh, yeah. Him."

"A few fun facts about Mr. Bonaparte. He was actually 5'6", which wasn't all that short for his day. And I don't think you're 6'6" Mr. Quint, so your height excuse doesn't hold water."

Informing her that Quint was actually my first name seemed unnecessary. She was in her own world and it wouldn't register anyway.

"Speaking of water," she continued. "Napoleon's last battle was, of course, Waterloo. After that defeat, he was no longer going to control Europe and he was never the same man."

"Don't you mean me?"

"What?"

"You said 'He was never the same man.' But aren't I him?"

She leaned over and patted me on the shoulder again. I couldn't tell if she was trying to hit on me or my past lives. It was hard to tell with Clementine Ya.

"I'm going to keep my eye on you," she said for a second time.

I had to bring this back to Henry or I was going to sprint out that door in a few seconds. I figured I would try a different route.

"Who was Henry in his previous life?"

She laughed.

"C'mon, that's an easy one. He was the world-famous baseball player, Lou Gehrig."

It took all the strength I had to not bust out laughing. It was less that she said Lou Gehrig and more the utmost confidence she had that she was correct. Clementine Ya should have been a stand-up comic.

"Yeah, I can see the resemblance," I said, playing along.

"Duh. Anyone could."

"Did he like playing with Babe Ruth?"

"Who wouldn't love that roly-poly? He could hit the ball really far."

"So I've heard."

"So, you're a baseball fan?"

I was at my wit's end.

"Sorry, Clementine, but I came here to discuss a poker player you may have met when you and Henry went to the home of Tom and Krissy Butler. His name was Frank Manning. Do you remember?"

"Of course. The poker player was Jim Thorpe in a past life."

"I'm noticing a lot of athletes."

"Duh," she said as if it was the most obvious thing ever.

Probably not many women her age still have "Duh" in their repertoire. It's one of the many things that differentiated Clementine Ya from normal people.

"Do you know how Henry and Frank knew each other?"

"I imagine it's through their past lives. I'm sure Jim Thorpe and Lou Gehrig met at some point and they kept the friendship going in their next lives."

If I had a drink, I'd undoubtedly have spit it up. This was some next-level comedy, even though Clementine wasn't in on the joke.

"I'm talking about in this life. Did they say why or how they were friends?"

For the first time, she looked as if she was taking my question seriously.

"I can't remember. Do you want me to bring out my tarot cards?"

I'd heard enough.

"No, I don't want any freaking tarot cards. If you know anything about the poker player, tell me now. If not, I'm getting the hell out of here."

"This outburst doesn't surprise me. Napoleon was known for his temper."

I literally threw my hands up in the air. I'd tried to behave, but at this point, I'd heard enough.

"You're batshit crazy and I can't waste any more of my time on you."

With that, I stood up and made my way toward the door.

"Just because you won't acknowledge your past doesn't mean I'm crazy."

"You keep on believing that," I said, and exited the premises.

Sophie and I met up that night and after discussing Clementine Ya, made our way to my bed and passionately made love twice.

I'd performed pretty darn well. Napoleon would have been proud.

"So, what's next?" Sophie asked as we sat in bed.

"Are we doing the right thing?" I asked.

"Do you mean by sleeping together?"

"Yes."

"Are you afraid this is just me emotionally reacting to my father's death? We've been through this, Quint."

"I'm not sure exactly what I think, but I want to make sure you're not feeling pressured to do this."

"I'll assume that's a joke. I'm the one who came on to you. And by the way, we dated at one point, so this isn't creepy in the slightest."

"Alright, just making sure."

"Such a guy thing to do," Sophie said.

"What's that?"

"Ask if we are doing the right thing after having sex twice. If you were so worried, you would have asked beforehand."

I looked over at her and laughed. She had a point.

"You got me there."

"Now that we've got that cleared up, I'll go back to my original question. What's next?"

It seemed she asked the question every time we met up. Obviously, it was warranted. She wanted to know how her father's investigation was proceeding.

"I'm going to find out more about what the police have learned."

"I thought you didn't want to deal with them because of my father's warning."

"I've got my ways around it," I said, thinking of Paddy Roark.

"That's good to hear. I think I may call the police myself today and find out if they've discovered anything."

"Good. You should. It's your father and they would give you more information than anyone else."

"Do you still think his death is related to this poker player and the guy named Needles?"

"Would be a pretty darn big coincidence if not."

"I wish I could help. I've never heard of either of them."

"No problem. That's why I'm here."

She leaned over and kissed me.

"Would your father keep things from you, Sophie?"

I'd decided to broach the subject I'd promised not to.

"What do you mean exactly?"

"If he was in any sort of trouble, would he tell you?"

"We were pretty close as far as fathers and daughters go, but I'm sure there were some things he'd rather not tell me."

"Like what?"

"I don't know. Isn't that kind of the point? I wouldn't know what they were."

"Sure. I just meant what in general he'd keep from you. Women after your mother? Finances? Other jobs he had?"

"He had a few other girlfriends after my mother passed, but none that lasted very long. He loved to live on that boat and I think most of the women got tired of it after a while. As for his finances, he had a 401k and I'm guessing a few hundred thousand in it. I'm meeting with the executor of his will tomorrow."

"Will you be getting the money?"

"I assume so. I'm his only child."

"Sorry I had to ask that."

"It's okay. I don't give a shit about the money. I'd send it all back for one more week with him."

I nodded.

"I wish I could see him again too," I said. "He was larger than life. And obviously, he had something very important to tell me."

"You have no guesses who he was referring to when he referenced a whale?"

"Absolutely no idea, but it's undoubtedly connected. In fact, it didn't even sound like Henry knew himself. I think he had a suspicion but hadn't been able to confirm it yet."

"That's my read on it also," Sophie said.

"If your father was going to keep a secret from you, who would he tell? Who was he closest to these last few years?"

Sophie leaned back and thought long and hard about it.

"He had a fishing buddy. He went to Alaska with him for a week-long expedition. He's the only one I can think of."

"Do you remember his name?"

"Artie Morton. He's getting up there in age too. Probably approaching eighty. The guy thinks he's still twenty-one and in a fraternity though. Quite the character."

I laughed.

"Funny immature or annoying immature?"

"He toes the line."

We smiled at each other, knowing we had similar senses of humor.

"Do you have his number?" I asked

"Yeah, I think my father gave it to me at one point. I'll check my phone when we get out of bed."

Our post-coital, still-in-bed talks, had to be amongst the strangest in history.

"Did the police say when they are going to give you Henry's phone and other belongings back?"

"They didn't."

"It's been less than a week so they are probably still scouring through it, hoping to find something, but I'd ask them today. Hopefully, you'll get it back sooner than later and maybe we'll discover something the cops couldn't find."

~

Sophie left an hour later. She gave me Artie Morton's number on her way out.

I reached out to him and he agreed to meet me. Once I said that I'd be buying lunch, he asked if we could do it on Friday. I had no idea why.

I'd find out soon enough, and calling him a character had been a vast understatement by Sophie.

CHAPTER 8

"Henry Madsen was an all-time great guy and I miss him dearly!"

Artie Morton was eighty going on thirty-two. Or twenty-two. Sophie wasn't lying.

The guy had more energy than me and he was almost twice my age. He had long, curly white hair that looked a bit out of place on a man his age, but he rocked it with confidence.

We were having lunch at a North Berkeley restaurant and Artie was already on his second drink. When I'd arrived, he was having one at the bar and he'd ordered one as soon as we sat down to eat. I wasn't much of a day drinker but ordered a glass of wine. I wasn't one to miss a party.

"His daughter told me that you were probably closer to him than anyone else."

"That's true, at least later in life. And obviously, he loved Sophie the most, but a daughter is different from a best friend."

"How long had you known Henry?"

"Only about five years, but we'd become fast friends early on. I'm sure there were guys he'd known twenty years who never got as close as us."

"Why do you think that was?"

"We met each other within a year of both of our wives having died. I think that was a big part of it. We'd kind of look at each other and say, 'Now what?'"

"How did you meet exactly?"

"It's a funny story. We were at a local bait and tackle shop. Not many of those left. I turned a corner too quickly and bumped right into him, knocking over everything in his hands. He had an old school salmon eggs jar that shattered on the floor along with his styrofoam container holding nightcrawlers, emptying its contents. The little buggers were squirming all around. He looked at me like he wanted to fight. Imagine that! Two old fuckers going at it over some spilled bait. Anyway, cooler heads prevailed and once we started talking, realized we were both going fishing that day and ended up joining each other."

"What a great story," I said. "The last time I ever talked to Henry I was actually out fishing."

"Do you go often?"

"Very rarely these days. I went with my father a lot when I was a kid, though. Fond memories."

"I feel like it's a dying art. Fishing was a big thing back in my day. Especially amongst fathers and sons."

Artie took a sip of his drink and I took a sip of my wine.

"Did you guys catch anything that day?" I asked.

"Several. We kicked ass. Which led us to set up another fishing excursion the next week. Once he divulged that his wife had just passed, it was inevitable we'd become good friends."

"Old timers' male bonding."

Artie Morton laughed. I usually wouldn't call someone old whom I'd just met, but Artie already felt like an "old" friend. I could see why Henry liked hanging out with him.

"What did you guys do besides fishing?"

"We tried to get laid. Almost always unsuccessfully."

I laughed, in spite of myself.

"Hey, it's not easy getting old," Artie said. "You'll find out your equipment doesn't work like it used to. It will happen to you if you're lucky enough to grow old."

"Yeah, it sounds like a blast."

Artie laughed.

"Better than the alternative," he said and then raised his glass. "To Henry."

We clinked glasses and took a sip in honor of our mutual friend.

The waiter came back over and I ordered a Croque Monsieur. Artie went with the soup of the day and another cocktail. It appeared Artie was on an unhealthy version of a liquid diet.

"Henry talked about you by the way," he said, taking me by surprise.

"Really?"

"He updated me on all your cases. I know about Charles Zane out on the Pacific. I know about that serial killer you brought down. The one who killed that young kid from Berkeley."

"Ronnie Fisk was the kid. Leonard Rolle was the killer. He killed many more kids sadly," I said.

"And Henry couldn't shut up about the Bay Area Butcher case."

"Yeah, he called me quite a few times once that one was over."

"Ending on the Golden Gate Bridge. How cinematic. They should make a movie about that one."

"My face is out there enough as it is," I said, and Artie laughed.

"Yeah, but you could get a little of that Hollywood money."

"I'd be just fine with that."

We took another sip of our drinks.

I was having a blast talking with Artie Morton, but we hadn't really gotten anywhere per my investigation.

"Do you have any idea why anyone would want to kill Henry?" I asked.

"Well, we both know that Henry liked to, and pardon the expression, rock the boat. I was just sure that's what got him into trouble."

"I'd have agreed fifteen years ago, but you think he was still doing that at seventy-five?"

"Oh, yeah. I'm not sure that ever goes away. You should have seen the two of us out together. Trouble with a capital T!"

Artie continued to make me smile.

"I have no doubt. Any guesses on what boat he may have rocked a little too hard?"

"He'd piss off the people who owned the Berkeley Marina, always complaining that it was getting too busy and there was going to be more and more accidents, but I don't think he'd be killed for that. He had an occasional fight with this guy Ed Keener who owned a boat a few down from Henry, but Ed didn't have anything to do with this. I was told he was out of the country."

"By who?"

"The guy who runs the dock. Ivan, or something like that. Size of a bear. You should go meet with him."

"I will. Does anything else jump out?" I asked.

"I've been racking my brain since I heard the news. Nothing though, I'm sorry. As I said, Henry could get fiery, but he'd usually be friends with the guy five minutes later. Kind of like when we met. He wanted to kill me when I first knocked over his salmon eggs and nightcrawlers, and then, an hour later, we're fishing together. So no, I don't know why anyone would want to kill that old man. And yes, I say that, knowing I'm an even older man."

Our food arrived. It hadn't been more than eight minutes since we'd ordered. The advantage of merely ordering a soup and a sandwich. The waiter wasn't going to get off that easy though.

"I'll take one last cocktail," Artie said.

"Same thing?" asked the waiter.

"Always."

Artie looked in my direction.

"I don't always drink like this, I promise. Today is a Friday and it's the only day of the week I drink anymore. Of course, I do like to throw them back rather quickly. Gets me home and in bed early and keeps me out of trouble. You don't want me rolling around your local bar at 10 p.m."

Artie Morton was a treasure. I could sit and laugh at his stories all day.

And now I knew why he'd requested we meet up on a Friday. All his drinks would be on my dime.

"I beg to differ," I said. "You'd be a blast late at night."

"Is that an invitation?"

"You're damn right it is."

Artie lit up. He seemed genuinely touched.

My thoughts went to Kincade's. I can't believe we were forty-five minutes in and I hadn't asked him about Frank Manning. Or Needles, for that matter.

"Have you ever heard of a bar called Kincade's?"

"Of course. You don't live to be my age and not know the famous local bars."

"Did you ever go there with Henry?"

"Come to think of it, we did go there one time."

"Whose idea was it?"

I could see Artie trying to remember, but he couldn't place it. It was the first time he'd acted his age.

"I honestly don't remember. Probably his idea, because that bar wasn't one of my regular stops."

"So it must have been a Friday you went there," I said.

"Why would you think that?"

"Because you said you only drink on Fridays."

"Oh, that. I only started that last month."

I laughed for probably the fifth time. Artie joined in. He must have been a wrecking ball in his younger days.

"I'm trying to better myself in my old age," he said.

"Never too late, right?"

"Indeed."

"Do you remember if Henry met up with anyone else that night at Kincade's?"

As Artie was thinking about it, I realized I was loitering around the subject instead of just asking the question.

"Allow me to rephrase my question," I said.

"You sound like a lawyer."

I nodded. I'd heard that a few times over the years.

"Have you ever met a guy named Needles or someone named

Frank Manning? He was a poker player."

I had absolutely zero reason to suspect Artie of anything, but I still looked closely at his reaction when I dropped those two names. People give away a lot, especially in their initial response, and even though it was a million to one that Artie was involved, I instinctually judged his reaction.

There was a flicker of recognition in his eyes.

"Henry had mentioned someone named Needles a few times. I'm trying to remember when exactly."

I was starting to wonder if Artie's drinking might have been affecting his memory.

"Take your time," I said.

And he did.

Just when I thought it was a lost cause, Artie jumped to attention.

"I remember now!" he exclaimed with the vigor of someone on his third Gin & Tonic. "I met Needles one time."

"At Kincade's?"

"No. It was at a San Francisco Giants game. I don't think it was planned. In fact, if I remember correctly, Henry wasn't that happy to see him."

"It seems like that's something you would have remembered. What took so long?"

"It was random. We ran into him at the concession stand. And because it took a minute to remember he'd introduced himself as Needles, you dodo bird."

Being called a dodo bird by an inebriated octogenarian was an all-timer.

"Fair point. How could you tell Henry wasn't happy to see him?"

"You know Henry. He loved to talk people's ears off. Not this time. He was all about getting this Needles guy to move on."

"How long did this last?"

"Not long. A minute."

"Did Henry say anything about him once he left?"

"No. The awkwardness continued."

I took another bite of my sandwich and Artie took another sip of his soup. The drinks were going down quicker than the food.

"I'm still surprised how well you remember a one-minute conversation."

"It was so out of character for Henry. That's why."

"How long ago was this?" I asked.

"Six months or so."

"And Henry never mentioned Needles again?"

"Not a word."

If Artie was correct and he had indeed met Needles, it proved that Henry knew him. But now what? It's not like the meeting itself gave me any clues as to why either of them would be murdered. Or, under what circumstances they had become friends.

Artie took two big spoonfuls of his soup. It was as if he knew this lunch was coming to an end.

"Is there anything else you can tell me about Needles? Or about Henry?"

"Nothing more about Needles. What more do you want to know about Henry?"

"Anything that you think might get me closer to finding his killer."

"Are you close?" he asked.

"I'm a thousand miles away."

Artie smiled.

"That doesn't sound so far. You'll get your man eventually."

"Let's hope so."

I took another bite of my sandwich, saw the waiter, and asked for a check.

"Let's do this again," Artie said.

"Alright, if you're buying next time."

"Deal, but I'll make sure it's not on a Friday."

CHAPTER 9

It had been an interesting few days.

Yancy Quizenberry. Clementine Ya. Artie Morton.

And Erika Manning, who was the most normal of them all.

But where had all these eccentrics gotten me? Not very far.

What to do next?

I pondered the possibilities.

It was time to focus on Needles, a.k.a. Rupert Shinn. I now assumed - if Artie was correct - that he and Henry knew each other. I would circle back to Henry and Frank's friendship, but for now, Needles had my full attention.

I needed to talk to the people close to him.

Needed knowledge on Needles, you might say.

I was able to find the number to the Shinn's landline - yes, some people still had them. It was registered to Angela and Rupert.

I'd called the number twice, hoping to speak to Angela Shinn directly. When she didn't answer either time, I left a message. She had not returned my call so I decided it was just going to be easier to make a house call.

~

"How can I help you?"

A woman who looked to be in her mid-fifties answered the door. She was wearing a red windbreaker and jeans. What she wasn't wearing was a smile. In fact, quite the opposite.

"I'm a friend of Henry Madsen's. Do you know who that is?"

She paused a second too long. That's all I needed to know. My intuition took over from there.

"I've never heard that name in my life," she said, entirely too loudly.

Her adamant response only furthered my opinion that she knew him.

"I think he was an acquaintance of your husband's. And by the way, I'm very sorry for your loss."

I was a day late and a dollar short with my apology.

"He wasn't an acquaintance of my Needles."

Jeez, even his wife called him Needles. There had to have been some awkward moments with that nickname over the years.

"How can you be so sure? There must be some acquaintances of his that you've never met."

"Only distant acquaintances. Are you investigating my husband's murder?"

"Yes," I said.

"So you're with the police?" Mrs. Shinn asked me.

"Not exactly.."

"Not exactly? What the hell does that mean?"

Angela Shinn was playing hardball. From what I'd gathered about Needles, Angela probably wasn't far off.

"I'm not a police officer, but I'm trying to find out who killed your husband and my friend, Henry."

"Do you have a police badge or something?"

"No, only police officers carry those," I said sarcastically.

"You know what I freaking mean. A badge or piece of paper proving you are who you say you are."

She made "freaking" sound more menacing than "fucking."

I probably should have been smarter than to cross Angela Shinn, but it was already too late.

I took out my P.I 's license and handed it to her.

She snatched it out of my hand and quickly grabbed her phone, taking a picture of the license.

She looked at it, handed it back, and said, "Consider yourself marked, Quint," and then slammed the door in my face.

On Wednesday, I caught my first little break.

Sure, I'd done a lot of interviews and met the aforementioned cast of characters fit for a Scorsese movie, but I'd yet to really get anywhere. That changed when I met with Igor - yes, Igor - Smyth. He sounded like Russia had sex with England and they named their baby after their carnal interlude.

Igor was one of the people in charge of monitoring the Berkeley Marina. Artie Morton had suggested I go see him and I obliged the old man.

I'd driven to Berkeley early that day and walked down towards the marina itself. I was greeted by the aforementioned Igor, a man who looked to be about 6'4" and - if I had to guess - two hundred eighty pounds. And honestly, I was probably underestimating his dimensions. Igor might well have weighed more than three bills. He was in the vicinity of sixty years old and had old-school mutton chops.

"I know who you are," were the first words out of his mouth. I couldn't place his accent. It was half Eastern European, half New Orleans and I'd never really heard anything like it.

"Are you sure you've got the right guy?" I asked.

"Quint Adler, right?"

"How did you know?"

"When you jumped on Charles Zane's boat, it was probably the most attention this marina ever received."

"You've been here that long?"

"Shit, that was only like five years ago. I've been here over thirty."

That's when I looked at his name tag and saw his odd name.

"What's your job title, Igor?" I asked.

It came off as rude, but I was genuinely curious.

"Director of Security. Some people like to try and jump on boats that aren't theirs."

It took me a second to realize he was referring to me when I'd hopped on Zane's boat.

"You must moonlight as a comedian," I said.

Igor laughed and his whole body shook with him.

"Don't tempt me," he said.

I looked around and didn't see a chair. Was poor Igor always standing?

"So are you on your feet all day?" I asked.

"No. I've got a few chairs and a table down yonder, but I saw this suspicious-looking guy coming this way, so I walked over here."

I got this joke right away.

"I'd be weary of him," I said, referring to myself. "He's super-duper sketchy."

I then experienced his full-body laugh a second time. Igor was pretty easy to make laugh.

"What are you here for?"

"I was friends with Henry Madsen."

"Oh shit, you were?"

"Yup. I actually found his body."

"Damn. I'm sorry. That's probably the second most attention this marina has ever received. And you've got a connection to both."

This time he wasn't joking, but it wasn't exactly an accusation either. More like he was just stating facts.

Someone approached us, said hi to Igor, and kept walking down towards their boat. Igor was obviously pretty well-known after working here for 30 years.

"I really liked Henry," he said as the man meandered down the dock.

"Have the cops been by here lately?"

"I haven't seen them. Why?"

"Just wondering if they are still investigating."

"I'm sure they are, but I haven't seen them. I'd sure like to know who would kill that sweet man."

"That's what I'm trying to find out."

"A couple of the old regulars down here have brought up having a little memorial for him out on the water."

I gave him my card.

"Let me know if that is going to happen. I'm friends with his daughter and I'm sure she'd love to be here as well."

"You got it."

"And there are no cameras here?"

"Not on the marina itself. I imagine there's more sex - and other untoward things - on these boats than we'd guess. I doubt the boat owners would want cameras on them at all times."

I'd have placed the odds of Igor using "untoward" at a thousand-to-one.

"Makes sense," I said.

"Plus, my job would almost become redundant if they had recordings of everything that went on down here."

I smiled.

"I'll be out of your hair in a minute, Igor."

"No problem."

"Just a few more questions. Do you know someone named Needles or a man named Frank Manning? He played poker for a living if that helps."

"I don't screw around with no poker players or no bookies. As a younger man in the 80s, I liked to bet on the AFC in the Super Bowl. Ended up getting me in trouble for a stretch."

I didn't bother explaining to Igor that the only similarity between poker players and bookies is that they involve gambling.

"Okay. And how about the other guy?"

"What was his name again?"

"Needles."

"Doesn't ring a bell."

I grabbed my phone and went to my photos. The first photo that came up was of Frank, and even though he said he didn't know him, I showed him the picture anyway.

"No, I'm sorry. Never seen that guy."

I found my picture of Needles and showed him that.

"I know that fucker," Igor said.

It was as colorful as he'd been the whole conversation. He obviously didn't like Needles.

"How do you know him?" I asked.

"He rents a spot down here."

"Is it near Henry's?"

"It's relatively close."

I'd never thought to ask anyone if Needles had a boat at the Berkeley Marina.

"Do you know if they interacted?"

"I never saw it, but they probably crossed paths. Their boats were somewhat close and these docks are narrow. They would have passed each other walking on the docks. Of that, I'm certain."

Igor waved at another boater.

"Why did you hate Needles?"

"He's a rude asshole. The type of guy who walks in the middle of the dock and has other people wait until he passes. Most people here - myself included - despise that shit. We're supposed to be a family out here at the marina. He doesn't want to be part of that family."

It didn't seem like Igor knew that Needles was no longer alive. I decided not to tell him. Not yet, anyway.

"I'm surprised you didn't know his name when I first brought it up. Seems like you'd know everyone here."

"There are two reasons. He didn't introduce himself as Needles. His name was like Roger or Rumple or something weird like that."

"It was Rupert."

"That was it. That's a weird ass name if you ask me."

"And what was the second reason you didn't know his name?"

"Huh?"

"You said there were two reasons."

"Oh, yeah. It's because your guy Needles was rarely down on the docks. I think he just joined a few months back. I saw him at most two or three times."

"Can you ask around to see who he hung out with?"

"You sure ask for a lot, Quint. A bit pushy."

He had a sly smile as he said it.

"Guilty as charged," I said.

"I'll see what I can do."

"I appreciate you helping me out."

"Maybe throw me a few crumbs as you investigate. I'm not above hearing a little gossip about what went down with Henry."

"I'll keep you posted for sure," I said. "One last thing. Can you think of a boat owner who knew both Henry and Needles?"

"Let me think."

Igor paused for a good fifteen seconds, looking up at me once something clicked.

"There's probably a few, but Blaine Travers would be as good a guess as any. He has a boat between the two and I'm pretty sure I've seen him talking to your guy Needles before. I 100% know that he was friendly with Henry."

"Can you point to where his boat is?" I asked.

He pointed down toward the general vicinity where Henry's boat had been docked. It was hard to be too specific from where we were standing.

"I can do you one better. He comes here every Monday and Friday at eight a.m. to take his boat out. He's been on that same schedule for years."

It was a Wednesday so it looked like I'd be waiting a few days.

"Thanks, Igor."

"You're welcome. Anything else?"

He'd given me more information than I could have expected.

"No, that's good. I'll probably be seeing you soon. Are you going to be here Friday at eight?"

"How else do you think I know that Mr. Travers was always here at that time? It's because I'm here too, not because I'm some mind reader," he said and let out one final belly laugh.

I patted him on the shoulder and turned to go.

"See you Friday, Mr. Private Eye," he said.

Thursday was uneventful and I returned to the marina early on Friday. Our dinner with Tom and Krissy was later that night so it was going to be a busy day.

Igor was standing at his post and we engaged in some small talk when I arrived. He even offered to tell Blaine Travers that I wanted to talk to him. I thought it would be better if I approached him myself. If Igor spoke to him first, he'd likely have his guard up. That's not what I wanted.

Igor gave a more specific description of the boat this time, and as I walked towards it, I passed Henry's boat in the process. I wondered when the police - or the marina itself - were going to come to pick it up and either give it to Sophie or sell it. I hated still seeing it there because it reminded me of how he met his brutal end.

I had the same question about Needles' boat. I was still surprised that Igor hadn't been alerted.

Blaine Travers's massive speed boat was yellow and white and stood out from most of the others. There were lots of blue, black, purple, and red boats, but his was the only yellow one I'd seen. It left an impression, that's for certain. Whether that was a good thing or not, I'd leave to the boating fashionistas. Personally, I thought it stood out like a sore thumb.

"Mr. Travers," I said.

He was standing on the second level, a coffee in hand. He was probably around sixty with mostly gray hair and a killer tan. He looked like he'd spent his whole life on the water. He looked like George Hamilton, only the tan was likely real.

"Call me Blaine. How can I help you?" he asked.

You can often tell how a person is going to respond to your questions by his initial response. If you get a *'What the hell do you want'* or a *'I'm Mr. Travers, what is it to you'* then you know you're in for a long day. His *'Call me Blaine. How can I help you?'* was very benign. That boded well for our conversation to come.

It was the polar opposite of the first meeting I'd had with Angela Shinn.

"I'm an old friend of Henry Madsen's and was wondering if you had a few minutes."

"I've got more than that for an old friend of Henry's. Although I have to say, you look like a young whipper snapper. How long could you have known him?"

With that, he jumped down to the dock and guided me up to the boat. We both took a seat, with me facing the helm of the boat and Blaine facing me.

He motioned for me to talk.

"I actually knew Henry for over fifteen years. I was kind of his protege at *The Walnut Creek Times* earlier this millennium."

"I know who you are. Quint, right?"

I was surprised, but I guess I shouldn't have been. A lot of people seemed to know who I was these days. Igor Smyth was proof of that.

I extended my hand and said, "Nice to formally meet you."

"My boat, *The Canary*, was docked here during that whole Charles Zane event too."

His comment should have flooded Charles Zane thoughts back to my brain, but all I could think was that his boat was named *The Canary*. Had he named it that because it was painted yellow or had he picked the name first and then painted it yellow after the fact? It was the whole chicken and the egg argument all over.

"That feels like a lifetime ago," I said.

"And yet, here you are, back again."

It sounded sarcastic, but Blaine said it with a smile and I don't think there was any malicious intent.

"Here I am."

"So what did you want to know about Henry?"

"Let's start with the obvious. Do you have any idea why anyone would want to kill him?"

"I can't help you there. Sorry. He was a great old guy. Everyone seemed to like him."

"Did Needles like him?" I blurted out. So much for working my way into the conversation.

"How do you know Needles?"

The way that he said it made me think he didn't know Needles had been murdered. It made sense. If Igor didn't know, maybe Blaine didn't either. My guess was that Angela Shinn was keeping her husband's death on the down low. I wanted to know why.

It made me realize that I had seen basically next to nothing as far as media coverage of Needles' death. I'd found an article in the online edition of *The San Francisco Chronicle,* but that was it. Nothing on the news. Not that every murder in the Bay Area had to be covered, but if someone took a bullet to the brain, you'd think the media would give it a little airplay.

It only furthered my opinion that something was fishy.

"Did you know that he is deceased as well?" I asked.

He shook his head in disbelief.

"You're kidding. Two dead from our little marina down here."

"Yup. And Needles was murdered as well."

I had no explanation as to why I'd told Blaine this news but not Igor. It just seemed right to tell him in the moment.

"Jeez. You're just a barrel of good news, Quint."

I smiled, in spite of myself.

"I'm sorry."

"Don't sweat it. So, let me guess. You're trying to figure out if these two murders were related?"

"It certainly crossed my mind," I said.

"Shit, it just crossed mine and I found out about it ten seconds ago."

"How well did you know Needles?"

"Not very. We'd say our pleasantries when we saw each other on the dock. I think I met his wife once as they were getting on his boat."

His wife. The one, the only. Angela Shinn.

"You'd exchange pleasantries? I was told that Needles wasn't the friendliest guy on the dock. That he'd walk right in the middle, forcing people to wait until he passed."

"Let me guess. You've talked to Igor. That guy loves to gossip."

I'd found the same to be true but didn't want to break Igor's trust.

"No, it was other people around the docks."

Blaine smiled.

"Sure, Quint. I believe you."

I wanted to change the subject from Igor.

"So, you and Needles were affable?"

"Well, I wasn't going to invite him out to dinner, but we were cordial enough."

"Do you know if he and Henry ever talked?"

"It would be hard not to with their boats this close. Maybe it was just "Hi" and "Bye" though."

"So you never saw them having a long conversation?"

"No. Sorry if that's what you were expecting to get from me."

"I don't know what I was expecting," I said honestly. "It doesn't sound like Henry had an enemy in the world. None of this makes any sense."

"Maybe he was killed in the crossfire."

"Getting strangled while alone on your own boat hardly sounds like crossfire," I said.

"That's not what I mean. Maybe he saw or heard something he shouldn't have. The crossfire of other people's wrongdoings. That's what I'm suggesting."

It made some sense. Maybe Henry saw Needles doing something illegal on the docks and whoever killed Needles felt it necessary to take out Henry as well. It was as good a theory as any.

"Maybe you should be the P.I."

Blaine laughed.

"Too much work. I prefer hanging out on my boat."

"Are you taking it out today?"

"I wanted to, but the seas are going to be rough this morning. I'm waiting to get a better report before heading out."

"Do you go out alone?"

"Usually. Sometimes I'll take out my wife or some friends, but that's never as peaceful as when I go it alone."

"I hear that," I said.

"How is Henry's daughter taking this?" he asked. "I know he just had the one kid."

"It's hard on her. I'm hoping to give her closure if possible."

"Closure won't bring her father back."

"I know, but if you had a family member murdered, wouldn't it drive you nuts knowing the killer was out there roaming around free?"

"Yeah, I guess it would. I didn't mean to be combative."

"Don't worry about it," I said. "I'm just trying to protect her."

I didn't like what I'd said. It sounded too personal; like we were a couple.

"You know, from one friend to another," I said.

I was making things worse. It was time to change the subject.

"Did you and Henry ever do anything outside of the marina?" I asked.

"We probably went out and had dinner or drinks about six or seven times over the years. So no, we weren't super tight, but we always had fun when we were together."

"Henry liked his beers."

"He sure did. And if you're including the days where I either had beers on his boat or he had beers on mine, then we are talking about thirty-plus times. Maybe we were closer than I even realized."

"I wish I could have a beer with him one more time."

"I do too, Quint."

No one said anything as we both took a few seconds to think about our friend.

"So, how is your investigation going?"

"Calling it an investigation is almost giving it too much credit."

"What do you mean?" he asked.

"Well, I've talked to like five or six people, but I'm literally stuck in first gear."

"You have to start somewhere."

"True. But I hope to move into second gear before too long."

"Touché. Look, I'm sorry I couldn't add much to the mix. Henry was a good guy. None of this makes any sense."

"I've told myself that fifty times."

Blaine was a nice guy, but this conversation wasn't going anywhere.

"I appreciate your time," I said.

"Next visit, swing by sometime after noon. Any time after that is beer o'clock for me."

"Consider it done. Thanks, Blaine."

"Good luck, Quint."

I walked back up the dock, said a quick goodbye to Igor, and headed toward my car.

CHAPTER 10

I knew within five seconds of our dinner at Tom and Krissy's that they were going to be on their best behavior.

As I re-introduced them to Sophie, neither one made a comment like, *'Nice to see you guys back together'* or *'You guys are such a cute couple.'* Considering her father had been murdered, it would have been in bad taste, but Tom Butler liked to poke buttons, so I wasn't putting anything past him.

It was the warmest night of the year thus far and we had dinner in their backyard.

Sophie wore a casual blue dress with a white jacket. Sure, it was warming up, but it was still April, and a jacket made sense. Krissy was in an orange dress and both Tom and I had on khakis and a dress shirt. Sophie had thought we looked good. Possibly over-dressed for a home-cooked meal, but Sophie hadn't seen them in years and wanted us to look good.

There was the expected small talk for the first twenty minutes of the dinner. Our initial dish had been served: a delicious cream of asparagus soup.

As we began to eat, Tom broke up the small talk.

"Sophie, I just wanted to let you know that we will do anything we can to help catch Henry's killer. If you want us to publish a story about it or if you want me to lean on some people I know at the *East Bay Times*, I'm a phone call away. Obviously, you're in good hands with Quint, but if we can play a part ourselves, just give me the word."

"Thanks, Tom. I can't think of anything at the moment, but I'll let you know if something comes up."

I was pretty sure Sophie and I were the only ones who knew about Henry's fax. I certainly hadn't told anyone, and as much as I trusted and respected Tom and Krissy, I wouldn't break Sophie's trust. It would have to be her who brought it up.

"Have you made any progress on the case, Quint?" Krissy asked me.

"I've been talking to a lot of people and a few have been helpful, but nothing even approaching a smoking gun yet."

"Any suspects?"

"No."

"Well, we have faith in you, Quint," Tom said. "It's still really early on."

A few minutes later, Krissy took our soup bowls. We offered to help, but she said she had it under control. She returned ten minutes later with our entree: Mushroom Risotto.

As she set our bowls down, she answered the question we were all thinking about.

"So, I cheated a little bit. There's this Ina Garten recipe for Risotto where most of the time you are cooking the rice in the oven and then you finish it in the pan. That's how I was able to finish up a risotto in ten minutes."

"I thought you were just a magician in the kitchen," Tom said.

"I'm reminded of *My Cousin Vinny*," I said. "They put someone on the stand who says he can cook grits in ten minutes. His fellow Southerners shake their heads in disbelief."

I got a few courtesy smiles, but I don't think any of them got my reference.

"It looks delicious, Krissy," Sophie said.

It really did. The steam was coming up from the plate and there was a little parmesan cheese on top that was melting in real-time.

We all waited a solid minute until we took a bite. The steam served as our little warning.

I raised the spoon to my mouth first and blew on it for just a brief second. I'd be the guinea pig, but I didn't want to be the guinea pig with a burnt tongue.

It was excellent and I told Krissy so.

"Thanks, Quint."

Sophie and Tom followed me in taking a bite.

"Wow!" Sophie exclaimed. "It honestly tastes better than when people spend forty-five minutes stirring the rice themselves. I want this recipe."

"You got it, Sophie."

It was a mutual admiration society but not unfounded. The risotto was top-notch.

No one spoke for the next minute or so as we savored the gourmet meal in front of us.

"It's delicious, honey," Tom said to his wife.

Sophie took a quick glance at me. She didn't have to say a word. I knew what she was thinking: That Tom and Krissy still had a great marriage after all these years.

She ran with it.

"What's your secret to a long, happy marriage?" Sophie asked, to neither one in particular.

"Good food, good wine, good sex, and some good alone time," Krissy answered.

Sophie laughed.

"I'm glad you added the last part. You were laying it on pretty thick."

"It's true though. Alone time matters."

"It gives me relationship goals. More time away from Quint."

Krissy laughed quite loudly.

Tom had a nefarious little smile. I knew he was going to jump at the chance. He'd been so good all night, but the devil on his shoulder made his first appearance.

He pointed to the both of us.

"Is that what this is?" he asked. "A relationship?"

"We're in the early stages and not ready to label it yet," Sophie said and grabbed my hand before continuing. "And it's not like we left on bad terms the first time. It's almost like we just took a long break."

"You guys were such a cute couple," Krissy said. "Sophie, you look the exact same. Quint, you've got a few gray hairs now, but you're still aging like a fine red wine."

"What gray hair?" I said and put my hands on the hair above my ears; the only place my grays showed up.

"It happens to the best of us. Father Time is undefeated," Tom said.

"You look to be holding it at bay," I said to him.

Krissy jumped in.

"That hair dye Touch of Grey deserves an assist as well."

We all laughed.

"Shots fired," I said.

"The truth comes out," Sophie added.

"Guilty as charged," Tom said. "You'd asked about the keys to a good marriage earlier. Having a wife who busts your balls and keeps you on your toes always adds a little spice."

"I'm nothing if not spicy."

Tom and Krissy had invited me and Sophie over in hopes of getting a little info on how our relationship stood. It had turned into a study of why they had lasted so long together.

We were all winding down on our risotto.

"How's your guys' appetite doing? I've got dessert all lined up, but I promise it's a very small portion."

I was starting to get full, not that I would ever tell Krissy that.

"Can't wait," Sophie said.

It turned out to be something called an Angel Pia which tasted boozier than the wine we were drinking. It was a combination of eggs, sugar, vanilla, cream, and some sort of booze. I was guessing it was rum.

She also brought coffee to the table.

"That was the perfect size," Sophie said and I half expected a *'That's what she said'* from Tom, but he held his tongue.

"You liked it?" Krissy asked.

"What's not to like? A great dessert with a hint of alcohol," Sophie said.

"A hint?" Tom interjected. "Yeah, like Lenny Bruce's stand-up had a hint of satire."

"Are you trying to age yourself with Lenny Bruce references?" Krissy asked.

Sophie grabbed my hand and smiled brightly. We were having a blast.

And Krissy wasn't done.

"What, were Atilla the Hun jokes not on the bingo card? They are about as current as Lenny Bruce ones."

Sophie spoke next.

"Whatever age-reversing qualities Touch of Grey gives you gets nullified by Lenny Bruce references."

We all laughed. Tom spit up a little of his water.

"I can't top that," he said.

"Not today, not ever," his wife chimed in.

~

We stayed for about fifteen more minutes and thanked them immensely before we left. Tom and Krissy had us promise to do it again in two weeks and we agreed. We'd had a blast, it's not like they had to twist our arms.

As I drove Sophie and myself home that night - and we reminisced on the evening - it certainly felt like we were starting to become a couple again.

I was happy about it; I mean there was no doubt I was falling for her a second time around.

~

After Sophie left the following morning, I wasn't sure where I wanted to head with the investigation.

The most obvious lead was Needles, but if I confronted his wife again, she'd probably call the cops. That's not what I wanted.

Or was it?

I know what Henry had said in the fax, but maybe ruffling some feathers was exactly what I needed.

~

Approaching Angela Shinn at her front door a second time wasn't advisable, so I came up with an alternative plan.

I parked my car outside of her house at 8:30. I hoped she was a morning person and would head out to the store/gym/bank before long. I was willing to sit there all day if I had to, but that sure wouldn't be ideal.

By 10:30, I started cursing myself. She hadn't left.

I called the Shinn's house line and when she answered, I hung up, but at least I knew she was there.

Mercifully, at 11:23, the garage door opened and she backed out into the street. Once she got to the end of the block, I pulled out and started following.

If Needles and his wife had been involved in some money-making scheme, she hadn't spent it on a new car. She was driving a Buick straight out of the 1990s. And I don't mean vintage and cool. I mean old and dirty.

She drove slowly and it was easy to keep my distance without fear of losing her. She put her blinker on way too early and was a passive driver. If I hadn't known better, I might have assumed she was a nice, polite, older woman; the polar opposite of the nasty woman who took a picture of my driver's license.

After about eight minutes of tailing her, she made her way into the parking lot of a Trader Joe's. This was perfect. If she'd gone to a salon or a bank or something a bit more private, it would have been tougher to approach her. A big grocery store would be easy.

I let her walk in first and then followed a minute later. I grabbed a shopping cart and put a few ingredients in it. She probably wouldn't believe this meeting was random, but I at least wanted to make it look as if it was.

I pounced when I saw the opportunity. She was in the corner of the store looking at some pre-marinated pork tenderloins. No one was within ten feet of her. That may not sound like much, but in a Trader Joe's, that's about the most alone space you're going to get.

She saw me approaching and after a second for it to click, she started shaking her head in disgust.

"Wow, this is some wild coincidence," I said.

"I doubt that," she muttered.

"Why would you doubt that? This is my favorite TJ's in all of the Bay Area."

"I heard you lived in Walnut Creek."

She'd been studying up on me.

"You're making my point. Why else would I travel this far if this wasn't the best TJ's in a twenty-mile radius."

She didn't enjoy my rationale.

"What do you want?" she asked.

Her face told me she just wanted to get the hell out of there.

"Actually, I want one of those pork tenderloins you're staring at."

My sarcasm was once again lost on her.

"I mean, what do you want with me?"

"I have no idea what you're talking about. As I said, this is just a random coincidence."

She said nothing so I continued.

"You know what a coincidence is, right? It's like when two men are killed who both had boats docked within fifty yards of each other. That would be a big coincidence. So big, in fact, that people might not even buy it. They'd think their deaths were likely related."

Her eyes turned steely.

"What the fuck do you want?"

I almost rattled off a few other Trader Joe's items, but the time for sarcasm had passed.

"I want to know why a woman whose husband was murdered is being so standoffish to a man who is trying to find out why he was killed."

I used standoffish instead of several other dirtier words that were more warranted.

"Maybe I'm scared."

"Of me?"

"Of the people who don't like you out there investigating."

This put a new wrinkle on things, if true. She was trying to pretend she was the victim. I wasn't buying it. Not yet, anyway.

"And who might that be?" I asked.

She let out a wry smile.

"You're so out of your league. Go back to Tee-Ball. This is the major leagues."

"See, when you say things like that it makes it hard to take your whole '*I'm the victim*' act seriously."

"Believe what you want, Quint who lives on 1716 North Main Street."

It sounded very much like a threat.

And it only got worse.

"Did you follow me from my house?" she asked. "Maybe I'll have someone follow you from outside your place. Would you like that? I think I could make that happen."

"You're sounding less and less like a grieving wife."

"Think whatever the fuck you want, but I loved Needles."

A woman with her young son had closed to within about five feet of us and looked in Angela's direction when she dropped the F-bomb.

"Clean up your language," the woman said. "I've got a child with me."

"Fuck him and fuck you," she said.

I was taken aback, and that wasn't easy considering how she'd acted to this point.

"And fuck you too!" she yelled at me.

With that, she left her full shopping cart and started walking briskly toward the door.

"She seemed nice," the woman said, and I couldn't help but burst out in laughter.

CHAPTER 11

Sophie and I went out on the town Friday night.

I'm not saying it was earth-shattering news, but with the exception of going to Tom and Krissy's, we'd mostly just hung out in my apartment. I wasn't sure if that was due to the convenience of my place or whether subconsciously, we weren't ready to be seen out in public, basically admitting that we were together.

I'd suggested walking around Walnut Creek and maybe grabbing a bite. She'd eaten before coming over so we agreed on a cup of coffee and a shared dessert.

La Scala was a coffee shop that was a few blocks from my apartment. I frequented it regularly.

We each got a respective Americano and split a Tiramisu. The plate sat in the middle of us and we took alternate turns digging in with our forks. It felt like something a couple would do. Was that what we slowly - er, quickly - were becoming? Had become?

As usual, Sophie read my mind.

"Sharing food is pretty intimate, don't you think?" she asked.

"Agreed. Especially dessert."

"You're right. Not sure why that is."

"Dessert means you're close to finishing up and going home together. It's more romantic than sharing a charcuterie board."

"That sounds like some made-up bullshit," Sophie said and laughed. "But I like it!"

"Watch. Next time we'll share a charcuterie board and see if you find it romantic when I'm reaching over you to grab a piece of salami. Plot twist: The answer is no."

Sophie started laughing and a few patrons looked over at us. We were having a really nice time. We'd proven that we were compatible - and then some - in bed, but being out on the town felt somehow different.

"You know what?" Sophie asked.

"What?"

"I don't want to hear anything about your investigation when we get back to your place. We can do that on Tuesday. And Tuesdays going forward. Fridays will be our days to hang out without the burden of talking about my Dad."

"If that's what you want," I said.

She leaned over and kissed me on the lips.

"It is," she said.

Maybe I had a recency bias, but I couldn't remember the last time I'd had this much fun on a date. Sure, I'd dated Cara off and on for several years, but it was never this romantic. There was always a little tension between us. I felt at ease with Sophie. We had better playfulness.

"Are you sure we're going to find things to do at my place without talking about my investigation?"

Sophie smiled seductively at my leading question.

"Oh, I can think of a few things. I'm going to rock your world."

If this was a movie, this would have been the moment I'd have yelled, 'Check, please!'

I did the real-life equivalent, grabbing Sophie's hand, and leading her out the door and toward my apartment.

∾

The next morning - after Sophie left - I exited my apartment and headed toward my office. Last night had definitely been a turning point in our relationship. We acted - and felt - like a couple. It was now full steam ahead.

As I approached my office, I realized I hadn't been there in several days. I'd been spending so much time on Henry's case that I'd put my other cases on the back burner. It made me ponder why I even paid rent in the first place. I could always meet potential clients at a coffee shop if need be.

Look at Mickey Haller, the eponymous character in Michael Connelly's *The Lincoln Lawyer*. He worked out of his Lincoln Town Car. I could do the same with my car. Although I had to admit, *The Camry P.I.* didn't have quite the same ring to it as *The Lincoln Lawyer*.

The reason I went to the office on this day was to spend some time on my other two active cases. I'd been neglecting them. Yes, Henry's death was far more important to me, but these people had paid me. Not that I was overcharging or committing any malfeasance, but it was still a bad look. I vowed to spend more time on them in the coming days.

I grabbed my mail, entered my office, and took a seat at my desk. There were three messages on the office phone. I gave every client my cell number and told them that was the easier way to get ahold of me, but not every client remembered that, and I still got the occasional call on the office line.

I clicked play on the answering machine.

"Is this Quaint Ladder? If so, contact us at 888-828-8282 to collect your grand prize."

I quickly pressed the fast forward button although I suddenly wanted to buy a racehorse and name him Quaint Ladder. That may have been my new favorite way in which my name had been butchered. I'd gotten some interesting spellings of my first name at coffee shops over the years, but the last name elevated this one.

The second message also told me I'd won a prize. I was killing it this morning.

The final message proved to be altogether different and it left me in a rotten mood.

"Quint, this is Gary Howard. I hired you to find my wedding ring. I know you said to call you on your cell phone, so that's exactly why I called you on this line. I was hoping that you wouldn't answer. I wanted to tell you that you're fired. I read a little article in our local paper that you're investigating the death of a friend of yours. Is that why you haven't called me with an update in three days? That's terribly rude. I hired you because I thought we'd interact daily with any progress. That's been far from the case. Your mind is elsewhere, and for that reason, you're freaking fired! If you haven't worked the hours we outlined in our first meeting, please mail me the remainder of my down payment. Goodbye."

I sat back in my chair and cursed myself. He wasn't wrong. I'd spent way too much time on Henry's case. I had my reasons, but that didn't excuse me for effectively just tossing aside my other two cases.

The call didn't hurt because he was yelling at me with great vitriol. It hurt because he was right.

I beat myself up for another minute and then remembered he'd said there was an article about me in his local paper.

That's just what I needed. In a case where I was supposed to be laying low, I was now having articles written about me.

I googled my name and the article popped up immediately.

It was in the *East Bay Times,* not exactly some small-time newspaper. It had a large following. The other *Times* covered Contra Costa and Alameda Counties. The Berkeley Marina was located in Alameda County so I guess that's why they ran the article. I started reading. It was written by a man named Dexter Lund.

"Quint Adler, the reporter turned P.I., is at it again. The man responsible for catching The Bay Area Butcher, Leonard Rolle, and a few others, is now looking for the person responsible for Henry Madsen's murder. Who is Henry Madsen, you may be asking? He worked with Quint at The Walnut Creek Times many moons ago and apparently, the two were friends. From what I've been able to gather, Henry died a savage death aboard his boat docked at the Berkeley Marina. You may remember that's

where Quint first received attention, killing Charles Zane in a battle to the death out at sea.

Quint's cases are never boring, so I'll be keeping an eye on this one. Keep reading right here for more details as they come in."

"FUCK," I yelled at the top of my lungs.

I'd been hit by a stiff left jab by Gary Howard and then an overhand right by Dexter Lund.

The first I deserved. The second came out of nowhere.

Who the hell alerted this Dexter Lund that I was asking around? Angela Shinn was my first suspect, but there were several other possibilities.

However he found out the information, nothing good would come of this.

"At least he didn't refer to me as Quaint Ladder," I said, trying to get myself to laugh.

It worked.

CHAPTER 12

The next morning I returned to my office, assuming it couldn't have been any worse than the previous day.

I was wrong.

Hanging on my front door was a pinned piece of printer paper. I took it off and started reading it once I got inside.

"Quint,

Stop investigating this case. If not, you and Henry's daughter - or, should I say, your girlfriend - will not be long for this world.

Consider this your first and final warning.

You won't see us coming next time."

I read the note a second time, hoping to recognize anything that stood out; something that might lead me in the direction of who possibly could have written this.

I found nothing. It was printed out - not handwritten - so that made it nameless and faceless.

What clearly stood out was the author referring to Sophie as my girlfriend. Who knew that? Tom and Krissy were the only people. I hadn't even told my mother yet.

Sophie and I had held hands the other night when we went to La Scala. If we were being followed, they easily could have seen that. I don't remember seeing anyone outside of my apartment complex when we stepped out, but who knows...I wasn't exactly looking for one.

And then I remembered what Angela Shinn had said. Something to the effect that she might hire someone to follow me.

I wouldn't put it past her, but would she then write a letter and include the information about me and Sophie? That didn't seem too smart. No, Angela Shinn wasn't a rocket scientist, but I don't think she'd want to be so easily identified as the person who wrote the letter.

I racked my brain. No one else came to mind. I'd call Tom and Krissy and make sure they hadn't told anyone. It's possible they could have said it in passing to someone at *The Walnut Creek Times,* but unlikely. And even then, how would it get back to the people or person who killed Henry?

The other possibility was that Sophie told a friend, but the question still stood: How did it get back to the killer or killers?

I had to call Sophie. This was not going to be easy, but it would be wrong to wait until I saw her tomorrow. She had been specifically threatened. She had to know now.

She answered on the second ring.

"Hey, Quint."

"I have a question, Sophie."

"Shoot."

"Have you told anybody about us?"

"No one."

"Not even in passing? Maybe a quick reference to meeting up with me that someone might have misconstrued?"

"No."

"You're sure?"

"Quint, I haven't told a single person about us," she said forcefully. "Why?"

Here came the tough part.

I grabbed the letter.

"I received this letter a few minutes ago. It was pinned to the front door of my office."

I proceeded to read it.

After an agonizing ten seconds, she responded.

"I just had a shiver go up my spine. This isn't good."

"No, it's not."

"I'm assuming you asked Tom and Krissy if they told anyone?"

"I called you first. They are next."

"It had to be them. I know it wasn't me and I'm assuming it wasn't you."

"I haven't told a soul."

"How about the other night when we went to that cafe?"

"That's a possibility. I don't remember anyone looking at us suspiciously."

"Were you looking out for that?"

"No," I admitted, having already considered it.

"If that's how they knew, that means people are following us around. That makes it even scarier."

"Without question."

"What should we do? I'm sure they know where you live, but what about me?"

I hated having this conversation and especially how it was affecting Sophie. I just wanted to give her a hug, but I couldn't.

"Let me think about it. Would you consider moving in with me until this is over?"

"Are you sure it's not safer for me to stay out this way and not hang out with you?"

That stung. She was right, of course. Staying away from me was the smarter decision.

"That might be for the best, " I conceded. "This is so fucked up,"

"Maybe it's time to go to the cops, Quint. It's possible my father was mistaken about their part in this."

"He was pretty adamant."

"True."

An idea came to me.

"Can I call you back in thirty?"

"Sure. We're going to be alright, right Quint?"

"Of course, Sophie."

What else was I going to say?

I immediately called Tom and he denied telling anyone that me and Sophie were a thing. He said he'd ask Krissy, but he was sure she'd said nothing.

That's what I'd expected.

I hung up with Tom and immediately called Paddy Roark.

"Quint, how the hell are you?"

He always seemed to answer the phone the same way.

"I need a favor and it's a big one."

"Then you better tell me what it is before I say yes."

"I'd like to talk to one of the cops that you trust implicitly."

"That is a big ask," he conceded. "That doesn't mean I can't make it happen."

"The sooner the better, Paddy. I was threatened this morning along with a woman who matters greatly to me."

There was no use trying to avoid the issue of me and Sophie. The cat was out of the bag.

"I'll get on it and call you back as soon as I can."

"Thank you, Paddy. I owe you one."

"You may owe us two for this one."

"Two it is," I said.

I left my office and went home.

I sat on my couch, turned on some jazz, - my favorite album of all time, Miles Davis's *Kind of Blue* - and waited for Paddy's call.

It didn't come for almost two hours.

"Hey," I answered.

"Do you have a pen on you?"

I grabbed one from the desk in front of me.

"Yeah."

"Take down this address. 1919 41st Avenue. San Francisco. My friend's name is Lefty. Used to be a southpaw pitcher and the name stuck. Just pretend he doesn't have a last name and don't try to find it out. He'll meet you tonight at 6 o'clock at his house. Don't be late."

"I won't. Thank you very much, Paddy."

"Stay safe, Quint. You've got me a little worried."

I was about to respond when I noticed that Paddy had already hung up.

1919 41st Avenue was in the Sunset District, meaning I had quite the trek ahead of me. Luckily, driving into the city at five p.m. was going against traffic, but I couldn't risk being late, so I'd leave Walnut Creek by 4:45.

I arrived at 5:45 and found a parking spot relatively quickly, not always easy to do in San Francisco. I was told not to be late, but I also didn't want to knock on his door fifteen minutes early. I listened to sports talk radio for several minutes before leaving my car and approaching his door.

I knocked and he opened it so quickly I was sure he was just on the other side of it.

"You must be Quint," he said. "Call me Lefty."

He extended his hand and I shook it. I'm a pretty big guy, but he could have taken my hand off if he wanted.

"Nice to meet you," I said.

Lefty was of average height but built like a tank. He wore glasses and looked both bookish and intimidating; not an easy thing to do. He had blondish/reddish hair that was cut short on the sides.

"Come on in," he said.

I walked into a small house. It was two stories, but extremely narrow. The house was probably taller than it was wide.

Lefty motioned to a couch and I took a seat. He sat across from me. No offer of water or coffee. He was ready to get down to business.

"Our mutual friend Paddy tells me that you've found yourself in a sticky situation. Again."

I was surprised he'd included the last word.

"Paddy told me I had to add that," Lefty said.

I laughed.

"That sounds like him. That darn Irish sense of humor."

"Indeed. I'm Irish as well. So what exactly led you here? He didn't tell me much else."

"Does the name Henry Madsen ring a bell?" I asked.

"I don't think so. Should it?"

He was killed in Berkeley, so it wasn't the SFPD's jurisdiction. There was really no reason Lefty should have heard of Henry.

"He was a friend of mine who was strangled on his boat at the Berkeley Marina."

"I'm sorry. I do remember hearing something about it."

"And I'm a P.I. so I decided to start investigating."

"I know who you are. Continue."

"I've interviewed probably six or seven people close to the case. Most of them have been candid or, at least, polite."

"Who wasn't?"

I'd wanted to avoid talking about Needles and Frank the poker player.

I gave myself a few seconds to think. If I wasn't willing to discuss the whole case, then why the hell was I even here? If I was going to trust Paddy's guy, I had to trust him implicitly.

Plus, excluding Needle's wife wouldn't give Lefty the full range of suspects. It would be a half-hearted meeting on my part. I had to tell him everything.

"Alright, here's the thing."

I spent the next several minutes describing everyone I'd met and included the three deaths that I believed were connected. I told him about my run-ins with Angela Shinn. I even told Lefty that I'd become romantically involved with Sophie.

I finished by reading him the letter left outside my office.

"Someone's got a hard-on for you," he said.

"I know. Wish I wasn't so damn desirable."

Lefty smiled, which I took as a win considering he was a no-nonsense type of guy.

"Who knew that you and Sophie were a thing?"

I mentioned Tom and Krissy.

"No one else?"

"We didn't tell anyone else, but obviously, someone found out."

"Any guesses?"

"No. Except that, it's someone who wants this case to go away."

"I'd say that's a safe guess."

"One other thing I'd forgotten to mention. There was a small article written about me yesterday that said I'm out investigating this case."

"Whoever leaked that wants the opposite of whoever left the letter."

It took me a second to realize what he meant.

"The letter is hoping this case will go away," I said. "The article hopes to prolong it."

"You're pretty smart for a P.I.," Lefty said.

"And you are, for a cop."

He laughed. Maybe he was more down-to-earth than I'd given him credit for.

"You're lucky that Paddy and Dennis like you. They wouldn't come to ask me to help just anyone."

"They are good guys. I'm glad to have them on my side," I said.

"You should be. Now, what exactly do you want from me?"

"As I said, Henry didn't want me to talk to the cops. I would, however, love to get my hands on the police reports of the three murders."

"Isn't it two murders and an assumed drowning?"

"Maybe the police reports say that. It's not what I think," I said.

"This really is a big ask, Quint. I don't have jurisdiction over these deaths. They all took place in Berkeley. And it's not that easy to just ask a fellow cop for a police report without other people finding out."

"You said not easy, you didn't say impossible…"

I'd had a similar discussion earlier that day with Paddy, and he'd also called it a '*big ask*.'

"No, I didn't."

I didn't interrupt, waiting for him to continue.

"You're going to have to give me a few days."

"No problem," I said.

"And I'd suggest trying to lay low. If you're right and three people were murdered, you're dealing with a seriously fucked up person. Or people. And look after that woman of yours."

"I will."

"That's smart. Paddy gave me your number. I'll call you once I know more."

"Thank you, Lefty."

"Stay safe."

I'd heard that too many times lately.

I left my meeting with Lefty and went over our conversation in my head.

One thing stuck out.

He'd said that whoever gave the information to the reporter was hoping to keep this case afloat. They didn't want it lost in the vast array of crimes committed since Henry's death. They didn't want it relegated to the back pages or not in the news at all.

If Lefty was right - and I reckoned he was - I needed to find out who told Dexter Lund that I was investigating the case. It wasn't any of the "bad guys", whoever they were. The last thing they wanted was for this case to seep into the public's conscience. Thus far, Henry's murder had stayed pretty low-profile, which is exactly how they'd want it to remain.

It was time to meet with Dexter Lund.

It's highly unlikely he'd disclose his sources, but that doesn't mean I wasn't going to give it the old college try.

CHAPTER 13

I didn't have to travel far the following morning.

The *East Bay Times* was located in Walnut Creek. When I was at *The Walnut Creek Times*, we used to butt heads with their reporters from time to time. They were the more well-known, established paper and we were treated as the red-headed stepchild, or the middle child, or any other childhood stereotype that you wanted to use.

This sometimes led to confrontations if both papers' reporters showed up at the same story/crime scene. They got better coverage, more access to the police, etc. so we had to work just a little harder to get our story.

To go back to the childhood stereotype game, maybe we just had a bit of the little brother syndrome. Whatever it was, I had no love lost for the *East Bay Times*.

They were located on California Boulevard, within walking distance from my apartment, so I set out on foot. They leased a portion of a gigantic white building that sat yards away from one of the Bay Area Rapid Transit (BART) stops.

I walked in and was greeted by a secretary who had a snarl on her face. I could already tell that she hated her job.

"Can I help you?"

"Yeah, I'm here to see Dexter Lund."

She looked down at what was likely her calendar.

"Do you have an appointment? Cause I don't see one here."

And we were off.

"I don't, but he's going to be excited to see me."

The snarl only got bigger. The corners of her lips quickly went downward like they were the opposite of Salvador Dali's mustache.

"Why is that?" she asked, with all the enthusiasm of a salt shaker.

"Because he mentioned me in a recent article and now he gets to ask me some questions in the flesh."

My odd answer had befuddled her.

"Uh, hold on a minute," she said.

I could tell she was considering calling Dexter Lund on her phone, but likely didn't want me to overhear it.

Instead, she walked back through a large glass door. You could see people rummaging around and for a brief moment, I missed working for a newspaper. Because of the camaraderie more than anything else. Yes, I interviewed people all the time, but being a P.I. was often a solitary job. Working at a newspaper was anything but that. You were talking to friends every day, often all day. As a P.I., there were many days when I didn't talk to a single friend.

Miss Congeniality returned a minute later. That was my new nickname for her.

"Mr. Lund is willing to meet with you," she said.

"Should I just walk in?" I asked.

"No, please wait here. He's going to come out here and help you get in."

"Oh, thank god. Not sure I could have opened that big glass door all by myself."

I was being a jerk, but Miss Congeniality had brought it on.

"You must be quite the catch," she said to me.

I laughed.

I generally had a pretty mellow demeanor but had never been

one to run from a fight, either. I know those sounded like competing personality traits, but it worked for me.

And it's not like I wanted to get into a verbal sparring match with my new best friend, but here we were.

"My smoking hot girlfriend sure seems to think so," I said, despite knowing Sophie would have been embarrassed - and likely not impressed - by my comment.

Miss Congeniality just waved her hand at me, like she was shooing a fly away.

Dexter Lund walked through the front door and saved the two of us from continuing to act like children.

"Quint Adler, in the flesh," he said. "It's great to meet you. You're something of a local legend. Follow me."

I stopped one last time at the front desk before following him in.

"See, I'm a local legend," I said and gave Miss Congeniality a wink.

I was behaving like an infant, and honestly, kind of loved it.

Dexter Lund had jeans on, a black t-shirt, and bright orange glasses. He was certainly making a fashion statement with those. He led me to a cramped office with barely enough room for a desk and two chairs.

As much as I missed working for a newspaper, the digs weren't always the best.

"Sit down," he said.

I did.

"So what brings you here, Mr. Adler? I'm assuming it's because of my recent article."

"Call me Quint," I said. "And yes, it is."

"Is there something in the article that you are taking issue with?"

"No, nothing like that. I wanted to know how you knew I was investigating Henry Madsen's death."

"I've done a little reading up on you. You used to work for *The Walnut Creek Times*, correct?"

"That's right."

I knew where this was going.

"And were you in the habit of outing your sources?"

"No, obviously not."

"But you want me to out mine? Doesn't seem all that fair now, does it?"

I hadn't liked the *East Bay Times* before I stepped into their headquarters today. Miss Congeniality and Mr. Lund were only making it worse.

"I understand," I said. "But…"

I paused. As much as I wanted to tell Dexter Lund that I'd been threatened in hopes of learning his source, I couldn't give him that information. He'd run with it and that would be the topic of his next article. I couldn't do that to Sophie.

I decided to use a different strategy.

"What if I gave you an exclusive once this all comes to a conclusion?"

"What exactly is 'this all'?"

"Finding out who killed Henry," I said, keeping it as minimal as possible.

He didn't answer for several seconds.

"The offer still stands. An exclusive once it's over," I repeated.

He thought it over. Lund would sell out, I had no doubt about that. How much he would benefit would be the tipping point.

"How about an exclusive right now?" he asked. "You can tell me all the things you've learned about this case. And btw, I didn't post everything I could have. I heard you interviewed a few other people about someone else who was murdered."

That piqued my interest.

"Why did you withhold that?"

"A request from the person who gave me the initial information."

This was getting weirder and weirder. Why would someone do that?

"Do you know why?"

"I'm sure he has his reasons, but he didn't tell me."

"So it was a he?"

Dexter Lund smiled for the first time.

"You're good, Quint."

"Thanks. Does that mean you are going to give me the name of your source?"

He smiled again, but this time it was more of a painstaking effort.

"No, it doesn't mean that. And you never answered my question. Can I get an exclusive right now?"

"And for that, you'd give me your source?"

"Yes."

I pondered the offer. Obviously, I wouldn't be giving up everything I'd learned. I could just give him a few morsels. Was it worth it?

I needed to stall.

"What happened to never giving up your source?" I asked.

"Are you sure that's the best strategy? Pissing off the guy who might help you?"

I wasn't a fan of Dexter Lund. He was squirrelly. His eyes darting, his arms constantly moving. I don't know if he was on something or if it was just his personality. Either way, it wasn't charming. Quite the opposite.

"Point taken," I said.

No one said anything for a minute. He knew I was considering his offer.

Could I use this to my benefit by planting something in the article that would help me out in some way?

One part of my brain was telling me to turn down his offer. Anything that brought more attention to this case was a bad thing for me. And Sophie.

The other part told me that someone out there might be vital to helping this case move forward and it was important I knew who.

"Quint..."

"I'm thinking. Give me thirty seconds."

I finally realized what my answer was going to be. It had been staring me in the face, but I hadn't been able to see it. This guy was willing to sell out one of his sources and it had only taken a few minutes for him to get there. How could I ever trust a man like him?

"My answer is no," I said.

"What a tease."

I could have told him the real reason but decided against it. I might need Dexter Lund at a later time and didn't want to risk offending him.

It was then that I noticed him doing something with his right hand. I couldn't see below the table, but he was looking down to his right side and moving his right hand. The asshole was recording me! I jumped up from my chair and walked around to his side. Sure enough, he had his phone on and I could see the red button that signified something was being recorded.

"You're a piece of shit," I said.

I lunged for the phone.

"Security!" he yelled at the top of his lungs. "Security!"

He turned around and put his phone in a tiny safe he had directly behind him, shutting the door behind it.

There was nothing I could do.

I looked up and saw a bear of a man headed toward Dexter Lund's office.

"You really are scum," I said.

"Check out my next article. I'm sure you'll be the featured player."

"I take it back. You're lower than scum."

Bear, the Security Guard, entered the office.

"Is there something wrong, Dexter?"

"I'd like you to show this asshole to the door."

I was already going to be "featured" in Lund's next article. I didn't need a separate article talking about me fighting with a security guard at the *East Bay Times*. Especially a fight I was inevitably going to lose.

"I don't need any help. I'm leaving right now," I said.

Dexter Lund had a smile from ear to ear.

"I'd say come back any time," he said. "But you're persona non grata here, asshole!"

"We'll be seeing each other again," I said.

"That sounded like a threat to a member of the media. I might have to add that to my article."

I knew it would be best to keep my mouth shut going forward. I walked toward the door, raising my hands to show Bear that I wasn't going to do anything.

He followed me as I walked through the office and out the door, all eyes in the office upon me.

The last face I saw was Miss Congeniality who had a raised middle finger waiting for me.

Yup, it was one of those types of days.

CHAPTER 14

The following morning it hit me like a ton of bricks.

There was one other person who might have assumed that Sophie and I were dating.

In my conversation with Blaine Travers, I'd slipped and made a couple of references that could be construed as me dating Sophie. I tried to reimagine Blaine's face and whether my faux pas had registered with him. From what I remember, his face hadn't given anything away. That didn't mean much. He could have realized it after the fact or just had a good poker face.

My read on Blaine was that he was a solid guy and even though I was usually a good judge of character, I'd gotten a few wrongs over the years. And if Blaine was involved in sending a letter threatening Sophie, I'd been way off with him.

Was I crazy to suddenly cast dispersion on him? Probably. However, Blaine did have a boat within close proximity of two people who were killed. It wouldn't exactly be a shocker if someone around the docks either knew what happened or was somehow involved in the murders.

Maybe, just maybe, that was Blaine.

What should I do with this information? And that was being

generous calling it that. It was more like conjecture on my part. I was undoubtedly jumping the gun. Taking a shot in the dark. Hoping to find a needle in the haystack. You get the point.

I certainly didn't want to confront him. If he was truly involved in leaving me the letter, the last thing I wanted was for him to know I knew. If he/they/whoever thought I was getting close, they might carry out their threat.

And there was the other obvious reason. This theory of mine was unhinged.

I was acting a bit crazy.

Would it just be better to let sleeping dogs lie? To drop this case completely? No matter what happened, I wasn't going to be able to bring Henry back. The one thing I might inadvertently accomplish is getting Sophie and me an early one-way trip to meet Henry in the Big Casino, what Frank Sinatra called heaven.

I didn't know what to do.

There was only one right answer. I'd go with whatever Sophie decided. It was her father, after all.

"Fuck no! We're not letting sleeping dogs lie," Sophie said.

Well, that settled that.

"You do understand this puts us at risk, right?" I asked.

"Yes, I get that. We can't just drop the case. That would be akin to a country bowing down to terrorism. I won't be part of that."

It was as animated as I'd ever seen Sophie.

"I agree with you," I said, surprising her. "But I had to broach the subject. It would have been wrong for me to keep investigating without you knowing the potential risk. And it was your father, so you get to make the final call. Which you have."

"Thanks, Quint. And listen, I don't want you to be all gung ho and running around like a chicken with your head cut off. I want you to be smart and if possible, subtle. But I do want to keep investigating my father's murder."

"We are in agreement."

"Anything else?" Sophie asked.

"Don't we have enough on our plate?"

"Good point. I'll see you tomorrow."

I'd asked Paddy for many favors over the years.

Including two big ones over the last several days.

This would be the biggest of them all.

"Quint! How the hell are you?"

The familiar greeting.

"Are you at the grocery store today?"

"Sure am."

"Can I come see you?"

"This must be something important."

"It is," I said.

"Sure, come on through."

Paddy worked at a San Francisco Irish-themed grocery store called Boyle's several days a week. They had Irish beers, Irish whiskey, Irish butter, and Irish cheese. And I'm not talking run-of-the-mill stuff. I mean the ones that people drank in the old country. They also have every Irish food imaginable, although I'm not sure if that's a good thing. It's not exactly what the Irish is known for.

I don't know if Boyle's was a front for Dennis McCarthy to launder money or whether Paddy actually enjoyed working there.

Maybe a little of both.

I arrived at Boyle's an hour after leaving Walnut Creek. I'd caught some traffic on the Bay Bridge and it took a little longer than expected.

I saw Paddy standing near the front door and he led me down the now familiar path toward his office in the back of the store. I walked in and was surprised to be greeted by none other than Paddy's boss, Dennis McCarthy.

"Figured I'd invite the boss man," Paddy said. "Sounded like this might be important."

I shook his hand.

"Been a while, Dennis. How have you been?"

"The same," he said succinctly, but with a sly smile behind it. "Why change perfection?"

It was reminiscent of Yancy Quizenberry's response. Maybe being content in your life was something that happened as you aged. I certainly wasn't there yet.

"Must be nice," I said.

"Your problem is you worry too much. Which I'm sure is what brought you here."

"It is," I admitted. "Although, I think I have reason to be scared this time."

Dennis nodded.

"I'll be the judge of that."

"How much has Paddy told you?"

"A little bit, but why don't you tell me from the beginning?"

I spent the next ten minutes going over everything that had happened, starting with the phone call from Henry and ending with my conversation with Sophie in which she implored me to move forward with the case.

When I finished, the first thing he asked me came out of left field.

"Have you ever heard of Willow Tree's Golf Club?" he asked.

"Not sure."

"You've either heard of it or you haven't, Quint."

"No, it doesn't ring a bell."

"Well, it's an exclusive golf club out in Napa."

"Okay. And…"

"And…I'm getting to that part. Jeez, this guy," Dennis said as he looked over at Paddy.

"I'm sorry. Please continue," I said. It wasn't in my make-up to be quite so deferential, but with the favor I was about to ask, schmoozing was my best course of action.

"Anyway," Dennis said, pausing for full effect. "I once played a round of golf with Blaine Travers there."

I didn't say anything. Dennis continued.

"It came out of nowhere. We had a threesome ready to play and someone from the club came up and asked if we minded if this guy Blaine joined us as our fourth. The employee vouched for him and said he was a great player. I'm no slouch myself, but Blaine was even better than the guy had let on. If memory serves, he shot under par."

"How long ago was this?" I asked.

"Probably two years."

"Got to be honest, Dennis. I'm surprised you remembered his name after two years."

"That's probably because I didn't finish the story."

"I'm going to shut up now," I said, which drew a smile from Paddy.

"After we finished, we invited this Blaine guy to join us at the 19th hole for a few drinks. He accepted. One drink turned into three or four and we started talking about what we did for a living. As always, I said I worked in the gaming business and left it at that. The other two were my friends so they knew to keep quiet when it came to my profession. This guy Blaine was no dummy though. *'Ah, so you're a bookie'* was the first thing he said when I told him I worked in the gaming business. I didn't deny it. He wasn't a cop and didn't seem like the type of guy who would go squeal to the cops, so what did I care?"

Paddy chimed in.

"The cops love us, anyway."

"For the most part that's true," Dennis said.

"Did Blaine say what he did for a living?" I asked.

"Was in finance if I remember correctly. Stockbroker. Financial planner. CEO of some rich firm. Something along those lines."

"And that's how you remembered the name when I mentioned it?"

"He was a pretty memorable guy. I might have remembered him even if our conversation stopped there. It continued, however.

I told him to look me up whenever he was out in San Francisco. He told me if I was ever down by the Berkeley Marina, to let him know. He went out on his boat every Monday and Friday and he'd love to take me out. This applied to my two friends too, but I knew he was mostly referring to me."

"So that's how you remembered him. The Marina." I said.

"We eventually got there," he joked.

It was interesting that Dennis had crossed paths with Blaine Travers. It didn't move the needle, though. What exactly was I supposed to do with this info?

"Did you ever take him up on the offer of going out on the boat?"

"No, but do you think maybe I should now?"

Dennis let out a sarcastic smirk.

Now the whole story made sense. Dennis was using himself as bait in case I wanted to get some more information on Blaine Travers.

"This is your first senior moment, Quint," Paddy said and Dennis laughed.

"How was I supposed to know that's where he was headed with this?"

"I'm kidding. I didn't know that was going to be the quote-unquote punchline either."

"Looks like I fooled you both," Dennis said. "So, what do you say, Quint?"

"Thanks for the offer," I said. "But I think we should wait. I don't have enough on him yet. In fact, for now, it's just a suspicion and I have zero evidence he sent the letter or was involved in any of the murders."

"I agree, Quint. I wasn't talking about hitting him up tomorrow, but now it's something in your bag of tricks."

"Thanks," I said.

I still wasn't sure exactly what he could do if he got out on the boat of Blaine Travers, but Dennis did have a way with people. Who knows, maybe it would come in handy down the line.

"Now, what was the favor that you wanted?" Dennis asked.

I'd been so wrapped up in the story, I'd momentarily forgotten why I'd scheduled this meeting in the first place.

Then it came to me.

"I'm worried about Sophie," I started. "I can't look after her all day and if these thugs already killed three people, they are obviously capable of anything going forward. I worry about her every moment I'm not with her."

"You should worry when you are with her as well. Killing two birds with one stone and all."

"Thanks for making me feel better," I said.

"I wasn't kidding. It would be easier to take you out together."

"I can take care of her when we're together."

"I believe you're dumb enough to think you can," Dennis said.

He wasn't wrong.

"So, what do you think?" I asked.

"Think about what exactly? You're skirting the issue."

"Do you have someone who could look after Sophie from afar? Follow her around to make sure she's safe. I told you I was asking for a lot."

Dennis shook his head.

"You weren't kidding. This is a huge ask, Quint. We're not the police. We don't just have unlimited resources where we can lend you a guy or two to follow a woman around. And how long is it for? A day or two? A week or two? A month or two?"

"I don't know," I admitted.

"I'm not trying to be a jerk; just being honest. What if this case drags on for two months? You're a friend, and me and Paddy love ya, but I can't just have one of my guys be a chaperone for an undesignated period of time."

I knew there was one way to ensure this case didn't get protracted for too long: To keep pressing people's buttons. To keep my foot on the gas pedal. That might not be the safest route, but it would ensure we'd hit the finish line earlier than if I just stood on the sidelines.

"What if I asked for two weeks and after that, I'm on my own?"

Dennis looked at Paddy who gave him the slightest nod. Yes,

Dennis was the boss, but Paddy likely knew the day-to-day operations of their company better.

"We can give her protection for two weeks, Quint," Paddy said.

"Thank you. Both of you."

Dennis stared at me intently.

"In my business, if someone doesn't pay, it's a bad look. More than that, it gives other bettors ideas about not paying. And they have to know I will always pay on time. That I'm a man of my word. For that reason - and I know your situation is different - I'm not going to give you a day more than two weeks. I have to stick to my word. The same as I expect from my clients."

Dennis's face was very stern. This wasn't the affable friend I'd made over the years. This was the cutthroat, business side of him. A side I'd heard about, but had only seen once, years ago, when I first met him.

"I understand, Dennis. I'm just grateful for the two weeks. I won't ask for an extra hour."

"Good," Dennis said. "Cause you ain't getting it."

"I think your plan just changed, Quint," Paddy said.

"How is that?" I asked.

"To steal a poker term, you're going all-in. No more dilly-dallying around the case. You're going to start knocking on some doors."

"And maybe breaking them down," I said.

They both smiled.

"Take care of yourself," Dennis said.

"I can do that. It's Sophie I'm worried about."

"Just because you keep saying you can take care of yourself, doesn't necessarily make it true."

Was I putting off some false bravado? As I'd considered several times, three people had been killed. Was I out of my league just as Angela Shinn had suggested?

Dennis's voice interrupted me as my mind wandered.

"Before you leave, give me Sophie's address and her phone number. I won't have our guy call her unless it's absolutely necessary, but it's important he at least have it."

"I'll do it right now."

I grabbed a pen and a piece of paper and wrote both down. I had to look at my phone for her number and at one of her texts for the address. It was a small example of just how reliant we are on our phones these days.

"You want to pick up some corned beef and cabbage on your way out, Quint? The Irish think it's good luck. You may need it."

"Do you know how sick I am of people saying *'Stay Safe'* or *'Good Luck'*?"

"Then stop putting yourself in these precarious situations. You have no one to blame but yourself."

He was right, of course. That doesn't mean I liked hearing it.

It was time to get out of there. My request had been accepted, I didn't need to take up any more of their day.

"Dennis, I mean this with all sincerity: What can I get you for doing me this favor? I know I don't have the money that would do anything for you, but I'd like to do something. You're going above the call here."

"Do you know what you can get me?"

"What?"

"You can get me the guy who killed your friend."

I smiled.

"You're a gem. Thanks."

I stood to go, shaking both of their hands first.

Dennis gave me some sarcastic parting advice.

"Good luck, Quint! Stay safe!"

I was laughing as I left their office.

As I drove home, I debated whether I should tell Sophie I'd hired someone to follow her. I'd been upfront with her up to this point, but this was a little different.

On the one hand, she had the right to know. This was undeniable and there was no way I could sweet talk my way out of that fact. On the other hand, it would be better for her mental well-being if she didn't know. Who wants to think they need a "chaper-one" to follow them around town?

I flip-flopped several times.

In the end, I decided I had to tell her, despite knowing it wouldn't go over very well.

∽

She came over that night.

Sophie kissed me on the lips as soon as she entered my apartment. I'd finally connected my phone to the call box downstairs and now I could just buzz her in.

"It seems like it's been two weeks this time," she said. "And yes, I know it's only been three days."

"Listen, Sophie. We have to talk."

"Is it something new with the case?"

"Yes and no. Please, sit down."

We both sat.

"You're scaring me," she said.

"This whole case should be scaring you, Sophie."

"You know I'm being watchful."

"That's the thing," I said.

"What does that mean?"

"I'm worried that might not be enough against the type of people we're dealing with."

"I'm not just going to sit in my house and watch the world go round. I have work. I have friends. I have you!"

"I'm not asking you to be a hermit."

"Then what exactly are you asking?"

"Well, to be honest - and you may not like this - I'm not asking. I went ahead and did something without your approval."

She looked pissed.

"What did you do, Quint?"

"I guess there's no way to sugarcoat this. I hired someone to follow you around."

I didn't know how she was going to take this. She pondered it for several seconds.

"Follow me around?"

"Protect you, but from a distance."

"I don't have to meet with this guy?"

"No."

"I don't have to talk to this guy?"

"No."

"I basically won't know he's there."

"If he's good at his job, then yes."

"I guess it's not the worst thing."

I was relieved.

"Good. I didn't think you were going to take this so well."

"Is he handsome? Is a Brad Pitt lookalike going to be following me around?"

"You wish. I picked the ugliest guy they had. Can't have you fooling around on me."

Sophie laughed.

"He's probably got an eye patch."

"And a peg leg," I said. "Come to think of it, he probably won't be able to protect you at all."

She leaned in and kissed me.

"We sure find the weirdest things to laugh at."

"Ain't that the truth?"

Her face turned serious quite suddenly.

"So, what's next, Quint? Is this going to get dangerous?"

"It could. I wouldn't have hired someone to follow you around if I didn't think that was a possibility."

"I should probably be more scared than I am. Maybe that's because I feel safe with you."

"Thanks, Sophie, but there will be plenty of times when we're not together. And honestly, I'm no match for these people, whoever they are. They've killed three people. What have I ever done?"

"Prevented many deaths."

"I couldn't prevent your father's."

"Don't be ridiculous. That wasn't your fault. You weren't even there. And if you had been, there just would have been another dead body."

I'd been thinking about that a lot lately. If I'd arrived at the Marina a little earlier, could I have saved Henry's life? Or would I have been lying next to him, my neck at an equally odd angle?

"We'll never know," I said. It sounded a bit dismissive, but I didn't know what else to say.

"You didn't answer my question. What's next?"

"I'm going to hit them where it hurts."

"And where's that?"

"By using the media."

"You're going back to that slimeball Dexter Lund?"

"Not a freaking chance. We're going old school."

Sophie smiled.

"You're going to *The Walnut Creek Times?*" she asked.

"I sure am."

CHAPTER 15

Going to my old newspaper and asking them to publish an article on my investigation was a big risk.

When the killer - or killers - got wind of this, they were going to be livid. I planned on being interviewed and giving quotes. There'd be no guessing as to who had spearheaded the paper into printing this article. Yours truly.

They'd probably throw out the idea of trying to kill me. Shut me up forever.

And yet, I somehow believed the benefits outweighed all of that. First off, this case would suddenly get a lot more attention. That was important. If I was murdered, the killers would know the case would blow up. I hated acknowledging it, but I was somewhat of a local celebrity. My murder would be front page news and the lead story on the local news. It would be bad business to kill me. That would hardly be reassuring to Sophie (or my mother), but it gave me a slight reassurance they wouldn't do anything to harm me.

A second benefit I envisioned was that the killers might start making a few mistakes. When people get cornered, they tend to. They start turning on each other. Start talking too much. And if I wanted - no, needed - this case to start moving quicker, there was no better way than to put them on their heels.

Maybe I'd come to regret it.

Time would tell.

I met up with Tom at the entrance to *The Walnut Creek Times*. The familiar red awning had been freshly painted and the entire place looked brand new from the outside. They'd done a good job keeping the business looking modern.

"Isn't it nice to be home?" he asked.

"It always felt like it," I said.

"That's what we shoot for. How long has it been since you stepped foot in here?"

"Probably close to a year, I'd say. It's been almost four years since I stopped working for you."

"I remember. You had dreams of making it as a private investigator. Turns out, you were right."

"Thanks, Tom."

Had I made it? I guess so. It paid the bills (except for Henry's case) and I'd certainly accumulated a few high-profile cases in my short time as a P.I.

"Shall we," I said.

Tom opened the door and I made my way into the offices I'd worked at for well over ten years. I saw two familiar faces within the first second. It made me feel bad. These had been more than just my co-workers; they had been my friends. And I hadn't stepped foot in here for over a year. Nor had I been great about keeping in touch. I'd felt the same guilt when I was on the docks, waiting to meet with Henry. Sadly, that never happened. And one day, one of my co-workers - or me - might not be around. It was time to start keeping in better touch with my friends.

It was easy to blame it on being a P.I. and the somewhat solitary life that came with it. That wasn't the full story, though. I had enough free time. Blaming it on my job was just me looking for a convenient excuse.

"Quint!" Trent Buckley yelled, snapping me out of my stupor.

I walked over and gave Trent a bear hug. He started before me at the paper, so we'd worked together the entirety of my time here. So had Greg Alm who was standing behind Trent waiting for his own bear hug. Which I obliged him with.

I had to give Tom and Krissy credit. They had far less turnover than most newspapers. Trent and Greg had been there close to twenty years now. You didn't get that longevity very often in the newspaper business. Not these days, at least. Maybe back in the day, but the industry has changed so much and no one had any loyalty anymore. That goes for the writers as well as management.

"Are you ready for this?" Tom asked.

Trent and Greg nodded.

"Am I missing something?" I asked.

"I've decided that since you've known Trent and Greg the longest, I'm going to have them work together on this article. There's a lot here, Quint, and it would probably be too much for just one of them."

"No wonder you guys were waiting for me by the door. I should have known. This wasn't a courtesy hello. This was business."

They both laughed.

"It's a little of both," Greg said.

We walked toward the conference room. I saw some more familiar faces - including the long-time editor Jan Kingston - and said a few words, promising to come back after we'd finished up with our meeting.

The conference room hadn't changed much over the years. Not that I was expecting it to. It was what it was.

Tom took his forever position at the head of the table and we all fell into line, sitting in the seats closest to him.

"Without further ado Quint, why don't you present why this current case you're working on is worthy of a featured article?"

I stood up, which was probably unnecessary, and spent the next ten minutes talking about the deaths of Henry, Needles, and Frank Manning. I told them of every interview I'd conducted and even mentioned following Needle's wife around.

I told them of my relationship with Sophie. It was necessary because the Blaine connection was contingent on that, but I asked them to exclude my relationship with Sophie from the article.

"No one is going to care who I'm sleeping with," I said.

The truth was, I didn't want anyone to know. Was it because I thought I'd look tacky - or worse - for sleeping with the deceased's daughter? Maybe. I still hadn't worked through all of my feelings on that, despite Sophie having no problem with it.

I finished my summary and sat back down.

The only thing I hadn't mentioned was my dealings with Dennis McCarthy and Paddy Roark. Yes, talking to Lefty and hiring them to surveil Sophie was a big deal, but it's nothing the public needed to know about. If they were mentioned in an article, my friendship with Dennis and Paddy would be over in a New York minute.

I waited for Tom, Trent, and Greg's responses. It came soon thereafter and I instantly wished I'd never come here in the first place.

"So, all you have on this Blaine fella is that there's a chance he deduced you are sleeping with Sophie? And from there, you jumped to him either being part of the murder or - at the minimum - having sent you the letter?" Trent asked.

It was obvious they weren't as enthralled in my findings as I was.

"Yeah, I guess," I said. "There was just something about him that gave me pause. It's hard to describe. And he does have a boat near both Henry and Needles."

"So do loads of other people."

"True."

"And I'll bet there have been other people over the years that gave you pause."

"Also true."

"I doubt they were all murderers."

I was starting to get upset but held my tongue.

Shit, was my whole hypothesis based on me jumping to conclusions? Was there a single thread of evidence that truly connected Blaine to these murders? The faces in front of me would have said yes to the former and no to the latter.

I suddenly felt like an idiot. I despised the looks I was getting from my former co-workers. Even Tom looked dismissive.

"I'm sorry Quint, but I have to agree with Trent and Greg. There's not much here. Look, maybe we could publish an article saying that three suspicious murders took place in the span of twenty-four hours, but that's honestly about all you've got. As far as Blaine Travers goes? You've got nothing."

I was going to object, but why? Tom was correct.

And he wasn't finished.

"If you think we're going to publish an article saying the cops are somehow involved in these murders, you're crazy. There is zero evidence of that. I'm sorry, but Henry's fax doesn't count as evidence. Listen, you know I love Henry and I'd love to do anything to get the story of his murder out there. This isn't that story, though."

That all cut deep, but nothing like what Tom said next.

"What were you thinking, Quint? Truth was, you weren't!"

Tom was pissed, but then again, so was I.

"Listen, you're probably right," I said. "This isn't something you can publish. I'll tell you one thing, though. I'm right. Blaine Travers is involved and in one way or another, so are the police."

"How do you know this?" Greg asked.

"Intuition," I said and left it at that.

My temperature continued to rise. The anger should probably have been pointed inward, but I felt cornered and was lashing out. Just like I'd hoped the killer/killers would react once this article was published. The article that I now knew would never be published.

"And tell me once again how Frank Manning is tied into this?" Tom asked.

"Clementine Ya couldn't pay her marker so she drowned him," Trent said

All three of them started laughing.

I stood up. My emotions had gotten the best of me and I could no longer hold my tongue.

"Fuck you, guys," I said and walked toward the door as they screamed after me.

"Oh, come on Quint. Can't you take a joke?" Tom asked.

"I'm sorry. I had to," Trent said.

"Wait and see," I said. "I'll be proved correct."

"That's not the point," Tom said.

At least, I think he did. I was already slamming the conference room door.

With a scowl that would have scared little children, I walked through and then out of *The Walnut Creek Times*, ignoring the waves and greetings that came my way.

CHAPTER 16

I woke up the next morning in a haze.

It was like a hangover without the booze.

I knew I'd overreacted and would have to make things right. Just not today. Tom, Trent, and Greg had been pretty rude themselves. I'd be the better man if it came to that, but they wouldn't be receiving an apology this soon.

This case was driving me up the wall, there was no doubt about that.

However, time was of the utmost importance, so I couldn't just sit back and soak things in. There was a timer on how long they would look after Sophie. Thirteen days and counting to be exact.

I decided to take a shot in the dark and scrolled through my numbers.

"Hello?" a woman's voice answered.

"Erika, this is Quint Adler, do you remember me?"

"Of course."

"I have a question if you don't mind."

"Shoot."

"Did the police return Frank's phone to you?"

"Yeah, they did."

"Did they give you the code to unlock it?"

"We've been married a long time. Do you think I need that?"

Bingo!

"That's what I was hoping. You never know though. Some married couples probably don't want their significant other to be able to unlock their phone."

She laughed on the other end.

"I'm sure that's true. Me and Frank had a good relationship though."

"Sure seems that way. Can I look at the phone?"

"Yeah. Do you remember where the house is?"

"I do. Are you there now?"

"Yup. Swing by whenever you want."

I was there within the hour.

Erika answered the door and led me through to the living room. On the table in front of the couch were the phone, a pen, and a little pad of paper.

"You didn't have to do that," I said.

"In case you want to take some notes," she said. "I know everyone's got their cell phone for that now, but I'm old school, so there's a pad of paper if you want it."

"Very kind of you."

"Do you want some coffee?"

She'd already done quite a bit for me and I probably should have turned her down, but it sounded too good.

"That would be great."

"I'll be back in five or six minutes. You can get to work."

I looked down at the phone, which hadn't been unlocked.

"Erika, I think you need to unlock this."

"Oh, silly me."

She walked over, typed in the 6-digit code, and handed the phone back.

I went to his messages. There was no reason to scroll too far back. His final text messages were the ones I was most interested in.

His very last text was to his wife, saying he was going to go for a swim. Some people would argue that proved that Frank was going into the pool and he did likely die of drowning, or maybe had a heart attack in the pool and then drowned. I thought the opposite. Once Frank was killed, the murderer would have his phone and could easily text pretending to be Frank. And a text of this nature would lead people to believe he was going in the pool. It was the perfect front. My guess was that Frank did not send that text. I don't know if they persuaded him to give him the password or whether the phone had been on, but they got their hands on it. Of that, I was almost certain.

Furthermore, is texting your wife that you're going in the pool even a thing? Maybe, but it sounded a bit forced.

The second to last text was to a friend, telling him they should get together for a beer. Nothing to see there.

I started scrolling down, looking for anything that seemed out of place. There wasn't much. Certainly no texts about meeting at a secret rendezvous or incoming threats. There was a text to Yancy Quizenberry telling him that he'd be coming into Kincade's that night. Sadly, Frank wouldn't be going there anymore.

I'd never exactly been a barfly, but I'd been a semi-regular at some bars over the years. It was always sad when one of the regulars passed away. They are often what made these bars feel so homely. Kincade's would never be the exact same without Frank. Sure, it would survive, but a very small piece of it would be gone forever.

I'd scrolled down as far as two weeks before the murders. Nothing jumped out. He and his wife had a cute banter on the phone. I felt like I was spying on them, but I had to read this just in case something gave me pause.

I knew I'd gone back far enough through the texts.

I switched over to the phone calls.

There were no outgoing calls from his phone on the day he died. There were two incoming calls, however. One, from his wife, that he didn't answer. And a second one, from a 510 area code also went unanswered. Judging by the time, it was likely after Frank had passed away.

I wrote the number down. I wasn't going to call it right now from my phone and I certainly wasn't going to call it from Frank's. That would be more than a little suspicious, getting a call from a dead guy.

I scrolled down through a week of missed phone calls. There were several 800 or 888 numbers, but I ignored them. The 510 number was the only one that wasn't either an 800 number or a friend's name that popped up.

Erika came back in with my coffee.

"Thanks so much. I have a question."

"Hopefully, I have an answer."

"Was it odd for Frank to text you and tell you he was going swimming?"

"Yes. Completely out of character. It's one of the main reasons I think he was killed. Whoever did it probably texted that."

"I was thinking the same thing. Did you tell the cops that?"

"I sure did. They seemed to have their minds made up that this was an accidental drowning or a drowning due to a cardiac event."

"Have you looked at the texts yourself?"

"I looked at the first few and I had to stop. It was too sad. I was hearing his texts in his voice and it was just too much."

I looked over at Erika and tears were appearing in her eyes. She'd really loved Frank and I felt for her. I'd had quite a few girl-friends over the years - a few whom I'd really loved - but I'd never had a marriage that had lasted decades. That's a different type of love and Frank and Erika obviously had it.

"I'm sorry for this," I said. "Just one more question."

She just nodded. I showed her the 510 number.

"Do you recognize this number?"

"No, I don't," she said, wiping away a tear. "Hold on one second."

She came back with her phone and I saw her inputting the number.

"I don't have the number saved either. Do you want me to call it?" she asked.

"No, I'll take care of that."

The last thing I wanted was for Erika to get involved with this case. If this 510 number had anything to do with Frank's death, I'd rather be the one calling it.

"Is there anything else you need?" she asked.

"Not that I can think of."

I set Frank's phone back on the table.

"Why don't you take it?" Erika suggested.

"You're sure?" I asked.

"Yeah. Maybe something will come up and his other phone calls will become important."

"Thanks. I'll need that password again."

"It's 6-5-4-3-2-1. Pretty elaborate for a big-time poker player, huh?"

I managed a smile.

"I'll return it as soon as my investigation is over."

"If you want. As I said, it just makes me sad."

"I'll bet that down the line you'll enjoy reading some of the old texts."

Erika smiled.

"Yeah, you're probably right."

I stood up and gave her a hug.

"Go catch whoever did this," she said.

"I'm trying."

It felt like I'd now taken on Frank's case as well. Frank for Erika and Henry for Sophie. I didn't think that would be the case with Angela Shinn. She still hated my guts.

I was driving home when I saw the rarest of rare things on the side of the road. Rarer than a unicorn. Rarer than a Bigfoot sighting. Rarer than Haley's Comet.

I saw a pay phone.

I quickly pulled over and grabbed my notes next to me.

The pay phone took quarters. I honestly didn't know if it took one quarter or four quarters to make a phone call. I couldn't remember the last time I'd used one of these things.

It turned out to be fifty cents.

I dialed the number, thinking there was about a 75% chance that it would go to voicemail. If I didn't know the incoming number, I almost always just let it ring or pressed the button to end the call prematurely. Other people I knew answered their phones no matter what, so I guess it just depended on what type of person had called Frank on the day he died.

The phone rang three times and just when I'd given up hope, I heard someone come on the other line.

"This is Blaine Travers," the voice said.

I quickly put the phone back on the hook.

"Holy shit," I muttered to myself.

CHAPTER 17

Things were starting to escalate by the day.

It wasn't so long ago that I'd lamented that the first two weeks consisted merely of throwaway interviews. I'd never come close to suspecting anyone or really tying anything together, with some minor exceptions.

But now, in the span of a few days, Sophie and I had been threatened and I now had a viable suspect.

He was a tanned, handsome, rich guy in his sixties who'd likely spent most of his life on Easy Street. I should have been happy to go after someone like that. The thing was, I kind of liked Blaine Travers. Maybe I'd read him wrong and he was a complete asshole and possibly a killer. If so, this had been as far off as I've ever been on reading a person. Something I'd always prided myself on.

The fact that he'd answered the phone call certainly didn't bode well for his innocence. He'd had every chance to tell me he knew Frank, but he'd stayed mum. That was pretty incriminating. With all due respect to my people-reading skills, he was likely involved in this.

It was time to go pay him another visit.

Due to his Monday/Friday schedule at the marina, I had to wait a few days until I went and saw Blaine Travers.

He'd told me that any time after noon, he'd be willing to share a beer with me, so I decided to go later than I'd originally planned. As we all know, most people who have had a beer or three are more likely to gossip. Or, at least, to let a few things slip. That's what I was hoping for with Blaine.

I'd flip-flopped several times as to whether I should be confrontational or conversational with him. Yes, I was up against it time-wise, but finding out the connection between Frank and Blaine was huge. I didn't want to scare Blaine off by being confrontational right away. I wanted to keep that in my back pocket if at all possible.

If the conversation went sideways, then I'd go the confrontational route, but I wanted to start the conversation off as happy-go-lucky Quint.

Igor Smyth was there when I approached. For the first time, his smile seemed a bit forced.

"Everything okay, Igor?"

"There hasn't been a great vibe down on the docks lately."

"Why is that?"

"Ever since Henry died it hasn't felt the same, particularly the last few days. It just feels like there's a shadow looming over us."

Igor looked up into the bright blue sky. Spring had been officially here for a few weeks and the weather had finally caught up.

"Obviously, not literal shadows," he added.

"Maybe these sunny, cloudless skies are a harbinger of good things to come," I said.

"I hope you're right, Quint. I don't know, though. I feel like something more is going on."

"Is it just a feeling or do you know something?"

He paused for just a split second before answering.

"Just a feeling."

"Anything you want to talk about?" I asked.

"No," he said emphatically. "What brings you down here today?"

"I wanted to say hi to Blaine Travers and maybe have a beer with him. We had a nice talk last time and I just need to ask him a few follow-up questions."

"Blaine is a good man."

Apparently, Igor wanted to think the best of him just as I did.

"Does everyone like him down here on the docks?" I asked.

"Oh, yeah. He's been here as long as anyone. And you know, he's a pretty charismatic guy."

"So I've noticed."

"And people just kind of flock to him."

Igor looked down toward the dock.

"Look, there he is now. Hey, Blaine!"

I didn't want Blaine thinking I was potentially up here getting the gossip from Igor, so I patted him on the shoulder and headed down towards the dock.

"Good seeing you, Igor."

~

When I arrived at *The Canary*, Blaine was having a beer, just as I'd hoped.

"I told you, Quint. Any time after noon is happy hour for me."

"Care if I join you?"

"Thought you'd never ask."

He reached down into a cooler he had next to him.

"Corona or Bud?"

"I'm on the water surrounded by boats. Give me a Corona. It's more fitting."

"That's a fair statement. Me, I'm more of a Bud man, but I've always got a few options in this little cooler of mine."

I smiled.

"Here, take a seat," he said.

I stepped from the dock onto the boat. The sun felt warm on my back.

Blaine handed me the beer, but not before removing the bottle cap first.

I took a quick sip.

"Thanks, Blaine."

"You're welcome, Quint."

I couldn't tell if there was a glimmer of sarcasm in responding with my first name as I'd done with him. Maybe I was just looking for a chink in Blaine's armor and was trying to condemn him for what was just a cordial conversation.

We sat on the cushions that ran around the perimeter of the stern of the boat.

"Enjoying this weather?" I asked.

I was going the more conversational route as I'd planned out.

"Oh, yeah. A lot more fun taking the boat out when you've got sunny skies above."

"Are you taking it out today?"

"You're late, Quint. Pardon the pun, but that ship has sailed. I got back thirty minutes ago."

"Just you?"

"Just me and a few Budweisers. The best company a man can have."

"Some would say second best," I said.

"Depends on the day, my friend."

"Reminds me of a poster I had as a freshman in college. It said…"

"Man cannot live on beer alone," he said, finishing my sentence.

"Ah, you know that one?"

"I sure do. I may have twenty years on you, but that poster was a classic. I think my son had one if memory serves."

"How many kids do you have?"

"Two left. A boy and a girl. I had another son, but he died in a car accident about ten years ago."

"I'm very sorry," I said.

I meant it. I wasn't sure just how far involved Blaine was in all of this, but it didn't matter. Whenever you hear about someone losing a child, it's devastating.

He raised his glass up.

"To Richard," he said.

"To Richard," I echoed.

"So what brings you down here, Quint?"

I hated that we had to transition from the death of his child into what had brought me here.

"Just a few more questions about Henry," I said.

"Not getting anywhere?"

"I didn't say that. I've learned a great deal."

"Oh yeah, like what?"

He'd opened the door ever so slightly. Was it time to break on through to the other side, Doors-style? Maybe we'd gotten through the conversational part and it was time to transition to the confrontational.

"Like, that you were friends with Frank."

I guess I'd decided it was time.

His shoulders noticeably sagged.

Blaine said nothing, putting the beer to his lips. He proceeded to down the whole thing in one fell swig.

"It looks like I finished my beer," he said and let out a laugh.

He reached into the cooler and grabbed another beer. I was surprised to see it was a Corona this time.

"Fuck it, let's make it an island beer this time," he said.

He grabbed a bottle opener that was next to him and popped the cap.

I couldn't tell if Blaine was about to drop a truth bomb on me or whether he was just being coy. He didn't seem quite like the cool customer I'd met last time. My mentioning Frank had put him on edge.

When I'd first discovered that Blaine knew Frank, I was imagining Blaine as the ringleader of whatever was going on. That's the impression he'd given. He gave off the alpha male vibe, and if he was involved in something, he was probably into it up to his neck.

Now, as I looked across at him, he looked more like a man with too much on his plate.

"How did you find out?" he asked.

There was no need to lie.

"His phone. The police turned it back over to his wife."

"Fucking idiots."

"The cops?"

Blaine didn't answer.

"That call you got from an unlisted number on Wednesday. That was me."

"Since as far as I could remember, I always answered calls from numbers I didn't know. I realize I'm in the minority when it comes to that. I used to let it go to voicemail, but it was always spam or cold callers and they'd just leave a voicemail, prolonging this little charade for another minute or so. I preferred to just answer and hang up within a few seconds. Guess it cost me this time, though."

"I like the logic. Hang up on them before they can leave a voice message."

"That was the idea."

Neither one of us said anything. It's like we were at a standstill, both trying to figure out our next move. He budged first.

"From all I've read and from our brief visits together, I think you're a pretty smart guy, Quint. And your record speaks for itself. You're a damn good P.I."

I thought he was going to continue but didn't do anything for a few seconds, so I softly said, "Thanks."

I didn't want to do the talking at this point. I wanted to let him spill his guts. He looked like he wanted to.

"But, you're no match for these people," he said.

"Who are these people?"

A bird flew down and landed on the railing a few feet from us.

It stared at us with interest.

"Not here," he said.

"It wasn't the bird, was it?" I asked. "Surely, whoever these people are, they don't put hearing devices in birds."

Blaine smiled. His face looked tortured.

The bird flew off.

"It wasn't the bird, Quint, but it did remind me that these docks have eyes. And ears. But mostly eyes."

He laughed loudly when he said "And mostly eyes." I had no idea why.

"So if you want to talk to me," he continued. "We'll have to do it somewhere else."

"You tell me when and where."

"How about that bar you mentioned on your last visit? Kincade's. If I remember, they have a few booths in the corner that will give us some privacy."

"When?"

"How about tomorrow night at eight?"

"Sure. Is there anything you want to tell me before then?"

"My call to Frank was a warning that people were dropping like flies. I'd only met him a few days previous."

That explained why Frank didn't have his number saved.

"Anything else? We could do this all now."

"I'll see you tomorrow night, Quint."

With that, he shooed me away. I wasn't ready to go. He was so close to telling me something big and twenty-four hours felt like forever.

"Please go," he said. "Someone might be watching. No one will be watching at Kincade's."

"Alright."

I grudgingly walked up the dock and off the marina, my eyes darting around like I was being watched. Blaine Travers now had me on edge.

I'm sure I was just being paranoid.

Blaine was overreacting. I was sure of it.

Then again, what if he wasn't?

A lyric from Nirvana came to mind:

Just because you're paranoid
Don't mean they're not after you

～

I arrived back at my place and intentionally fell face-first onto my bed.

I wanted to sleep for the next forty-eight hours. This case had already taken quite a few unexpected turns and my talk with Blaine Travers might have been the strangest of all.

I'd gone into our meeting thinking that maybe Blaine was the one I should be worried about. That he was the "bad guy" I'd been searching for. If I was to believe him - and honestly, I did - it appeared he had been caught in the middle of something he'd never planned on being involved in.

I guess that would all be sorted out. At Kincade's of all places.

Sophie came over that night and I told her about my meeting with Blaine.

She wasn't her usual vibrant self and to be honest, neither was I. We shared some leftover pizza I had and then she went home early. No sleepover. No sex.

I couldn't wait for this case to be over.

It was taking a toll on me, on Sophie, and from the tenor of this visit, on our relationship.

I had a nightmare that evening.

It was the middle of a sunny day and I was looking directly at the sun. As much as I tried to look away from it, my eyes wouldn't budge. They just kept staring at it. I knew the harm that could cause, but I still couldn't avert my eyes. They were fixated. The sun changed from yellow to orange to dark red. And then, all of a sudden, the sun began to change and the center of it morphed into an eye.

Ever so slowly, I started being dragged toward the eye. I tried to look away and wrestle myself from the invisible force field that was pulling me toward the eye. To no avail. My eyes remained fixated on the eye as I headed towards it.

As I moved closer, the heat became unbearable. My arms started to burn and then my skin started to singe. I was burning alive. All the while, my eyes couldn't avert from looking straight in front of me. There was something about the eye that was mesmerizing. In an evil way.

When my skin started to melt off, I frantically woke up, tossing and turning in my bed. It still felt real for a good ten seconds, as most intense nightmares do.

After several minutes, I slowly started to calm down. I had no idea what the nightmare was meant to symbolize, but I knew what had been the precursor.

Blaine Travers mentioning the eye. Whatever the hell that meant.

Not much happened on Saturday. All of my eggs were in the Blaine Travers' basket. I had no idea what he was going to tell me. That he and Frank and Henry and Needles were all just in the wrong place at the wrong time. That Igor was actually a Russian spy doing away with them one by one. That there was a secret agency called *The Eye* that was killing all these people.

Everything was on the table in my mind.

PART TWO: ON BORROWED TIME

CHAPTER 18

I arrived at Kincade's at 7:40.

The bar was busy. It had a younger vibe than most times I'd visited. Maybe Saturday night was college night. Looking around, I felt old.

I hadn't forewarned Yancy Quizenberry that I was coming. I didn't want him making a big deal out of my appearance. My lone reason for coming was to talk to Blaine. Everything else was secondary.

Yancy must have seen me walk in because I saw him headed my way. He sure had a keen eye for knowing when friends walked into his establishment.

"What's up, Quint?"

"Hey, Yancy."

"Did you talk to your boss about doing that follow-up article about his place?"

I had brought it up to Tom, and honestly, hadn't thought about it since.

"I did. And Tom seems interested. I imagine I'll hear back from him soon and then I'll get back to you."

"That is awesome news, Quint. Just awesome. Should we cele-brate with a shot?"

I always secretly hoped that my interviewees were a drink or two deep like Blaine had been out on the docks. Like Artie Morton had been at our epic lunch. I didn't want myself to be. It might cause me to overlook something.

"Raincheck, Yancy. Actually, I'm here to meet someone and I was hoping we could have a booth that's a bit private."

"Say no more," he said. "Follow me."

He walked over to a booth in the far corner of the bar. It was really more like a little nook, which gave us more privacy. Yancy removed something from his jacket pocket. It was a little placard that said, *"Reserved."*

He set it on the table.

"These come in handy now and then," he said.

I smiled, appreciating the favor, but also hoping to end this conversation sooner rather than later. Plus, since I was now sitting at the table, I'm not sure the placards were necessary. Not that I was going to tell him that.

"You're the best," I said instead.

I could be a world-class kiss-ass when necessary. I could also be a world-class pain-in-the-ass. I guess you could say I was always an ass of some sort.

"And don't you forget it. So who are you meeting here tonight? Who is this mysterious guest? Some beautiful woman?"

"You're going to be disappointed if that's what you are expecting to see."

Yancy laughed.

"Sounds more like business than pleasure."

"It is."

"Then I will leave you be. Thanks again for reaching out to your old boss at *The Walnut Creek Times.*"

"You got it. I'll give him a call on Monday and see where we stand."

I knew where we stood. Tom was probably still pissed at me

from the other day and a follow-up story about Kincade's was the furthest thing from his mind.

"Great, Quint. Just great."

He turned to go.

"Are you sure you don't want a drink?"

I thought back to my preference for interviewees who were having a drink.

"You know what? How about a bottle of Bud?"

"Coming right up," Yancy said.

He came back and set the Bud bottle down and then let me be. Yancy could be a bit of a blowhard at times, but he could sense that my mind was on the meeting at hand and decided to give me my space. I appreciated that.

Blaine walked in five minutes later. Or, at least, I thought he had.

Turned out it was just a dead ringer for him.

I stood up and took two steps toward the door before I realized my mistake.

When Blaine hadn't shown by eight, I didn't think anything of it.

When he wasn't there by 8:10, I started to get a little worried.

By 8:20, I was fearing the worst.

By 8:30, after two unanswered texts to go along with the no-show, I was in full-on panic mode.

At 8:35 and 8:38, I called him. No answer either time.

And that's when I became truly concerned for Blaine's well-being.

"Fuck. Shit. Fuck."

I alternated swear words at my table.

At 9:00, I was just hoping for a miracle to walk through that door. It didn't happen, so a few minutes later, I walked out of Kincade's.

If I were a betting man, I'd have put it at 50/50 that Blaine Travers was still alive. I sure hoped I was wrong.

∾

I took a left as I exited the bar and walked toward my car.

I was five blocks down, in the closest spot I could find. Considering it was a Saturday night at nearly 8:00 in a busy district, five blocks was just fine with me.

The area in and around Kincade's was really busy, the definition of a bustling city. Bars, restaurants, coffee shops, etc. Where I parked - even though it was only five blocks away - was a barren street, no houses or apartments or bars or really, anything else. Just a few cars that would be picked up after they finished dinner or possibly left overnight if they had a few too many at Kincade's.

I couldn't stop thinking about Blaine. Was it time to call the cops? Despite my fears that I felt were warranted, it's not like I could tell the cops to put out an APB because someone didn't show up to a bar.

But he didn't answer my texts, either!

That wasn't going to make any difference. I'd have been laughed out of the precinct. I'd have to wait until tomorrow morning to notify them. Even then, they'd just assume that Blaine would eventually show up. After twenty-four hours, maybe they'd do something. I looked down at my watch. It was 9:12. Twenty-four hours felt like an eternity away.

I knew basically nothing about Blaine's life. I knew he had two living children and I think he'd mentioned a wife. Or had he? Regardless, I didn't have any idea how to get ahold of his loved ones.

Maybe I could swing by the marina tomorrow. I'm sure Igor - or his superiors - had contact info for people who docked their boats there. I could get his wife's number and call her. Hopefully, he'd slept through our meeting or had come down with the flu or something, and when she answered she'd put my fears to rest.

I'd keep trying his cell in the meantime.

I tried not to think about Blaine anymore as I inched closer to my car. It wasn't going to be productive - counterproductive actually - and would just lead to me fearing the worst.

I walked the final block and took a right. My car was about the sixth one in. I was now on that quiet little street and the city noise around Kincade's was a thing of the past.

When I was about thirty feet from my car, still walking in the middle of the road, I heard a guy on a bike about to pass me, so I moved closer to the sidewalk. It sounded like it had a motor, but it definitely wasn't an old-school motorbike. This was like the Prius version with a slow, low hum being the only sound. Maybe it was just a scooter.

Something told me to turn around and as I did, my eyes couldn't believe what they were seeing. The guy on the bike pulled a gun out of his jacket and pointed it at me. There was no mistaking what it was, nor what was about to happen. I noticed a silencer on the end of it. No one was going to hear shit on this quiet little street.

I cursed myself for not trying to find parking closer to Kincade's. It's funny what your mind will conjure up in a moment of panic.

I took off sprinting toward my car and the adjoining sidewalk, zig-zagging as I went.

When I got to within about five feet of my car, my plan was to launch myself in the air and dive behind it.

It would give me some cover and a fighting chance.

I never made it. A bullet penetrated my abdomen and I fell to the ground, landing on my stomach. I was only a few feet short of the refuge of the car, but that didn't matter anymore. I was now a defenseless animal who was about to be put out of his misery.

I waited for the second shot that was going to finish me.

Instead, I heard the guy walk over to me and stand there, hovering over me.

"Turn over," he said.

I knew I was going to die and probably should have just told him to fuck off, but I wanted to know who it was. I started to roll over, taking my sweet time. It was partially because I'd been shot and was in bad shape to begin with. I was also hoping for some miracle. Maybe an extra second or two would somehow make the difference. Probably not.

"Roll over right now or I'll shoot you in the back," he said.

I quickly finished rolling over.

I guess my mother is going to need a closed casket.

Not exactly what I wanted my final thought to be.

I looked up at the man who was going to kill me.

I had never seen the guy in my life. He was a white guy in his early thirties. Mid-thirties at the oldest. Why did this young man want to kill me? This certainly wasn't the evil genius who'd organized the deaths of multiple people. Was it?

He was wearing all black, including a turtleneck and a black beanie to match, which would make it tough to describe his facial features. Not that it really mattered. It's not like my corpse was going to be able to give the police a description.

"Who put you up to this?" I asked.

There were no houses or apartment complexes on this street. It's unlikely anyone had even heard the gunshot, especially since he'd used a silencer. No one was going to save me. I was going to die here.

"Do you really want to know?" he asked.

"Yes," I said.

He started his bike back up and pointed his gun at me. He was about to shoot me and then drive off into the night, never to be caught. I couldn't believe it was going to end like this.

"I was contracted to kill you by..." the man said.

Before he could utter the name - or pull the trigger - a gunshot hit the ground in between us. And then another one.

Before I realized what was going on, the guy who had shot me had taken off on his bike down the street.

I tried to look around to see who had shot at us but saw nothing.

Was it really possible I was going to live through this? I'd avoided being shot in the face by some miracle. But I'd still been shot and was surely bleeding profusely. I felt down on my right flank and felt the blood oozing out.

I needed to get the hell out of there.

I let out a scream. And then another. And finally a third.

I looked around again but didn't see the man - or woman - who had saved my life.

Where did he or she go? If they'd truly been trying to save my life, wouldn't they come to check on how I was doing?

Worry about that later! You need to get to the hospital!

I screamed again.

After what felt like five minutes - but was probably more like two - I finally heard some people talking nearby. I couldn't tell if they were thirty feet away or a hundred feet.

I screamed again.

That's when the pain started to really hit me.

I'd been shot but had managed not to focus on the pain with all that was going on. It was now unavoidable.

I was likely losing a lot of blood. I was alive, thank god, but I needed to get to the hospital quickly.

I told myself I couldn't pass out. I had to stay awake until those voices found me.

If I passed out, it was basically a death sentence.

I yelled as loud as my body would allow me.

And followed up with a second scream, somehow surpassing the volume of the first.

That's the one that seemed to do it.

The voices changed direction and I could now hear them walking toward me.

CHAPTER 19

I was alive.

I'd woken up in Summit Hospital in Oakland, just as I had on my 40th birthday. On that occasion, I'd only needed a few stitches due to a friendly scrape with my friend, Gerald Dugan. This time was a little different. It wasn't a cut; it was a bullet wound.

I was found on the ground by several good Samaritans who called 9-1-1, but apparently, there was already an ambulance on the way. Whoever had tried to save my life by firing at my would-be assassin must have called it. Nothing else made sense.

I'd caught another break as well. The bullet had done the old through and through, entering me through the back of my left flank and exiting through the front of my abdomen. The doctor said if the bullet had entered the same location on the right side of my body it would have punctured my liver and unquestionably ended my life.

I was pretty darn lucky to be alive.

The same can't be said for Blaine Travers. He was dead. Blaine had been shot three times in his car mere blocks from his house and almost certainly on his way to meet me at Kincade's.

The police weren't giving me any information, but Sophie had been able to put a few things together. She'd been with me every day since I'd been admitted to the hospital. The same goes for my mother.

Sophie told me that the man who killed Blaine was likely the same man who tried to kill me. They'd also traced the bullets from Blaine's body and the through and through on me to Needles' death. He'd been killed by the same gun.

Henry and Frank Manning's deaths were strangulation and drowning so there weren't any bullets to tie back to them, but I had to assume the police were looking at the same guy for those murders as well.

He hadn't been caught yet. Nor had the media mentioned any suspects.

It's not like Sophie gave me this information right away. Over the first two days, she'd probably told me twenty times what I really needed to do was rest. By day three, I'd worn her down and she relayed what the local news was saying. The cops continued to stay mum with her.

I'd undergone surgery within an hour of being brought to the hospital. A few blood transfusions were necessary as well. I was told I'd lost a decent amount of blood, but the ambulance arrived quickly enough that I was never in serious danger of dying. If the ambulance had been even five or ten minutes later, things might have been different.

I'd been told *'You are very lucky'* at least five or six times. It's hard to feel that way when you're stuck in a hospital room with a hole in your stomach, but it was true. I could have been Blaine, sitting in a morgue awaiting burial or cremation. Against all odds, I was still here.

My mother spent the first few days crying by my bedside. She spent the next two imploring me to drop the case. Even Sophie, who'd originally wanted to move forward, said that maybe it was time to throw in the towel.

I was conflicted. Obviously, the best decision would have been to run a thousand miles away from this case. Never to look back.

It wasn't that easy. This had already been personal with Henry's death and now they'd tried to kill me. It couldn't get any more personal than that. I wasn't sure if I could just suddenly drop the case.

'Hey guys, I know you tried to kill me, but why don't we just let bygones be bygones and forget about it? Are you cool with that?'

That was not in my playbook.

Now, would my injuries prevent me from continuing to investigate?

That was a different question and entirely plausible.

My fourth day in the hospital seemed to be a turning point. I was getting stronger and I could tell by the doctors' and nurses' reactions that I was on the mend. It wasn't anything they said per se. It was more their manner of speaking to me as if I was getting better and wouldn't be in the hospital much longer.

I knew I'd be getting out soon.

On my fifth day, that news came. I was going to be released the following day.

"I'm sure you'll be happy to get out of here," Dr. Aaron Rosen said.

He'd been with me since the night I was brought in. He was around my age with a short, military-style haircut. He was no-nonsense and while he may not have been your first choice of guy to have a beer with, he's exactly what you wanted in a doctor.

"I can't stay longer? I was just getting used to it here. That milk and jello combination for dinner really hits the spot," I said.

The unflappable Dr. Rosen managed a slight smirk.

"I'll tell your girlfriend Sophie to pick up some milk and jello to have waiting for when you get out."

The doctor had jokes.

"Don't give her any ideas."

"I'll have you in for checkups twice over the next month, but I think you're going to be alright, Quint. I've left you a pamphlet. It's basically just a list of things not to do. Take it seriously. If you rip those staples, you'll be right back in the hospital. And any setback will just push back your overall recovery time. Behave for two or three weeks and you'll soon be back to your old self."

"I can live with that. I'll catch up on all those TV shows that people just love to suggest."

"Good idea. You're going to be spending a lot of time at home, so that's the perfect hobby."

"How about sex?"

"Too risky. Too much movement. I'll reassess in a week or two."

"You're killing me, Doc."

"Two weeks without sex. I'm sure you've done that before."

"Too many times that I'd care to admit," I said.

The doctor laughed again.

"You're going to be just fine, Quint."

About two minutes after receiving that news, Dennis McCarthy and Paddy Roark walked into my hospital room for the first time.

"Look who it is," Dennis said. "The never-say-die kid."

"Don't make me laugh. It hurts like you wouldn't believe."

"Wait, laughing with a hole in your stomach isn't comfortable?" Paddy asked.

"You really do learn something every day," Dennis followed up.

They were trying to get me to laugh.

"You guys are assholes," I said.

Dennis raised his arms, signifying he'd stop.

"We just talked to the doctor on our way in. He said they're releasing you tomorrow."

"They'll give out my information to any old randoms."

"Random? I told the doc that we were Uncle Bob and Uncle Bill."

"I think I might start calling you guys that."

They smiled.

"Forgive me, Quint. I've never been very good in hospitals," Dennis said. "My default is to try and make the patient laugh. Unless it's truly a matter of life or death and it doesn't sound like yours is."

"I hope not if they are releasing me tomorrow."

"Will you need a ride home?"

"I'm sure Sophie will be taking care of that."

"You haven't tried to get her two time zones away from you?"

It sounded like a joke, but Dennis wasn't kidding.

"I mean, are these assholes going to come after me again? Surely, they have to lay low at least for a while?"

"I wouldn't put anything past whoever tried to do this."

I didn't respond.

"By the way, we met Sophie," Paddy interjected. "She's a gem."

"When was that?"

"Outside about five minutes ago."

"Did you guys introduce yourself as Uncle Bob and Uncle Bill?"

"Luckily that didn't come up. We just said we were long-time friends."

"I may or may not have mentioned you guys have helped me out. She might have been able to guess who you were."

"We can live with that. Regardless, it was a pleasure to meet her. I think she'll be joining you after we're out of here. She let us come in first."

"Do you still have someone following her around?" I asked.

"Of course," Dennis answered. "Your two weeks aren't up yet. I'm a man of my word."

"How about me?" I asked. "I'm starting to think maybe I could use some protection."

I saw Paddy give the slightest of glances toward Dennis.

And that's when it clicked.

"Fucking A," I said. "Was it one of your guys who stopped the guy from killing me?"

They looked at each other again, giving themselves away one too many times.

"C'mon, I'm not a dummy," I said.

"Shhhh," Dennis said, as he took his index fingers to his mouth. "You never know who is listening. Please, don't ever mention this again."

He was as serious as I'd ever seen him.

"I won't, but I owe you guys my life."

"That phrase is usually said as hyperbole, but in this case, it's 100% true."

"How can I ever thank you guys? Or your friend?"

"I already told you; by never mentioning this again."

"And maybe dropping this case once and for all," Paddy said. "This might be too much, even for you, Quint."

"I'm considering that option."

"Consider it seriously."

"Can I just ask a few more questions?"

"What do you want to know?" Dennis said, but he was no longer the cuddly, joke-cracking friend who'd first walked in.

"How can they have bullet casings and several different crime scenes and still not know who did this?"

"These are all good questions, Quint."

"Okay. And?"

Just then, we heard someone screaming from a neighboring room. The sights and sounds of a hospital were always changing. Just when you get used to the relative quiet, there might be a soul-piercing scream or a nurse running around looking for a doctor. At least I wasn't in the ICU. That was twenty times worse.

"And?" I repeated after the screams ended.

"And this guy is good at his job. Very good. You don't kill this many people without getting caught unless you know what you're doing. This guy was very careful. I heard you say he was dressed all in black and had a beanie on. Makes it that much harder to ID him. If they haven't caught him yet, I don't think they will. Unless he strikes again."

"And we don't want that," I said.

"No, we don't. I'm assuming the cops came in and asked you some questions?"

"Yeah, but it was on the first and second days when I was still pretty doped up. I don't remember a lot of it."

"Maybe for the best."

"Can we do a sit down once I get out? Maybe I could talk to your cop friend Lefty?"

"We'll see. As Paddy said, you should seriously consider dropping this case. As for now, stop thinking about having a sit down with us. Just worry about getting better."

"I am better. The doctor just told you guys I'm getting out."

Dennis ignored my sarcasm.

"We'll talk in a few days, Quint. Rest up. Don't do anything stupid."

"Like what?"

"Like trying to investigate this case with a hole in your side."

They turned to go and were almost at the door when I called them back.

"You guys, come here for one second."

They did.

I grabbed both of their arms.

"I promise this is the last time I'm going to mention it, but thank you. From the bottom of my heart, thank you. I'm going to assume they didn't catch your good samaritan?"

"No, they didn't, and they never will. Now, if you mention this one more fucking time, I'm officially ex-communicating you."

"Mum's the word from here on in."

"Goodbye, Quint," they both said and walked toward the door.

"Take care, Uncles Bob and Bill."

"You must be ready to get out," Paddy said. "Your cheesy sense of humor has returned."

∽

Early the next morning, I was set to be released. My favorite doctor had come by my room and told me I'd be getting out in fifteen minutes or so. I thanked him for everything.

A few minutes later I heard someone walking into my room. It hadn't even been five minutes since the doctor had left. I was getting released quicker than I'd hoped.

No such luck. The guy was a cop, wearing his Berkeley Police Department blues. I thought I'd answered enough of their questions. Apparently not.

"You must be Quint," he said.

"I am. And can we make this quick? They are actually releasing me in a few minutes and I can't wait to have some non-hospital food."

The man let out a big smile.

"I can't blame you for that."

He then extended his hand and I shook it.

"I'm Dean Graves. It's nice to meet you, Quint."

"Likewise."

"I'm not here to ask you any more questions about what happened. I know several of my fellow officers have already covered that."

"Then what are you here for?"

Dean Graves was probably about 6'3" and well-built. He had a quick smile to him but was also probably someone you didn't want to fuck with. At least he seemed to have a personality. I couldn't say that about most of the other Berkeley police officers I'd met.

"I just wanted to insure you that we are going to catch whoever did this."

"Thanks."

"I mean it. It's terrible what happened and I look forward to bringing the guy to justice."

"I'd sleep a little better at night," I said.

"I've got a feeling you'll sleep well for the next few days. That usually happens when people go from these crummy hospital beds to their own."

"A warm meal and my own bed," I said. "I can't wait."

"I won't keep you much longer."

"You're not just a regular beat cop, are you?"

I'm not sure if it's the way he carried himself, or whether it's the fact he had the gusto to come visit me before I left, but I knew this wasn't just a regular old cop.

"No. I'm a little higher up than that," Graves said, but didn't give me any more than that.

"Is it protocol to come talk to gunshot victims getting out?" I said.

I was being a bit sarcastic and I wasn't sure quite why.

"Maybe it should be," Graves said. "People are losing faith in police departments around the country. I think a little personal touch can go a long way. Don't you agree?"

A nurse walked in before I had a chance to answer.

"Which one of you is Quint Adler?"

"That would be him," Dean Graves said.

I couldn't help but laugh. What a silly question by the nurse.

"I'm here to finalize your release," the nurse said.

Dean Graves extended his hand a second time.

"Take care, Quint. I'll let you get home to that warm bed and a warm meal. I just wanted to reiterate that I'll make sure we catch whoever did this."

"Thanks. And I think you're right. A little personal touch from police departments could go a long way."

"Indeed. People often feel Persona Non Grata around police officers. I'm hoping to change that and bring back the trust in our fine profession."

With that, he waved goodbye to me, walked out the door, and the nurse approached.

I was walking out of Summit Hospital ten minutes later.

.

CHAPTER 20

A LITTLE MORE THAN A WEEK LATER.

"I can't tell if you're a genius or completely deranged."

It was Tom Butler on the other end of the phone. It was a Sunday. I'd been shot fifteen days ago and after six days in the hospital, I'd now been out for another nine days. I was getting back to my old self and honestly felt about 90%. Dr. Rosen still wanted me to take it easy for at least one more week, but I was getting the itch to get back out there.

I couldn't sit around my apartment for much longer. It was driving me bonkers. Bullet wound be damned. To pass the time, I'd tried a few T.V. shows that friends had suggested, but most of them just bored me. The exception was *The Bartender* on Hulu. It was exceptional.

"And what side did you land on?" I asked Tom.

"You knew something was askew with Blaine Travers all because of a knowing glance he gave you. That's the genius part of you, Quint."

I was no longer sure that was the case. Yes, Blaine knew a lot more than he originally let on, but I no longer thought he was the one who'd had someone follow me and Sophie around.

"And the derangement?"

"That you jumped to Travers potentially being the ringleader of all these murders. Seems like a quantum leap."

"I feel terrible about his death, but he was involved in this somehow."

"I know. And that's why I lean more toward the genius side."

"Not to be recognized in this lifetime. All I did was take a bullet for the team and no one has been arrested. Some genius."

"And that's the point of my call."

"I'm listening," I said.

"This may sound odd. You're a well-known private investigator at this point. You may consider this a step down. If you know what I mean."

"Actually, I have no freaking idea what you're talking about, Tom. Is this a riddle of some sort?"

Tom laughed.

"It sounded better in my head. I guess I better just come out and say it."

"Agreed."

"How would you like to come back to the paper for a one-time engagement?"

"To investigate this case?"

"Yes."

"You're not still pissed about when I erupted at you guys?"

"You're not still pissed that we needled you that day?"

"Fair enough. So we're all good?"

"We were all good ten minutes after that happened. And even if we weren't, this little gunshot to your abdomen would have made all of that moot. You know I love you like a son."

"Thanks, Tom. Is this the point where I'm supposed to say I look at you as a father figure...because I don't."

I could feel Tom smiling through my phone.

"You've become even more irascible," he said.

"Life is short. I guess that's hitting home lately."

"Let's not make it too short. A lot of people out there love you, Quint. I saw your mother the other day."

"Randomly?"

"No, I invited her to lunch."

"That was nice of you."

"You want some advice?"

I knew where this was headed, but I probably needed to hear it.

"Sure."

"Include your mother a little bit more in your rehab. She thinks she's being overshadowed by Sophie."

I figured that's what he'd say. He wasn't wrong.

"Thanks, Tom. I will. Now, let's get back to your offer. How does the paper help me get any closer to solving this?"

"Didn't you tell me the doctor wants you to lay low for a few more weeks?"

"A little less. I'm hoping for only one more week. I'm seeing him in three or four days."

"He probably doesn't want you leaving your apartment very often?"

"Basically, yes."

"Well if all you're doing is coming to our office, that's basically like being at home."

"I'm still listening."

"You may not be able to go out and investigate yourself, but you can delegate authority. I'll have a bunch of our other staff members do any leg work that you want. They'll be at your beck and call. You'd be running the show."

"I don't want to be putting them in harm's way. A lot of people are dead, Tom."

"Trust me, I've thought long and hard about this. I think they'd be safe. When a news truck or a cameraman shows up at a scene or to interview someone, people are less likely to act violently."

"There are examples of it happening," I said.

"True. There are also examples of people dying from stepping on a tack, Quint. We all take some risks in this life."

"And I'd come into the office for the next several days?"

"That's the idea. As you get stronger, maybe you'll be able to get out of the office. At some point, I'm sure you won't need us. But you're not ready yet and it's not just me saying that. Listen to your doctor."

"I'm intrigued," I said.

"I'm guessing you're a little more than that?"

"When would I start?"

"Tomorrow is a Monday. Seems as good a time as any."

"I'll be there. Thanks, Tom. A very big thank you."

"Let's catch these fuckers," he said.

I called my mother ten minutes later and invited her to lunch.

Well, I had her pick up the food and bring it to my apartment to eat, but it's the thought that counts.

Our lunch - a couple of In-N-Out burgers - was going well until I decided to bring up Tom's offer.

"You're not going to take it, are you?" she asked

"I think I am."

"You've gone insane, Quint. This case is going to kill you. Literally."

"I'm just going to sit at the office and delegate authority. I'm not going to be doing any investigating myself."

We were sitting at the little dinner table I had in the corner of my apartment. It looked out on the street below. Sophie and I usually just ate on the couch, but that felt a bit casual for my mother, so we sat at the table.

"You're supposed to be staying at the house for another few weeks. Or, did you forget what the doctor told you?"

My mother was usually a calm, mellow, polite woman, so for her to be fired up meant she didn't like this idea one bit. I guess I couldn't blame her.

"Two weeks would be the max, Mom. Plus, I'm not sure being at the office is any different than staying here."

"Of course it is. You won't be sitting in bed getting the rest you need. You'll be making speeches and gesticulating your arms to make your point, which could tear open your gunshot wound."

She looked like she wanted to cry. Knowing her son had suffered a gunshot wound was hard enough. Saying it aloud made it all the more real.

I patted my mother on the shoulder.

"Mom, I'm going to be just fine at *The Walnut Creek Times.* To be honest, it's probably safer than being here."

She looked up. That had connected.

"Really?" She asked.

"Yes. I'm going to be surrounded by twenty other people. Not here, alone and in bed."

"You don't think it's safe here? Now I'll start worrying about Sophie too."

"What about yourself?"

"I'm an old lady. I'm not going to spend time worrying about myself."

"But you're worrying about me."

"That's how it works, Quint. You'll understand one day when you settle down and have kids of your own."

It was the beginning of the speech I'd heard a thousand times. The truth was, I did have regrets that my mother wasn't yet a grandmother. It's just not something I wanted to talk about at that moment, so I decided to change the subject.

"They killed Henry, Mom. They tried to kill me. They've killed several others. I can't just sit in the bleachers. However, I'm not exactly playing in the game, either. The reporters of the paper will be doing that. Think of me as the coach, telling the players what to do. On the other side of the white lines, away from the violence of the game."

She smiled and that's when I knew I was wearing her down.

"You do have a way with words," my mother said. "No wonder you became a journalist. Why you left that to become a P.I., I'll never know."

"So I could get shot and have my mother deliver me In-N-Out.

It was all part of my master plan. Now take a bite. You've barely had any."

My mother took a bite and I did the same. I was almost finished already. I'd lost ten pounds in the hospital and had been eager to put it back on. I was close, having gained seven back. A lot easier to gain weight eating burgers than hospital food.

"Are you going to need rides to *The Times* and back?" she asked.

"No, the doctor said I can drive. Tom has a spot for me near the front."

"A handicapped one?"

"No. He offered that, but I felt odd taking it. I'm not handicapped and don't want to steal someone's spot who might really need it."

My mother looked like she wanted to get emotional again.

"You're a good man, Quint. Your father would be proud."

I still loved my father very much and missed him every day.

"Thanks," I said. "That means more than you know."

"And maybe he's your guardian angel up there. Making sure the bad guys don't get you."

"Then tell him to stop the bullets next time."

My mother started laughing, spitting up a little bit of her most recent bite.

"Jeez, Mom. Can't take you anywhere."

She lost it at that point. There was laughter, crying, and some other emotion I'm not sure I'd ever seen.

After a minute, she'd gathered herself.

"Please be safe, Quint."

"I will."

"I'm serious. These people are dangerous and I can't imagine having to live without you."

I leaned in and gave her a hug.

"I'm not going anywhere," I said.

Sophie came over that night.

Not that it was any big surprise. She'd been over every night since I'd been shot. That included my hospital stay. Even my mother had taken a day off now and then. For her own mental health more than anything else. She hated to see her only child suffering.

But there was no stopping Sophie.

Along with being there every night, she tried to swing by most mornings as well. She was still living at her place, however. I'd asked her to stay the night a few times, but she was probably afraid to bump into me as we slept. Or afraid I'd try to convince her to have sex, something she knew the doctor hadn't approved yet.

On this night, I buzzed her into the apartment complex and she used her own key to get in. She'd insisted that I let her make her own copy.

What if you can't make it to the door? What if you've fallen and can't get up? What if you're hurt and I can't get in the apartment?

Yes, they were all variations on the same concept; I couldn't get up and open the door myself.

"You look pretty good tonight," Sophie said as she walked in.

I was sitting up in bed.

"As opposed to every other night?"

"Why do you always try to use humor when talking about this injury?"

"It's preferable to talking about the hole in my side."

"Fair point. Do you feel like you're getting stronger?"

"You know that's the case because I tell you every time I see you. I'm basically my old self at this point."

"Not according to the doctor."

"What does he know?"

She smiled.

"There you go using humor again. And the doctor knows to safeguard patients who won't safeguard themselves."

"That hurts," I said.

She leaned in and kissed me. I tried to grab her and wrestle her down to the bed, but she was able to remain standing. I guess I wasn't at full strength. I'd usually be able to accomplish that easily. My muscles had likely atrophied just a bit.

"You don't want to join me in bed?"

"I want to more than you'll ever know."

"Then do it."

"You told me what the doctor said. He said it's just too risky. There's too good a chance of tearing the staples."

"I never should have told you that."

Sophie blushed.

"How much longer until we can have some fun again?" she asked.

I pretended to look down at what was a non-existent watch.

"Will you look at that," I said. "Five minutes from now."

"You're hilarious," she said sarcastically. "How long for real? Another week?"

"Pretty soon. He said it will happen before I'm given the overall clean bill of health. I think one more week. Tops," I said.

"Damn."

"I don't think I can wait a week."

"If I can wait a week, so can you," Sophie said.

"It's harder for guys to live without it."

"You're just like every other guy I've ever met. They all think that."

"What, it's not true?"

"We want it just as much as you horn dogs," Sophie said. "Trust me, I'd love nothing better than to jump on that bed and make love to you."

"Then why don't you? Let's break a few rules."

"I'm more afraid of breaking a few staples."

"Ouch," I said.

"What do you want for dinner," Sophie asked. "I don't feel like cooking, so let's do DoorDash tonight. How's Sushi sound?"

There's no way sex meant as much to women. Sophie had just proved it. A man could never transition that quickly from talking about sex to talking about what type of Spicy Tuna Roll to order.

"Sushi is fine," I said, resigning myself to another sexless night.

CHAPTER 21

I t felt like the early 2000s, walking into *The Walnut Creek Times* office for the first time.

Sure I'd been there a few weeks previous for the train wreck of a pitch I'd made to Tom, Trent, and Greg, but this was different. I was essentially an employee for the foreseeable future, which I hoped wasn't too long. I was grateful to Tom, I just didn't want this to be permanent. Or anything approaching it. One week even seemed like a stretch.

Despite all that had happened, I liked being a P.I. I didn't like delegating authority. I liked doing things myself. And despite Tom saying I was running things, I still answered to him and Krissy.

I walked straight in - we didn't have a Miss Congeniality manning the door like the *East Bay Times* - and headed up toward Tom's office.

I didn't get that far.

"Where do you think you're going?"

It was Tom's voice. He was on the ground floor with some of the reporters. His office was upstairs, but he had always spent a fair amount of his time mingling down here, not wanting to miss anything.

"I was heading up to talk to the boss," I said.

"And by that, he means Krissy," Greg Alm said, knowing what I was going to say next.

"Can everyone come over here please," Tom yelled, ignoring the fun Greg and I were having.

Six people co-mingled in the middle of the room. I knew three of them.

"For anyone who hasn't met Quint yet, take your time and introduce yourself at some point today. As I told you on Friday, there was a chance he'd be joining us today and here he is."

Tom hadn't broached the subject with me until yesterday so he must have been pretty confident I was going to say yes. He probably assumed being apartment-bound was driving me crazy. He wasn't wrong.

"If he asks you to investigate something, please do it. Assume that I've already given it my approval. I don't want you guys spending a lot of time going back and forth from him to me and wasting our precious time. We may only have him for a few days, so give Quint the benefit of the doubt. I promise he won't ask you to do anything he wouldn't do himself if he were able. Quint, would you like to say a few words?"

I looked out over everyone.

"I'm not sure I deserve this. I'm just thankful to Tom for giving me this opportunity, and I'm hoping we might be able to find some new information relative to my shooting and the murders of Henry Madsen, Frank Manning, Rupert Shinn, and Blaine Travers."

When I said each name individually, it made everyone realize just how much loss of life there had already been.

I continued.

"I've printed up several three-page summaries of everything I know about the murders."

I walked over to the table and handed a copy to the six reporters who were present. I then gave two to Tom.

"One for Krissy too."

"She wanted to be here, but something came up."

"No problem."

I saw everyone looking over the pamphlets.

"I've got a few field trips if anyone wants to volunteer."

They all raised their hands in varying degrees of anticipation.

I didn't want to play favorites, so I pointed at one person I'd worked with before - Trent Buckley - and a fresh-faced young woman in her twenties.

"What's your name?"

"I'm Lucy."

"Nice to meet you, Lucy. I'm Quint as you already know. I worked with Trent about a hundred years ago and I know I can trust him so I'm going to pair you two up."

I did the same with Greg Alm and a man in his mid-twenties I'd never met. Finally, I paired up Crystal Howell - the third person I knew - with another young woman in her twenties. The staff was certainly getting younger at *The Walnut Creek Times*.

"There are two people I'd like you to investigate today. One is Angela Shinn, the widow of Rupert, a.k.a. Needles. I've had two encounters with her and she's a piece of work. I doubt you're going to get anything from her but it's worth a try. The second is, sadly, another widow. Her name is Tiffany Travers and her husband Blaine was the one killed on the same day they almost got me. And then, the last two-person team can head down to the Berkeley Marina and interview anybody who is willing to talk to you. I'm guessing that's going to be tough, especially with the death of Blaine. Three people who had boats down there have now been killed. This isn't a coincidence, obviously. Maybe someone will be willing to talk about any potential connections."

"Do you care which teams go where?" Tom asked.

"No, I don't," I said, but then realized I did have one preference.

I'd printed out a small one-page sheet on both Angela Shinn and Tiffany Travers. I handed one to Greg and one to Trent, not even looking which went to which. Those two were interchangeable to me.

"That means that Crystal and…"

"Jen," Tom said.

"Crystal and Jen, you get to go to the marina."

That had been intentional, albeit something I'd thought up in the previous minute. Almost all of the boat owners seemed to be males. Crystal and Jen were both attractive and my hope was that they'd be more likely to talk to women. Maybe my view was a bit sexist, but I didn't think so. I thought it was just a good investigative technique.

"Is there anything else, Quint?" Tom asked.

"I think that's pretty much it for now. We'll reconvene this afternoon and see what you guys were able to find out."

I got a few nods and they left the office in pairs of two.

"Looks like we're off to a good start," Tom said.

For the next three days, I went into the office of *The Walnut Creek Times* and asked the six reporters to interview people related to the case. It was killing me not to be out there myself. I hated being a desk jockey. I hadn't always felt that way; I was a news reporter for over a decade, after all. My time as a P.I. had changed all that, however, and I now wanted to be out there in the field, investigating the riff-raff of our society. Getting my hands dirty.

By the end of our third day, as I sat in my apartment reading the day's interviews, I knew our little experiment was over.

It wasn't the fault of the reporters. They had done everything I'd asked of them. They'd been thorough and had at least tried to interview every person I'd asked. Some, like Angela Shinn, had given them the cold shoulder I'd expected.

So, no, it wasn't the reporters' fault.

I'm just not sure they were ready to get grimy; to investigate a murder is different than covering your local sports teams or a group of kids playing doorbell ditch.

Greg Alm, Trent Buckley, Crystal Howell, and the other three reporters who worked for me did nothing wrong. In fact, they interviewed eight people who, at least peripherally, were involved in the case. They didn't find any smoking gun, however. Nothing that really moved the needle in the case.

Who knows, maybe their interviews would prove invaluable down the line, but at the moment, they weren't supplying much in the way of evidence.

I knew I had to make a call to Tom Butler.

"Hey, Quint. Am I going to see you tomorrow morning?"

It was an odd opening. It's almost like he knew what was coming.

"I don't think so, Tom. I've got a doctor's appointment at ten."

"Is that the only reason?"

"No," I admitted. "Listen, I think you had a great idea, but…"

"I know, Quint."

"You do?"

"Yeah, I could tell you haven't exactly been enamored with my employees."

"It has nothing to do with them. They did everything I asked of them. I just don't think - and don't take this the wrong way - that they are willing to go all the way as a private investigator might."

"I hope you're not thinking about going back out there, Quint."

"I am."

"Shit, you really do have a death wish."

Tom was a great friend, but I didn't want to go down this road. I'd already heard it from Sophie and my mother; shit, even Dennis and Paddy.

"Thanks for all you and the reporters did, Tom. It means a lot."

Tom ended our phone call with a familiar refrain.

"Stay safe, Quint."

Dr. Aaron Rosen was waiting for me as I walked into Summit Hospital and knocked on his door.

"Jeez, you must be eager to see me," I said.

"Not exactly, Quint. I have another client who needs my help a little more than you right now."

"So you admit that I don't need your help anymore?"

"That's not what I said. How do you feel?"

"99.99%."

"Do you think you're ready to get those staples out?"

"That would be great."

"I think you're ready also. I'll have Nurse Adams take care of that," he said, although I had no idea who Nurse Adams was.

"Great."

"Listen, Quint. I really have to go. I have a surgery starting in fifteen minutes. I think you're going to be alright. I'd ask you to lay low as much as you can for the foreseeable future, but from what little I've got to know you, that seems unlikely."

"Is that your roundabout way of saying I've been cleared to return to my normal life?"

Dr. Rosen smiled.

"Yes."

He headed toward the door.

"Does that include sex?" I asked.

"Have at it, Quint."

I laughed.

"Thanks, Doc."

He shut the door and left his office.

I was then startled by a voice behind me. She must have snuck up on me.

"Hi, Quint. I'm Nurse Adams. You ready to get those staples removed?"

"I sure am."

CHAPTER 22

And then one day, everything changed.

And I do mean everything.

I was reading the police report about the murder of Henry for probably the fifth time when something clicked. The homicide detectives on the case were listed as Omar Shahin and Wade Watkins.

My mind tried to remember back to the day in question. There had been an intense, slender, bespectacled investigator and I was almost positive his name wasn't Omar Shahin or Wade Watkins. I wracked my brain for a few more minutes.

Detective Mixon!

That was it. I was certain.

Why wasn't his name on the police report?

He was the man in charge. Despite his small stature he'd given no doubt about who was running the investigation. I remember being perturbed by him in the moment, but thinking that he seemed quite proficient. I'd made a mental note that Detective Mixon was someone you wanted on your side.

And yet, it appeared as if he'd been taken off the case just as soon as he'd started it. I read over some of the other police reports that Lefty had procured for me. Maybe Detective Mixon had been reassigned to another murder in the investigation. I scanned over the police reports of Frank Manning and Rupert Shinn. Nothing.

Something stank and it wasn't the leftover sushi in my fridge.

I picked up the phone and called the Berkeley Police Department.

"Berkeley PD."

"Yeah, I wanted to talk to Detective Mixon."

"What is this regarding?"

I had to make something up on the fly.

"I'm a potential witness in a case he's investigating."

"He's out of the office right now, but you can leave a message with me."

"I'd rather talk to Detective Mixon."

"I can have him call you back if you'd prefer."

"Perfect."

"What's your name and number?"

It was time to quickly make up a name. I didn't want any record that a Quint Adler had called the Berkeley PD. I decided to give them Robert De Niro's character's name in *Midnight Run*, an all-time favorite movie of mine.

"Jack Walsh and my number is 925-555-2590."

I had to give them my real phone number if I wanted a callback. Hopefully, that wouldn't come back and bite me in the ass.

"Okay, Jack. I'll have him call you sometime later today."

"Thanks."

The call came less than an hour later.

I was in line at Sweetgreen, deciding to have a healthy lunch.

"I'll be right back," I said to the clerk, halfway through my order.

She looked at me like I was crazy.

I ran outside and ducked around a corner where people weren't conglomerating.

"Hello?"

"Is this Jack Walsh?"

"It is," I said, trying to change my voice ever so slightly. It had been over a month, but we'd talked for a long time that morning and I wanted a safeguard from him recognizing my voice.

"I heard you may have some information on a case of mine. More specifically, you might be a witness."

"That's correct."

"I'd love to hear what you saw. And what case is this, exactly?"

This wasn't going to work over the phone. I needed to see his reaction in person. It was also way too easy for him to hang up on me when I was forced to admit I wasn't Jack Walsh.

"I'll do it in person. I don't trust you guys over the phone."

"You have nothing to worry about, Jack. Let's just get this over with so we don't have to go that extra step and meet in person."

"Sounds like you're trying to get me to hang up. I would have thought you'd want to close one of your cases."

"Woah, Jack. Don't hang up. I'll meet you in person if you'd prefer. I just thought that it would be easier to tell me over the phone."

"If you say that again, I really am hanging up."

"Have it your way. Where and when would you like to meet?"

"Will it just be you?"

"Yes, Jack, but you are starting to scare me a little bit."

"You have nothing to fear. It's me who should be scared."

"Scared of what, Jack?"

It was blatantly obvious that he kept calling me Jack in hopes I'd start to consider him trustworthy. I knew exactly what he was doing. This wasn't my first rodeo.

"I'll tell you when I see you," I said.

"Okay. When and where?"

I almost said Kincade's, but with me having been shot leaving there and Blaine Travers having been killed on his way there, I was afraid that location would give him pause.

"Rooted Cafe in Walnut Creek."

I thought he might complain that I didn't pick something closer to Berkeley.

"What time?"

"Can you be there at eight a.m. tomorrow?"

"And this will be worth my time, Jack?"

"Yes."

"I'll be there."

Rooted opened at 8:00 and I was there before they opened the doors.

A lot of the coffee shop had communal seating and that wouldn't work for the discussion I was ready to have with Detective Mixon. There was a couch that sat by itself in the right corner of the restaurant, however, and that's what I planned on locking down.

At 7:58, they opened the doors and I set my backpack and laptop on the couch before even ordering a coffee. The speakers were playing *Right Down The Line* by Gerry Rafferty, an underrated classic.

As I made my way back toward the front to order my coffee, I saw Mixon walk in.

He looked just as intense as the day I'd met him out at the Berkeley Marina. He was wearing jeans, a white t-shirt, some wire-rimmed glasses, and a no-nonsense look.

It only took him a second to recognize me. It had been over a month since the lone time we'd met, but the fact that I was also a somewhat public figure surely contributed.

"Detective Mixon," I said.

"It was Quint, right?"

I leaned in and whispered.

"Today I'm Jack Walsh."

I looked at his face to try and read his reaction. I was expecting anger considering I'd convinced him to come to Rooted based on a lie. Instead, I saw admiration, as if he was impressed by what I'd done.

"You're living up to your reputation," he said.

"And what might that be?"

"That you like to rock the boat."

"Guilty as charged."

"How's the gunshot wound?" Mixon asked.

"So you have been following my case?"

"Don't tell anyone," he said and smiled.

"What kind of coffee do you drink?"

"Regular coffee. Black."

I smiled at the young female barista I recognized and waved at Mike, who managed the place. Rooted was one of several coffee shops I frequented regularly and the staff had always been great to me. I ordered my Americano and Mixon's regular coffee and walked him over to the couch.

"This will give us a little privacy," I said.

Mixon sat down and I went up and picked up our coffees a minute later.

I returned, took a seat, and set our coffees down.

"I have to say. I'm a little surprised at your reaction," I said. "I was expecting a little more pushback. You almost seem - dare I say - happy to see me."

"Jack Walsh is the character from *Midnight Run*, correct?"

"Yes."

"When I got off the phone with you yesterday, the name just didn't ring true. It sounded made up. And then it hit me where I'd heard it before. Great movie by the way."

"One of the best," I said. "Did you think it was going to be me?"

"Let's just say, you would have been on my shortlist."

I was flabbergasted.

"Why?"

"Because you're a good P.I."

"What does that mean exactly?"

"It means you wouldn't be covering all your bases if you didn't come back and talk to me."

"The truth is I'd read the police report on Henry's death probably five times until I realized you weren't on it."

"Not to butter you up, but looking at the police officers of record isn't exactly the sexy part of a police report."

"Fair point, Detective Mixon."

"Call me Tyler, since I'm not acting as a detective right now."

"You're not?"

"If I was, I'd have turned tail and ran when I first saw you."

"Well, thanks for staying, Tyler."

"Nice little coffee shop," he said, smiling at his own version of small talk.

"I like it here. So, are we ready to get down to this?" I asked.

"Get down to what, exactly?"

"I want to know why you were the first homicide detective at the scene and then seemed to have been relieved of your duties?"

"Did you enjoy being shot?"

"What's that have to do with anything?" I asked.

"Just answer the question," Tyler said.

"That would be a resounding no."

"Then why are you back out investigating this case? Because that's what you've got coming again. And I promise you won't live through the next one."

"I don't need a lecture, Tyler. What I need is an answer to my question."

He looked around the coffee shop really quickly, showing his first signs of nervousness. People were starting to file in.

"The powers that be must have thought my fellow detectives Omar and Wade would do a better job."

"I don't believe that," I said. "I had barely met you and knew you were a skilled detective."

"Listen, Quint. I'm going to warn you one more time: Stop investigating this case. You can't win."

"Who am I fighting? The devil?"

"Some might say that."

"Does the devil have a name?"

"If I told you, then I'm next on the chopping block."

"I will not tell a soul."

"We're meeting at a public place. He could easily find out. He has eyes everywhere."

I thought back to Blaine Travers's comment. Had Blaine been referring to someone who has eyes everywhere?

"Who's he?" I asked, knowing he wasn't going to give me what I was looking for.

"You're so far out of your league," he said.

I'd heard that earlier on in this investigation. I didn't like it any better this time.

"I'm not some Triple-A baseball player or D-league basketball player," I said. "This isn't my first rodeo."

He didn't respond.

I took a sip of my coffee, hoping we could reset to a few minutes ago when Tyler Mixon seemed to be on my side. Something had changed. Maybe the consistent stream of people walking into the coffee shop had spooked him.

"Would you rather talk outside?" I asked.

"That would only be worse. There's more people out on the street than in here."

I thought back to something earlier in our conversation.

"There's one little thing I don't understand."

"What's that?" he asked.

"You're obviously being standoffish and don't want to give anything away."

"Thanks, Captain Obvious."

I ignored his attempt at sarcasm.

"And yet you came to this coffee shop knowing full well it might be me."

He didn't respond right away. I think he was trying to think of some way to talk himself out of this.

"I thought there was an outside chance, but I certainly didn't know it was going to be you."

"Outside chance? That's not what you said. You said I was on the shortlist of people you suspected."

"I know what I said," he said, becoming flabbergasted.

I could have buried him, saying something like 'It doesn't seem like you do know what you said,' but I thought this was my chance to kill him with kindness instead.

"Listen, the reason I called you here today is that I thought you came across as a very adept detective. You handled everything at Henry's crime scene just the way I'd want a homicide detective to do so. Your subordinates respected you and seemed eager to follow your lead."

"Thanks," he almost whispered.

"Which was why it came as such a surprise to discover you'd been replaced. Why replace an excellent detective?"

I'd hit him with a brutal 1-2, a scathing putdown, and then an honest compliment. People didn't know how to react when hit with those in rapid succession.

"I was as surprised as anyone," he said.

I was pretty sure Berkeley's Chief of Police was named Gary Laughlin.

"Did the word come from Laughlin?"

"It came from the top."

"So, Laughlin, right?"

"For a smart guy, you're very naive when it comes to this case."

"Help me out then."

"Laughlin is just a figurehead."

"Then who is pulling the strings?"

"This is where I walk away," he said and I could tell by his eyes that he meant it.

He was the no-nonsense Detective Mixon again; no longer Tyler.

He stood up, peering down at me. He leaned in closer as he whispered his parting shot to me.

"Please, for the love of God, don't contact me again. They will kill me. I've given you more than enough going forward, but you're on your own from here on in."

"You won't hear from me again," I said.

He scurried out the door, covering his face in the process.

I walked back to my apartment and saw that I'd received a text from Sophie. She said I'd seemed a little distant over the last several days.

She had a point. I'd been so wrapped up in my arrangement with *The Walnut Creek Times,* and now I was out doing my own investigating again. I dove headfirst back into the case and my relationship with her had been put on the back burner. It was my fault.

I called her.

"Hey, Quint."

"You're right. I've been a bad boyfriend. Let's go out to dinner tonight."

"You sure? It's not one of our assigned nights."

"Assigned nights sounds like something a married couple of thirty years sets up. We can go out when and where we want. How about I'll come to you? Can you be ready by 6:30?"

"Sure. Thanks for this, Quint."

"You got it. See you tonight."

Range Life was a great restaurant near the train tracks in Livermore, a city only about ten minutes from where Sophie lived in Pleasanton. I'd taken my mother there once and a few friends another time. Both times I'd left thinking it was one of the best meals I'd had in years.

Here's hoping it would go three for three.

I picked up Sophie at exactly 6:30. I walked to the door and handed her twelve red roses that I'd picked up on my way over.

The letter said, "*I'm so sorry. I promise to be better going forward. Love you.*"

She smelled the roses and then read the letter.

I thought she was going to cry, but instead, she just hugged me.

"I love you too," she said. "And I don't mean to be the nagging girlfriend, I just felt like our days were losing some of their luster."

"You're not being the nagging girlfriend. I was being the ungrateful boyfriend."

She leaned in and hugged me a second time.

One of the things I loved about Sophie is how quickly she'd forgive me. As we headed off toward Range Life, we were as thick as thieves again.

I did the ordering for the two of us.

Sophie had never eaten here and allowed me to pick our courses. The restaurant itself was quaint, with probably only about eight tables in the inside area and four or five outside.

We were given a table smack dab in the middle of the restaurant. It was definitely a change from the clandestine coffees I'd had with Detective Mixon and others. For those, I was looking for a corner table or something with privacy. Not tonight. We were stuck in the middle; clowns to the left of us and jokers to the right.

I ordered a salad that had Stracciatella cheese, grapes, arugula, and toasted pecans. I'd periodically look at Range Life's menu online, and while it changed a lot, Stracciatella was almost always on the menu. I couldn't blame them. It was one of the richest cheeses I'd ever had. And I don't mean the price. I meant the creaminess.

"This is delicious," Sophie said. "The cheese is outrageous."

"I've now had it all three times I've been here."

"Who have you taken here before?"

"I took my Mom once and a few friends and I came out here about six weeks ago."

"Right before we started dating again," Sophie said and smiled.

She just as easily could have said, 'right before my father was killed' but I'm glad she hadn't.

"I'm so happy you're back in my life," I said.

"So am I. I can't wait until the investigation into my Dad's murder is over so we can actually focus on being boyfriend and girlfriend. I feel like it's constantly hanging over us. And listen, you know I loved my father with all my heart. I'm not dismissing his death. Not at all. I just don't want it to be all-consuming for the months to come."

"I agree, but if we never catch the people responsible, it will only get worse."

"You're back investigating it on your own, aren't you?"

Sophie had always been good at reading me. This night was no different. Detective Mixon was really my first foray back out into the field and Sophie had already caught me. I hadn't made a conscious decision not to tell her. I just hadn't gotten around to it. It had only occurred earlier that morning, after all.

"I met with someone this morning," I said. "I've interviewed so many darn people for this case, but this was different. This one may have been important. Very important."

"And you weren't going to tell me?"

"You said you didn't want daily updates."

"True, but if it's really important, I'd like to know."

"I met with the detective who was the first to arrive on the scene of your father's murder."

I was starting to wish we'd gotten a corner table after all. I tried to keep my voice down as I discussed my meeting with Tyler Mixon.

"And what did he have to say?"

Mixon's paranoia was getting the best of me. I grabbed Sophie's wrist and leaned in closer, giving her a kiss.

"We'll talk about it on the ride home. I don't want to do it here."

I kissed her a second time and then let go of her hand. She could tell I was serious.

"So, how about those Yankees?" Sophie said.

I laughed. That had always been my go-to line when I wanted to change the subject and now she was using it as her own.

"Still loving the salad?" I asked.

"You kidding me? I'd have this fed intravenously every day if I could."

Our entrees came next. I'd ordered two and asked the waiter if we could each get a plate to share the dishes.

One was a local Halibut Crudo served with a fruit called Pomelo and an onion-based Verde sauce. The second was a beef tartare that came with crispy shallots and a Chimichurri sauce.

They were delivered together and Sophie went straight for the Halibut. She loved nothing more than fresh raw fish and from my understanding, Crudo was just the Italian name for raw fish.

"My God, Quint, this is perfection."

Looked like my restaurant choice had been a winner.

She tried two bites of the beef tartare, but she was so taken with the Crudo that it was almost as if we'd ordered our own separate entrees. The tartare was great, so I was fine with our little arrangement. More so, I just wanted Sophie to be happy.

"Thanks for all this," Sophie said. "I needed it."

"So did I," I said. "It's quite an improvement over what I was eating a mere two weeks ago."

"If you ever end up in the hospital again, I'll sneak in some food from here."

She was smiling, but I couldn't help but think of Detective Mixon's warning that I was risking being shot again. Then again, if he was correct, I wouldn't be ending up in the hospital. I'd be at the morgue. I told myself we were having a lovely time and not to focus on the case. That was always easier said than done.

"Don't bring the Halibut Crudo. You'll probably just end up eating it all."

Sophie laughed; a little louder than she expected.

"Sorry," she said unnecessarily.

"Don't be. I love your laugh."

She put her hand over mine.

"Will you stay the night at my place?"

When it came to staying the night, we almost always stayed at mine, which considering she had a house and I had an apartment, was an odd choice.

"Of course, I will."

She leaned in and kissed me.

Ten minutes later, we were sharing their signature dessert,

something called *Milk and Honey*. It was Malted Milk Ice Cream with Honeycomb and Olive Oil.

Like the rest of the dinner, it was delicious.

We paid the bill and walked out of Range Life arm-in-arm.

CHAPTER 23

I woke up sore the next morning.

Two rounds of lovemaking - hey, that's what Sophie called it - had made my arms and shoulders feel like the jello I ate in the hospital.

Sophie was already getting ready for work.

"I'll see you tonight?" she asked, knowing what the answer would be.

"Of course. Let's eat in," I said.

"That's fine, but you know it won't be as good as last night."

"That's for sure."

"I've got a busy day, Quint. I have to run. You know how to lock up."

"I do. See you tonight."

I grabbed my cell phone from the nightstand. It was 7:45. Rarely did I sleep in that late.

A wonderful dinner and some great sex helped do the trick.

I felt more like myself than at any other time since getting out of the hospital.

$\sim$

I left a few minutes after Sophie and headed back to Walnut Creek.

It took me twenty-five minutes and once I arrived home, I was already back on the case.

After my meeting with Mixon yesterday, I believed a break-through was close. I had to tread lightly because I was dealing with some extremely dangerous people, but for the first time, I felt like I was getting close.

The question was, what to do next? Part of me wanted to ask Dennis and Paddy if I could meet with Lefty again. They'd been pretty adamant that I drop this case, however, and I'm not sure they'd grant me that wish. They'd already given me way too much rope over the last several weeks. And I wasn't even including the fact that they had saved my life.

I could Google something like 'Who is the real Chief of Police of Berkeley?' but that wasn't going to get me anywhere. I needed to talk to someone who was ingrained in the department. And Detective Mixon was now off the board. I had to respect his wishes. He'd had every chance to name-drop the person he believed had him replaced. It was obvious he was scared of the guy.

Did that person have anything to do with the murders? It was far from certain, but it was as good a lead as any. I was starting to think that Henry's request about not involving the police was spot on.

As I continued pondering what to do next, a crazy thought came to mind.

I looked back over my recent call log and found the number I was looking for: The Berkeley Police Department.

"Berkeley PD," the monotone voice answered.

"Can I talk to the boss man?" I asked.

"Are you referring to Chief Laughlin?"

Here came the moment of truth.

"That's a good one," I said. "I'm talking about the guy who actually runs things."

The voice on the other end didn't respond for a few seconds. If it was possible to have a staredown over the phone, then that's what this felt like.

For a split second, I thought my genius plan was going to work. I was already patting myself on the back.

"I'm sorry, what did you say your name was?"

And just like that, I knew it was over.

"I'll call back later," I said and hung up the phone.

While I hadn't been successful with my little ploy, I'd gotten close. And I could tell the dispatcher knew who I was referring to, even if I didn't.

I had another idea which was a lot more dangerous than talking on the phone.

Should I be doing it? No. Was that going to stop me? Also no.

Within twenty minutes of my phone call to the Berkeley PD, I was off to the brick-and-mortar edition of the Berkeley PD. I'd been there several times over the years and knew it was located on the 2100 block of Martin Luther King Jr. Way in Berkeley.

I parked a half block up the street, near where the officers parked their cars. It would be a good spot to intercept them.

I didn't have to wait more than a minute before two of Berkeley PD's finest headed in my direction. I got out of my car as they approached, pretending to be walking toward the precinct.

When they got within twenty feet, I approached the older of the two, hoping he'd be more likely to talk. He was probably forty-five while the younger one was in his mid-twenties. From my history, it was the younger recruits who were more tight-lipped. Once people got older, they tended not to give a fuck. That was probably true in most parts of life.

I had on a ball cap that I'd lowered pretty far down over my face. I didn't want anyone to recognize me.

"Hello, officers. I was told to come here and talk to the boss. Do you know his name?"

"The Chief's name is Gary Laughlin."

I laughed.

"No, my friend said it's the guy who ran the place. Not the chief."

The older cop looked at me and I thought we might be at another standstill like with the dispatcher.

Instead, he laughed.

"You must be talking about Dean Graves."

Bingo!!

And then I realized that I recognized that name. Holy shit! He'd been the guy who came and visited me at the hospital. If he'd done that while being part of the plot to kill me, we were talking about a real sociopath.

"Thanks so much," I said, trying not to get distracted by this new information.

The officer laughed again, but this time it seemed more muted.

"Just don't tell him I told you that."

The younger officer looked up at his superior. I read the expression as consternation, but maybe it was just because I was on edge myself. If Dean Graves was the person that Detective Mixon wouldn't name by name, I had reason to be scared. And it would explain the younger officer's look.

The two cops took a left and went to pick up their car. The younger one turned around and stared at me as I walked down the block. I didn't like it one bit. This was more ominous than his earlier expression.

I kept walking past the police station and took a right, ensuring that I wouldn't see them once they drove away.

I waited longer than was likely necessary before I headed back to my car.

I started up the car and started heading back toward Walnut Creek.

It was time to find out a few things about Dean Graves.

I arrived home, ate some smoked salmon, and even had a few blue-berries. I don't know if there was any truth to those two foods being good for your brain, but I could have used the increased acumen.

After an hour, here's what I'd found out about Dean Graves:

He was born in 1988, which made him either thirty-four or thirty-five years old. I couldn't find an exact date of birth.

He was born in San Bernardino and then his parents moved north to Sacramento when Graves was five. His family remained in Sacramento where he graduated from American Legion High School in 2006.

There wasn't much in his bio from 2006 until 2010 when he joined the police academy in Sacramento. After two years there, he took the same job in Berkeley. It didn't say if he asked for a transfer or just moved to the Bay Area and reapplied down here.

He made quick advances through the ranks.

Graves was a detective by 2012 and a sergeant by 2014. In 2015, he was promoted to lieutenant. I didn't know everything about police hierarchy, but I knew it usually took more than four years to make lieutenant.

His next step was to make captain in 2020 - another really fast progression for somebody that young.

Since last year, Dean Graves had been the assistant to Chief Gary Laughlin.

Any way you looked at it, Dean Graves had a meteoric rise.

I Googled 'Dean Graves arrested' 'Dean Graves bully' 'Dean Graves in trouble' 'Dean Graves reprimanded' and five other similar types of searches, but nothing came back of import. He had either stayed out of trouble or knew how to keep bad news off the internet.

I read up on Chief Laughlin as well. He was fifty-three years old and seemed to have a sterling reputation. He'd grown up in Berkeley and risen up the ranks at a much more deliberate pace than Dean Graves. I wonder if there was some jealousy on his part; thinking Graves hadn't put in his time.

Then again, Graves was listed as the assistant to Chief Laughlin, so it's likely they had a good relationship. Or, maybe Graves was tired of playing second fiddle. This was a guy who had risen up the ranks at record speed. Being stuck in neutral probably didn't fit his personality type.

But even if all of my conjecture were somehow true, how the hell did the murders of four people - almost five - lead back to Dean Graves?

I didn't know, but I knew one thing for certain.

I wasn't going anywhere.

I was back on the case and loving it.

CHAPTER 24

My next order of business was to find out a little more about Dean Graves.

I decided to impersonate a member of the media. If Henry Madsen were still alive he'd probably have joked that I managed to do that for over ten years at *The Walnut Creek Times* and I would have laughed my ass off. Damn, I missed that guy.

I dialed the number of the Sacramento Police Department. Calling the cops and pretending to be someone I wasn't seemed to be my M.O. lately.

"Sacramento PD."

"Hi, my name is Jack Walsh and I'm a reporter down here in Berkeley."

Jack Walsh had worked once already.

"Congratulations," the voice said.

We weren't exactly off to a great start.

"Anyway, I'm doing a profile on Dean Graves and I was hoping to do an interview with a few of his former co-workers with the Sacramento PD. Is there any way you could send me in the direction of one of your older officers?"

"Are you calling me a graybeard?" he said and cackled at his own joke.

"You worked with Mr. Graves?"

"I sure did."

"I don't believe it," I said. "You sound like such a young man."

I could schmooze with the best of them.

"I'm in my forties, so maybe not young, but not a graybeard yet, either."

"Shit, I'm in my forties also. We're basically kids."

My schmoozing continued.

"What paper do you work for?" he asked.

"*The East Bay Times*," I said, hoping he wasn't googling Jack Walsh along with the paper and coming up empty.

"I've heard of the paper. What has Dean done now?"

"Oh, I'm sure he's still probably up to no good, but this is just a profile we're doing on him. Nothing specific."

"Dean was born up to no good," he said.

This was working out better than I expected.

"Would you care to elaborate?"

"You're not going to quote me on this, are you? He's got a vengeful side to him."

"I don't even know your name," I said.

I'm glad I hadn't asked him when the conversation started. It was working to my benefit.

"Let's keep it that way," he said.

"So, what would you like to say about Mr. Graves? This is your chance to get back at him."

I was goading him on, hoping he'd take the bait. He not only took it, but he ran with it.

"I thought he was an asshole from the start. He had no respect for his elders. Always looking to rise up the ranks. The guy had just started and everything was already political to him. If you want to run for office or advance when you get older, that's fine, but learn how to be a cop first. It's like he wanted to become Chief of Police before making his first collar."

"From what I've heard, not much has changed."

"A leopard doesn't change its spots, especially the mean SOBs."

He certainly wasn't hiding his opinion of Dean Graves. He despised the guy.

"Why did he leave Sacramento after only two years?"

"He got off easy if you ask me. He should have lost his job in my humble opinion. He and his partner - another crazy fuck - arrested these Hispanic guys in a tough part of town. They roughed them up, using their batons way more than necessary. Think Rodney King. The idiots still had their dashcam video on which caught some of the beating. Luckily for Graves, the dash cam only caught his partner doing the beating. Anyone who saw the video knew that Graves was just off screen doing the same exact fucking thing, but without the video, he was on better ground than his partner."

"So, what happened?"

"Well, Graves had made friends with a few powerful people during his time here. While they knew they couldn't keep him on the force since his fellow cops had lost respect for him, they allowed him to save face and just resign from the force. As I said, he should have been fired. They just let him resign and next I heard he was moving down to the Bay Area. It took quite a few of us by surprise to discover that he'd caught on as a cop down in your neck of the woods. But without him beating up those Hispanic kids on video, it's not like you could just ban the guy from all police departments."

"What happened to his partner?"

"He got fired."

"Do you remember his name?"

There was a pause on the other end. I took my time to thank my lucky stars. This dispatcher was a godsend.

"Timothy Vale, I believe."

Before I got a chance to thank him, he kept right on going.

"He was almost as big an asshole as Graves. I know this was only fifteen years ago or so, but police departments were very different back then. Trust me. There's no way Dean or Vale would

PERSONA NON GRATA 199

have been let in. They were not good people, and the two of them together were a menace."

"Any idea what happened to Vale?"

"Honestly, I don't think I've heard his name since. And I'm just fine with that. I'm actually surprised I even remembered it."

"Wow, I've hit a nest egg with you," I said, probably sounding a little too eager.

"I've been waiting to get back at Dean Graves for fifteen years. I hope your article turns into a hit piece."

The voice laughed on the other end. "Hit piece" hit a little too close to home for me.

"Did Graves do something singular to you or was he just an asshole overall?"

"Treated my friends like shit. Treated me like shit."

"How did this guy ever become a cop?"

"I asked myself that question a thousand times. The truth is, there are people who really love Graves. He can be very charismatic when necessary. And people are very loyal to him. I always kind of thought of him as a David Koresh type. While most of the world looks at him and says, '*Who does this guy think he is?*', he still has a strong and loyal following. There were plenty of people in Sacramento who would have run through a wall for Dean. I'm sure it's the same way down in Berkeley."

"So Dean Graves is like a cult leader?"

"That may sound crazy, but it's really not that far from the truth."

For the two minutes I'd met with him, he certainly had a charisma to him.

"I understand what you're saying."

"Good. Just don't use my name."

"I won't. It will be like this conversation never happened," I said.

"That's fine with me."

"Anything else you'd like to add?"

"I'll check out *The East Bay Times* in a few weeks. If this phone call helps take Graves down, let me know. I'll pop some Cristal or whatever type of champagne the young kids drink these days."

"Sounds like a party. Thanks for your time."

"You got it."

I hung up the phone, not believing my good fortune.

Getting closer to a potential murderer was a good thing, right?

CHAPTER 25

You know when your mind is razor sharp? When every decision you make feels like the right one? When your brain feels like a well-oiled machine? Sure, it usually doesn't last too long, but it sure is nice while it does.

That's how I felt at the moment.

I was making a lot of brash decisions, but they all seemed to be the correct ones.

Calling the Berkeley PD and impersonating someone else. Doing the same thing with the Sacramento PD.

If those were thinking outside of the box, my next decision was way, way, way outside of the box.

I remembered Tom Butler saying he couldn't decide if I was a genius or completely deranged.

This would be the litmus test for that.

∼

I headed over and parked my car in front of my favorite woman's house: Angela Shinn.

She'd had it in for me since the beginning.

I was now going to find out how she reacted to two little words.

She left her house within thirty minutes of my arrival. Luckily, I wasn't going to be sitting out there all morning. To my surprise, she headed to the same Trader Joe's I'd confronted her at several weeks previous.

I made sure she couldn't see me as I followed behind her into Trader Joe's. I was wearing a San Francisco Giants hat that I'd pulled down over my face. Another thing I was getting used to.

She was looking at avocados and rolling one around in her hand as I made my way within twenty feet of her. I was behind her and there was no way she could see me.

Now was as good a time as any.

"Dean Graves," I said.

It was loud enough for the people around us to hear, but I didn't yell it.

If you yell something, people might jump from being scared. I wanted to see if Angela Shinn reacted based on the two words I'd said, not on the volume of those words.

Within a split second of me saying his name, Angela quickly looked to her left and right. There was no mistaking what had happened. She was reacting to the name. And this wasn't a reaction, like, 'Hey, Dean is here.' It was more visceral. More menacing. More reflexive.

She quickly realized the voice had come from behind her and started to turn around.

I was too quick. I'd already ducked behind the next aisle.

I took the long way around - avoiding Angela Shinn altogether - and walked out of Trader Joe's a minute later.

I'd obtained the information I wanted.

I did the same thing to both Tiffany Travers and Erika Manning over the course of the next several hours. One was at a bank and the other was at a sporting goods store.

Neither one reacted even one iota. I'd said it loud enough that they would have flinched if they knew the name. I was convinced neither one knew who Dean Graves was.

Both times I left without them realizing it was me who'd said it.

If someone says the name of someone you know, you're going to have a reaction. It's impossible not to. And yet, neither Tiffany nor Erika moved a muscle.

That was not the case with Angela Shinn.

She was involved in this; one way or another.

I just knew it.

It might have seemed a bit excessive to call out *'Dean Graves'* at a bank, grocery store, and a sporting goods store.

After all, I prided myself on reading people's reactions in person. If that were the case, shouldn't I just have name-dropped Graves at their respective houses and judged their reactions?

Usually, I would have. However, these women had been questioned so much lately, by the police, reporters, and even me, that maybe they'd been able to perfect a steely demeanor and show nothing when asked a question.

That's next to impossible in the scenario I set up.

You're basically naked with your emotions at that point. If you know the guy's name, there's no way you're not going to react.

So I'd went with what some might consider an outlandish plan.

And it had worked.

"Does that mean Angela Shinn is involved?" Sophie asked.

She hadn't been at my place for two minutes and we were already talking about her father's case.

After telling her about my meeting with Detective Mixon, our twice-a-week updates were a thing of the past. She wanted to know anything and everything.

"If you're talking about the murders, then not necessarily," I said. "I guess she could be getting bribed to shut up. Maybe she knows why her husband was killed and Graves is paying her off."

"Is that what you think?"

"I don't know what to think. Shit, maybe Graves isn't even involved."

"Is that what you think?" she intentionally repeated.

"No. I think he's neck-deep in this thing. I actually doubt he's the guy going around killing people, but who the hell knows?"

"Scary to think there's more than one person you have to worry about."

"For all I know, there could be ten people in on Henry's murder."

"It kind of feels conspiratorial, doesn't it?" Sophie asked.

"I think you're spot-on. Theoretically, one person could be causing all this death and mayhem. And yet, with four murders, it just feels like more people would have to be in on this. I don't know if it's two people or ten people, but I agree with you about it feeling conspiratorial."

"Do you think the Chief of Police is in on it?"

"Everything I've read about him seems to suggest he's an honorable man."

"Do you put stock into all that you read?"

"It's a fair point, but I still don't feel like he's involved. I have nothing to hang my hat on; just call it a hunch."

"If you were a woman, that would be called intuition."

I leaned in and kissed Sophie. She looked beautiful. No, she was beautiful. That sometimes got lost on me with everything that was going on lately.

"Why didn't you confront Angela Shinn after she reacted?"

"And say what? I still don't know how she and Dean Graves are connected."

"But now you know they are. In one way or another."

"Yes."

"So, what's next?"

"The age-old question. I'm not going to confront Dean Graves yet, that's for sure. He's my number one suspect - and if I'm right about that - I need to keep my distance. The last thing I need is for him to know I'm on to him."

"That's why you didn't let any of the widowers see you? In case it got back to him."

"Nailed it again. You're getting good at this P.I. work."

"If you can do it, it must not be all that difficult."

"Ouch," I said as I leaned over and kissed her again.

She pushed me away after a few seconds. I'm sure we'd be continuing later, but for now, she had another important question to ask.

"Do you have enough to go to the cops?" she asked.

"No. Not even close, really. I have Detective Mixon alluding to the fact that someone besides the Chief is really running the Berkeley PD. I have a few of BPD's finest basically confirming that. Then I have an old Sacramento cop saying Dean Graves was a bad seed over ten years ago. And finally, I've confirmed that Angela Shinn knows Graves in one way or another. What I don't have is one single thing that connects him to any of these murders. No, I can't go to the police. And honestly, I'm not even sure I'd want to. Dean Graves is a cop and I'm sure he's got scores of friends on the force. Probably knows a lot of cops in neighboring cities as well."

"Eventually you're going to have to go to the cops," Sophie said.

"Don't be so sure," I said and told her another one of my hare-brained schemes.

CHAPTER 26

I got a phone call the next morning from a number I didn't have saved.

Usually, I wouldn't even answer it, but with all that was going on with the investigation, I decided to pick up.

"Hello?"

"Is this Quint Adler?"

"Yes, it is."

"This is Angela Shinn."

I was shocked. That was the last person I thought would be calling me.

"What can I do for you, Angela?"

"We need to talk," she said, sounding nervous. She spoke quietly, the opposite of the abrasive woman I'd met in person.

"I'm busy for the next few hours, but I could meet this afternoon," I said.

"Alright. Do you want to come to my house?"

I didn't know who Dean Graves was surveilling, but I couldn't take the chance Angela Shinn was one of them.

I thought of places I knew near her. Something small and tucked away from any crowds.

"There's a tiny Chinese restaurant named Tang's a few miles from you. Do you know where that is?"

"Yes."

"I'll meet you there at noon."

"Okay. I have one other question."

I could barely hear her. This was a 180-degree turn.

"What is it?" I asked.

"Are you the voice I heard scream a name at me the other day?"

It was obvious this was the reason she'd reached out to me. I thought it was equally obvious that she didn't want to say the man's name over the phone. It would have been logical to mention Dean Graves by name, but she'd intentionally left his name out.

"Yes," I said.

"That's what I figured."

"Anything else?"

"No, just wanted to make sure it was you."

"I'll see you at noon."

"Alright."

Tang's was a cozy little restaurant with only about six tables. I'd eaten there a handful of times with a few friends who lived close by.

The food was great and I always left happy, though that wasn't the reason I'd set up our meeting there. Coffee shops were too out in the open. It would be easy for someone to blend in and try to listen in on our conversation. Tang's was different. If anyone walked in and they weren't there to eat, I'd know in seconds.

Angela Shinn walked through the front door a few minutes after noon. She was wearing a black tracksuit and a black hat. She looked like someone who was trying to avoid detection.

She didn't see me at first, because my table was tucked in the corner, wrapped behind the front door.

"Angela," I said.

Yes, I was guilty of using her first name to gain her trust, just as people had tried on me. I wasn't above such trivialities.

"There you are. I'm glad you showed," she said.

"Of course. Have a seat."

She did.

"I'm going to order food, Angela," I said. "If you don't want anything, obviously I understand, but since we're here and taking up their space, I feel obligated."

"I'll get a small appetizer or something."

She looked at the menu and thirty seconds later, a waitress headed in our direction.

"Welcome to Tang's. What can I get you guys?"

She poured us water as she waited. I realized Angela wasn't ready to order, so I took the lead.

"I'll take the Walnut Shrimp with a side of white rice."

"Got it. And for you, miss?"

"I'll just take an order of potstickers."

"Of course. Do you guys want anything else to drink or are you good with water?"

"I'm good," I said.

Angela Shinn said the same.

When our waitress left, I turned toward my guest.

"I'm sorry I shouted Dean Graves's name at you. It was kind of a dirty trick."

"Pretty smart idea if you ask me. It's hard not to react when you don't see it coming."

"That was my thought process."

"So, what do you want to know?" she asked.

"I want to know everything," I said.

It may have sounded snide, but I meant it. I didn't want her to limit the scope and potentially leave something out.

"I don't know where to start," she said.

"How about with your husband's murder?"

"Alright. First, you have to promise me something."

"Anything."

"You cannot and will not use my name. I don't know what you

are going to do with this information, but just make sure no one knows it's coming from me. If you do, I'll end up as dead as my husband. If they got to him, they can certainly get to me."

"I will never mention your name specifically and I'll do all I can to make sure we safeguard where we got the information you give me today."

"Okay. Thanks. Alright, are you ready?"

"One last question."

"What?"

"Why did you come to me?"

"Because I couldn't risk you continuing to approach me in public."

"I understand. Alright, the floor is yours," I said.

Angela Shinn took a sip of the water in front of her as if knowing she'd become parched as she spoke.

"First off, I just wanted to say that I loved my husband. We had a nice life together and he was very protective of me. He'd do anything for me. Was he a saint? No. I think we both know that. He was mixed up with some shady people over the years. Organized crime, drug dealing, bad cops. You get the idea. He tried as hard as he could not to bring his work home with him. He knew I hated it, but he thought it was the only thing he was good at. He wasn't the smartest guy who ever lived and he was never going to be a doctor, lawyer, or professional of that sort. Shit, Needles never even graduated from high school."

I nodded but didn't interrupt. It was always hard to know the protocol when someone was going to be speaking for a while.

"His latest enterprise actually sounded safer than a lot of his previous jobs. He was going to supply security for a police officer. At least, that's what he told me. It begs the obvious question: Why would a cop need his own protection? I assumed it wasn't protection per se, but more likely, some sort of information gathering. Maybe get dirt on a rival. Those types of things. That's what Needles was best at. He worked for a well-known criminal in San Francisco at one point and his main job was to find something out about his rivals. Something scurrilous. Something disreputable.

Now, in the criminal world, doing things disreputable is almost par for the course. But certain things are beyond the pale. Ratting, for one. If someone is labeled as a rat, he loses all respect in that world. Being gay is the same. Sure, our country has come a long way and there's not the stigma there once was, but in that world, you'd rather be known as a sadistic killer than rumored to be gay. Which brings me to what happened down at the Berkeley Marina."

Our waitress brought over the potstickers and set them down, saying my entree would be up in two minutes.

Their service was fast; almost too fast. I could tell that Angela Shinn was about to drop a bombshell and I didn't want an interruption of any kind. I had to keep her eyes on the prize.

"So, you were saying," I tried leading her back.

"Yes, where was I?"

"You were talking about what happened down at the Marina."

"Oh, right. So this cop that Needles was working for decided he wanted to get some dirt on another cop. By the way, I found out all this information after the fact. Needles never would have told me the specifics while he was on a job. Obviously, something went wrong out there and when he got scared, he spilled the beans to me. I'll get back to that.

The rumor was that this other cop was gay. As I said earlier, our society has come a long way. But cops consider themselves macho much in the same way that people in the criminal underworld do. While no one would care if an accountant came out as gay, it's different if you're a Mafia Don or the Chief of Police."

I couldn't tell if Angela intentionally dropped the Chief of Police bombshell or if it just slipped out, but I certainly wasn't going to interrupt her. I was hitting the Mother Lode.

"If you're the man who is in charge of a bunch of cops, being gay would be looked down on. That's just the way it is. They didn't have any concrete evidence this guy was gay, though. Just a bunch of rumors. So, Needles' new employer asked him to try and get concrete evidence on him. Which leads us back to the Berkeley Marina. Well, hold on. Not just yet. The Berkeley PD was hosting an event earlier that night. Needles had an idea. It involved hiring a gay guy to seduce the Chief of Police."

It hadn't been a slip. She'd intentionally said the Chief of Police; although I noticed she still wasn't dropping Dean Graves as Needles's employer. Assuming it was.

"As I said, Needles had done a similar job during his time working for organized crime. In fact, he'd kept in touch with the guy over the years. His name was Allan. Needles wasn't homophobic and had no problem with the guy. So he asked Allan if he was interested in doing another job. He was. I imagine they were paying him pretty good money. And I never met Allan, but apparently, he was a very attractive man and Needles said he knew he'd charm the pants off the Chief. Literally. Needles had told his employer that if the Chief fell for Allan that he could set up a rendezvous on the Berkeley Marina for later that night. Needles was going to let Allan use his boat, and obviously, he'd hired a photographer to get pictures of what occurred."

I don't know what I'd expected coming into this, but it certainly wasn't this. The murders were simultaneously getting more complicated and at the same time, coming into focus.

"Allan did his job. I guess the Chief fell for him at the event. I imagine it was all done very subtly. After all, the Chief is married so you couldn't risk outwardly flirting. They managed somehow because they set up a rendezvous for later that night.

Needles had shown Allan the boat earlier that day so he knew where to take the Chief. He'd given him the keys and stocked the bar in case they wanted to have drinks once they got there. To loosen the Chief up, obviously. As for the photographer, he was going to be ready. Needles would call him when he knew Allan and the Chief were on their way. The photographer told Needles to tell Allan to try and turn the light on once they arrived at the boat. The pictures would turn out better."

I continued to be amazed by all I was hearing.

I saw the waitress bringing my food over. She set it down and looked over at Angela, who hadn't touched her food, but the waitress didn't say anything.

"You can continue," I said.

"So Allan and the Chief met at the Marina that night. Needles was there somewhere, watching from afar. He said it was a shit-show from the start. Both Allan and the Chief were already drunk and making a lot of noise. They were able to make it on the boat and Needles could see the photographer taking pictures about twenty minutes later. Allan must have got the Chief in some compromising situations. An hour later, Needles saw Allan and the Chief leave the dock. His plan had worked. Or so he thought…"

For the first time, Angela took a bite of her food. I did the same, but kept my eyes on her, pleading with her to continue the story. She did.

"The next day changed everything. Needles went down to the dock and before he got to his boat, he saw Henry Madsen and Blaine Travers having a beer together on one of their boats. There was a third guy that Needles mentioned, but I can't remember his name. I think Needles told me his name, but for the life of me, I can't remember it. I'm not going to recreate the whole scene since I wasn't there, but either Henry or Blaine had seen Allan and the Chief the night before. They prodded my husband, trying to get more information about what went down. It was Needles's boat, after all. They had seen the photographer as well and knew something was amiss. I guess it didn't really matter whether it had been Henry or Blaine who had seen it. They'd obviously told the other one. And the third guy now knew."

For the first time, I felt like talking.

"I'm sure it was Henry who saw it. He slept on his boat every night. Blaine just docked his there."

I was also 99% sure that Frank Manning was the third guy there.

"Okay. So it was probably Henry who was kind of egging on Needles for more information. Obviously, he wasn't going to say anything. These guys didn't know how big a story this was. If Needles said anything, it would be a death sentence. Needles said he started walking away from the guys and toward his boat, when Henry said something that changed everything. *'And I'm pretty sure one of the two guys was Gary Laughlin, the Chief of Police. It was dark so I can't be certain, but it sure as hell looked like him. What the hell are you mixed up in, Needles?'* At that point, Needles knew he'd have to go to his employer and tell him. To this day, I wish he hadn't. He'd probably still be alive and so would the others."

A tear rolled down Angela Shinn's cheek. She wiped it away.

"I'm sorry," she said.

"Don't be. You're being very courageous right now."

"If Needles had never told his employer about Henry and Blaine and the third guy, he'd probably still be alive," she said, basically repeating herself.

"When did your husband tell you all of this?"

"That night. He'd met with his employer after his run-in with those three at the marina."

"Do you think he knew he was in trouble?"

"Yes. There's no way he would have told me otherwise. He'd always tried to keep his professional life separate from our personal life. Now, my guess is he wasn't that scared after his talk with Henry. He probably thought there was some amicable way out of all this, but after he met with his employer, he must have gotten spooked. Maybe he knew at that point that there would be bloodshed."

"So, this guy likely killed Henry, Blaine, the third guy, and Needles all to cover up what happened out there?"

"Yes. I'm sure Needles' employer was afraid that Henry or Blaine would tell someone else and ruin everything. As you know, it's hard to keep a secret with two people. I imagine Needles' employer thought it was inevitable the secret would get out."

"With all due respect Angela, you can stop saying 'Needles' employer.'"

Another tear rolled down her cheek. She stared at me intently.

"Dean Graves. Is that better?"

That was the final straw, even though I knew it was coming. Everything had come into focus. All because of this brave woman in front of me. I'd been wrong about her.

"I understand why you were so brief with me in our earlier interactions," I said.

"If Dean Graves thought I was talking to you, I knew I'd be a goner. But then, when you said his name at Trader Joe's, I knew this was all coming to roost. Might as well tell you everything so you wouldn't confront me in public again."

"Have you told me everything?"

She spent several seconds thinking.

"No, I guess I haven't. Needles said they knew a newspaperman who was going to publish the photos of the Chief of Police and include some of the rumors about him in the article. And then..."

"And then, Chief Laughlin would be forced to resign and Dean Graves would take over."

"Bingo," Angela Shinn said.

I was completely floored.

"Jesus H. Christ," I said.

I didn't often use that phrase, but this warranted it.

Angela took a bite of her food, likely out of nervousness more than anything else.

An idea rattled around in the back of my brain.

"Do you know what newspaperman they were going to use?"

"I can't remember, but I do know it was someone at *The East Bay Times.*"

"Might it have been Dexter Lund?"

"Yeah, that sounds right."

The same guy who had written an article about me investigating Henry's murder was going to publish an article essentially ending Gary Laughlin's career. This didn't make a lot of sense. The article about me would keep the murders in the spotlight, which was the last thing Dean Graves would have wanted.

Had there been another article about my investigation?

If so, I hadn't heard about it.

Had Graves gotten to Dexter Lund and told him to stop publishing articles about the murders?

I still had so many questions.

"Is there anything else you can remember?" I asked.

I'd learned more than I thought possible. Now I was just getting greedy.

"I'm pretty sure I've told you everything."

"Thank you so much."

"You're welcome."

We both took a bite of our food.

"Listen, Angela, I'm going to leave in a few minutes and I'll be heading out the back. This place is as hidden as you could hope, but it's still probably better if we aren't seen leaving together. Just in case. I'd wait a few more minutes until you leave."

"You're scaring me."

"I'm scared too, but I'm telling you, no one saw us meet here today. There's literally no one else in the restaurant besides the staff."

"Okay. You'll keep me updated on the case?"

"I think it's better if I don't."

"Yeah, you're probably right. I sure hope you catch this asshole. Do you think you have enough to bring him down?"

"I've got a much better chance than I did twenty minutes ago and that's all thanks to you."

She looked petrified. I grabbed her hand. It was amazing to think this was a woman I couldn't stand as recently as four hours ago.

"It's going to be okay," I said.

"Are you sure about that?"

It looked like I was going to end our conversation with a lie.

"Yes," I said.

PART THREE: THE POWERS THAT BE

CHAPTER 27

To say things were moving fast would be a vast understatement.

Everything was coming to a head. For better or worse.

I didn't feel any reason to stop now so I drove straight from Tang's to the offices of *The East Bay Times*.

Much to my chagrin - or was it delight? - my old friend Miss Congeniality was at the front desk. The last time I'd seen her she was flipping me off as I was being escorted off the premises. Good times all around.

She recognized me instantly and gave me a little hiss, or at least that's what it felt like. She was like a cat ready to pounce.

"It's so great to see you again," I said.

Yes, sometimes I liked to kill people with kindness, but this was all sarcasm. I accentuated '*So great*' to cement my point.

"What can I help you with? I'm sure this will be good."

She was enjoying this game of sarcasm as well.

"I need to see our mutual friend Dexter Lund."

"I don't think he's a big fan of yours."

"Is he a fan of being arrested?"

"Excuse me?"

"You're excused," I said, once again, behaving like a child in front of this woman. "If you don't bring Mr. Lund out here, I'm going to call the cops and tell them all the illegal shit he's been up to. You see, Ms. Congeniality, your newspaper is a cesspool of halfwits."

I didn't even know what I was saying. All I knew was that I was fired up and not holding anything back.

"A cesspool of halfwits, huh? Wow, you must have been a really awesome writer at *The Walnut Creek Times*."

"Ah, you know who I am. Have you been stalking me?"

"More like keeping track of a train wreck."

My life was anything but a train wreck, but I had to hand it to Miss Congeniality. She wasn't some wilting flower. She was giving it back as good as she was taking it. Maybe better.

"You have too much free time on your hands," I said. "While I'm out doing things, you're on your keyboard, going along for the ride that is my life. Not actually part of it, just making little snide remarks from afar."

"Actually, I'm saying them right to your face."

"That you are," I said. "Now, can you please call Mr. Lund on your little phone there? You're free to repeat the whole '*getting arrested*' thing."

She stared at me, not exactly sure what to do.

"Call him," I said. "If not, I'm going to make a scene."

I saw her press a button or two and then she started talking.

"It's that guy you had kicked out. He's saying some crazy things. I think maybe you should come out here."

She hung up the phone.

"Thank you," I said with actual sincerity.

She didn't respond, but she didn't make a face at me either.

Baby steps. We'd be best friends in no time.

A short time later, Dexter Lund walked to the entrance of *The East Bay Times*. He was wearing slacks, a dress shirt, and a tie. Last time he'd dressed very casually. Maybe he had a big meeting today. Not that I really cared.

"What the hell do you want?" he asked.

"I want to talk to you," I said.

"Why the hell should I?"

Hell was his word of the day, apparently.

"Because I know some information that you'd rather I didn't."

"I highly doubt that," he said, but his voice belied his strong words.

"Alright," I said. "I'm going to start spelling a word and you can stop me any time you want."

"This should be good," he said.

Miss Congeniality looked at us. She was fascinated by this verbal duel we were having. It was like Hamilton vs. Burr but we'd substituted guns with words.

"G," I said.

"Oooh," he said and started fake shaking like he was nervous.

"A," I said.

"This is silly," he said.

"R."

He looked at me but didn't say anything. I think he knew where this was going.

"Y."

"You're crazy, Quint."

"First letter, last name. L."

Dexter Lund raised his hands in surrender.

"Okay. Okay. I'll talk with you."

I looked over at our mutual friend. She was dumbfounded. To be fair, without knowing what was going on, anyone would be similarly dumbfounded.

"Do you want to do this in your office?" I asked.

"No. Let's take a walk."

Miss Congeniality's face dropped. She had no idea what she'd just witnessed, but she knew I was winning. I was the Aaron Burr of this verbal duel.

"Alright. Let's do it," I said.

Dexter Lund led the way and I followed.

〰

"I don't know what you think you know about someone named Gary," he said, once we were fifty yards from their office and no longer within earshot of anyone.

"Don't treat me like an idiot and I won't treat you like one," I said.

"What Gary are you talking about?"

"See, that's what I'm referring to. And you know who I'm alluding to. Gary Laughlin. The Chief of Police of Berkeley."

I yelled those last two sentences. It was time that Lund understood how serious I was.

"Shhhh. Please don't yell. You've made your point," he said. "What information do you think you have on him?"

"I'm going to tell you this one last time, Dexter. If you treat me like a moron one more time, I'm going to the cops myself. Assume I know everything because I do, but just to throw you a little crumb, I'll say this. Mr. Laughlin's sexuality was what was at issue."

Dexter Lund dropped his head just a fraction. It was nothing drastic, but I noticed it.

"Okay," he said. "How did you find out?"

"You have zero chance of getting that information from me."

I was reminded of our last meeting where I was trying to find out who'd fed him information on me. The info that had led him to write an article on me. The ones that appeared to have stopped thereafter.

"You said you're not going to the cops, right?"

"It's contingent on how this conversation plays out."

Dexter Lund led us up a slight hill that veered away from downtown Walnut Creek and away from any potential crowds. He didn't want anyone to see us together.

"What do you want to know?" he asked.

"How did it all start?"

"I received an anonymous email asking if I wanted to be part of a huge story."

"And you said yes?"

"Obviously. I'm trying to make a name for myself. Any reporter would have done the same. At that point, I had no clue what exactly they wanted me to do. I just knew I was interested."

"What happened next?"

"I continued to have a back and forth with the anonymous emailer."

"What did they say?"

"They said they were going to soon have pictures of the Chief of Police with another man. And wanted to know if I would publish them."

"And you said yes?"

"I did. I know it wasn't the most ethical, but there's no doubt they would have found someone else if I'd said no."

"I'm just here to get the details. I'm not going to judge you."

Dexter Lund was a snake for agreeing to post pictures that were obviously taken without the Chief of Police's consent. He worked for a reputable paper, not the *National Enquirer*.

"I appreciate that," he said, not realizing I was very much judging him.

"So, what happened next?"

"I agreed to run the article along with the pictures, assuming the photos clearly showed it was Gary Laughlin. We set up a day where they would forward me the pictures and I told them I'd need a day or two to write the article and publish it."

"Was it a problem getting the higher-ups to agree on running it?"

"No. They knew it would sell tons of copies. They were on board."

"So, this email account sent you the pictures?"

"Yes. They were a little hazy, but you could tell it was Laughlin."

"How many pictures were there?"

"They sent probably ten over and I told them which three I planned on using. They were fine with my choices."

Dexter saw an unoccupied bench.

"Can we sit? All this walking and talking has me a bit gassed."

"Sure," I said.

We both sat down. No one was within thirty yards of us.

"Why didn't you run the article?" I asked.

"I got a call the night before publication, saying I had to stop it. At all costs. So I called one of the editors and said they couldn't print my article. I made up a story that there were discrepancies I needed to address. They knew this would be a hot-button article and they had no choice but to pull it. If you have any discrepancies in a story that big, you're just asking yourself to get sued."

"What happened next?"

"They pulled the article and I emailed the person I'd been dealing with. They told me I could never post that article. They were very adamant about that. They said some bullshit about there being legalities involved."

"They'd basically said the same thing that you'd said to your bosses."

"Pretty much. Only I didn't believe my anonymous source. The reasoning sounded hollow. They knew all along those pictures were going to be taken without his consent."

"Do you still have the pictures?" I asked.

"Yeah."

"On your phone?"

"Yes. I can pull them up."

Through Angela Shinn, I learned that these pictures took place on her husband's boat. The question was whether I could prove that. If the pictures just looked like they were taken in a random living room, it would be tougher to tie all of this together.

"Please do. I'd like to see them," I said.

Dexter paused, not pulling out his phone immediately. I could tell he regretted telling me he had them on his phone.

"I'll gladly go to the police if you prefer," I said.

I think Dexter Lund knew what he'd done had been completely immoral and might ruin his career in the newspaper business. If someone had sent him the photos of Laughlin, he would have been within his rights to post them. He'd gone a step further, however. He was dealing with the people before they had even taken the pictures. He was part of the conspiracy.

He grudgingly grabbed his phone and scrolled through his pictures.

"Here are the three I'd chosen to use."

I looked at the photos. There were two on a couch and one on a bed. It was Gary Laughlin - of that, there was no doubt - with a man who was probably twenty years younger than him. They were clothed in the pictures, but there was no doubt of what they were up to. I didn't care about that. I was trying to see if I could verify these pictures were taken on a boat.

The one on the bed was inconclusive. All you saw was a bed and the two men. It didn't pan out to show the whole room. The bed looked to be quite small like one you'd find on a boat, but that was hardly incontrovertible evidence.

The first picture of them on the couch was also unconvincing. It was too focused in on them kissing.

The third picture was different. They were still kissing, but it was a landscape-style photograph and you could see more of the background. I scanned it, looking for something to prove this was taken on Needles' boat. And then I saw it.

In the bottom right corner of the picture, something you had to strain to see, there were two life jackets stuffed in a little cubicle. Once you saw it, there was no mistaking what they were.

I debated whether I should show it to Dexter. I was convinced he wasn't part of the murder conspiracy, but does that mean I should share this bombshell with him? I'm sure most people would have advised against it. As was often the case, I had a different take on things. If he realized just how deep this conspiracy ran, he'd do anything to keep me from going to the cops.

"Look at this picture," I said, handing him his phone back. "What do you see?"

He looked at it for a good thirty seconds.

"Two guys kissing," he said.

"What else do you see?"

"I don't know."

"Look at the bottom right."

It took him ten more seconds to see them. They truly were difficult to see.

"Okay. I see two life jackets. Is that what you're talking about?"

"It sure is," I said.

He looked up at me.

I'd said *'It sure is'* in a manner that denoted its importance.

Slowly but surely, he started to realize the relevance.

"Wait. This happened on a boat? Was it at the Berkeley Marina? Are all these murders related to this picture?"

I merely nodded.

"Holy fuck," he said. "This wasn't what I signed up for."

"It doesn't matter. You're in up to your neck now."

"Who did all this? Who was that anonymous emailer I was talking to?"

That was information I was not willing to divulge. It was either Dean Graves or one of his subordinates, that much I was certain of.

"It's better you don't know," I said.

"This is fucking crazy."

"Hopefully, if this thing blows up, you're not involved more than you're letting on."

"I'm not. I promise."

I had him on edge which is exactly what I wanted. I had some more questions and I needed him to tell me the truth.

"Who told you that I was investigating the murder of Henry Madsen?"

"I can't give away my sources."

"Shut the hell up, Dexter. You almost sold him out a month ago when I first met you. And you were going to post pictures of the Chief of Police in compromising positions. Stop with your holier-than-thou bullshit."

He looked like a young puppy who'd just been reprimanded.

"His name was Mixon. He was a detective with the Berkeley Police Department."

That actually made sense. Mixon was pissed he'd been relieved of his duties so he wanted the Henry Madsen case to stay in the public eye. He probably wanted me to get to the bottom of it.

Maybe he suspected Dean Graves of being involved but thought it would be too risky to investigate himself.

"Now we are on to the million-dollar question, Dexter. Why did you only write the one article about me?"

His face went ashen white.

"Answer me," I yelled.

"The anonymous email account said to stop."

"That's it?"

"They used more colorful terms. Said I'd never work again. They'd tell my higher-ups that I'd set up the Gary Laughlin pictures myself. Things like that."

"And you never put two and two together? That the death of Henry Madsen and the pictures of Gary Laughlin might be related?"

"I honestly didn't. I never noticed those life jackets until today. I just figured they were taken in a regular old house."

"Hmmm," I said.

My response put Dexter further on edge.

He stood up from the bench.

"What the hell? I promise I never saw those life jackets and what if I had? Was I then supposed to make the leap that it was related to Henry Madsen's death?"

"Lurid pictures are taken on a boat and then several people around that dock get murdered. It would have sounded pretty darn suspicious to me."

"Stop!" he yelled. "I swear to God I didn't know."

I believed him, and yet, he'd still done several scumbag-ish things. I wasn't going to let him off easy.

"When was the last time you were contacted by that email?"

"I could look."

"Please do."

Dexter scrolled through his phone.

"Several weeks back. It was a follow-up email just making sure I wasn't going to publish any more articles about your investigation."

"I want you to send them an email right now," I said.

My plan - and I'd only come up with it seconds before - was to have Dexter send an email saying he was starting to suspect that the photographs of Gary Laughlin and the Berkeley Marina murders were related. It was time to play offense.

"What do you want me to say?" he asked meekly. He didn't want to send an email; that much was obvious.

I thought about it.

Dexter Lund was a jerk, but he didn't deserve to die. I'd be putting him firmly in the crosshairs of Dean Graves. I couldn't do that.

"You know what, I'm not going to have you email him just yet."

"Thank God," he said.

There had to be a way I could use Dexter Lund to my advantage, but I couldn't think how.

This time, I got up from the bench and started walking around.

"What are you doing? he asked.

He was a nervous wreck.

"Getting the blood flowing. You know, thinking on my feet."

I asked a question, not even sure exactly where I was headed with it.

"How much editorial control do you have?" I asked.

"As far as what?"

"I'm assuming you can't just publish any article without it being reviewed."

"Correct."

"If - and this is hypothetical - you were to publish an article accusing someone of the Berkeley Marina murders, what's the likelihood it would get approved by your bosses?"

"Unless you had irrefutable evidence, extremely unlikely. That's another lawsuit waiting to happen."

"And Gary Laughlin was different because you had the pictures?"

"That's right," Dexter said.

I didn't know what to do. I was thoroughly convinced that Dean Graves had spearheaded these murders, but I didn't have a smoking gun. Far from it.

The likelihood is that Graves had someone else to do the killings. He'd surely have an alibi for the nights in question. Plus, he obviously had a lot of cops on his side. The killer could have been anyone.

"Is there anything you've left out?"

I'd asked Angela Shinn the same question about an hour ago.

"No. There really isn't."

"Do you have a business card?" I asked Dexter. "If I call, you better answer."

He grabbed a business card from his wallet.

"Here you go."

I did the same.

"Call me if you can think of anything else and I do mean anything," I said.

"Alright."

"And listen, I wouldn't tell anybody about our conversation. Your anonymous email account is a very dangerous person. He has eyes and ears everywhere and you don't want him on your bad side."

"I won't say a word," he said.

For once, I believed him. I'd scared the shit out of Dexter Lund.

"Let's head back," I said.

We started walking back toward *The East Bay Times.*

This was crazy.

CHAPTER 28

When I arrived home, I was hit with a jolt of a thought.
It's probably something I should have considered when I first found out about Dean Graves, but at least it had finally come to me. Better late than never.

I googled a name, hoping to see a face I'd recognize. After ten minutes of searching, I couldn't find any digital footprint for the guy. I wasn't surprised. If my assumption was correct, this guy would do anything possible to prevent his face from being on the internet.

There was one place that I hoped still had a picture.

I called the Sacramento Police Department.

"Sacramento PD," a woman's voice answered.

"Hi, my name is Jack Walsh. I called you guys about three or four days ago and talked to a man who'd been on the force for a long time. Do you know who that might be?"

"We've got quite a few dispatchers," the voice said. "And several of them are long-time officers. In fact, some who are hurt on duty and don't want to leave the force, work as dispatchers."

That made sense.

"What if I could tell you the exact day and time?" I asked.

"Sure, I could find him that way."

I thought back a few days. It wasn't easy with all that was going on. Every day had been feeling like a week.

It was the same day I'd met with Detective Mixon. The day after I took Sophie to Range Life. Which had been an unplanned Wednesday dinner.

"I'm pretty sure it was this last Thursday," I told the dispatcher. "Around 1:30 p.m. or so."

I'd met Mixon that morning and then confronted the two officers outside of the Berkeley police department. I'd returned a little after noon and surfed the internet for an hour before calling the Sacramento PD. 1:30 sounded about right.

"You're probably referring to Gil then. Gil Jones."

"Is he on right now?"

"No, but he is later this afternoon."

"What time does he start?"

"You've sure got a lot of questions, Mr. Walsh."

I'd only said my name once, at the beginning of the phone call. My guess was the dispatchers were taught to write the person's name down right away. If not, this woman had an exemplary memory.

"I just had a good talk with Mr. Jones and wanted to thank him personally."

"Well, that's a nice thought. Gil is a good guy. He starts at three today."

"He sure is," I said. "I'll call him later. Thanks for your help."

I ended the call.

I reminded myself not to tell Gil Jones that I now knew his name. That had been something he didn't want to divulge. So I wouldn't ask to be transferred to him and give myself away. They couldn't have that many dispatchers on at once. I'd call until I heard his voice, which I was pretty sure I'd recognize.

At 3:15 I called the now-familiar number.

The first call was answered by a woman and I actually thought it might be the same one I'd talked to a few hours earlier. I hung up.

The second call wasn't Gil Jones either. It was a much younger man's voice.

The third was another woman.

How many dispatchers did they have on at once?

Finally, on the fourth ring, I recognized the voice.

"Sacramento PD."

"Hey, I know this voice," I said.

It only took him a few seconds.

"The Berkeley reporter?"

"That's right. Good memory."

"Did you randomly get me again?"

There was no point in lying.

"Actually, I called a few times, waiting for you to answer."

I didn't lie, but I did leave out the fact I knew his name and could have easily just transferred to him.

"Must be important," he said.

"I'm close to finishing up my article on Dean Graves, but I'm missing one thing."

"What is that?"

Here it was. The moment of truth. The reason I'd tried to find someone on the internet and been contacting the Sacramento PD.

"I couldn't locate a picture of Timothy Vale, the old partner of Graves. I searched online and nothing."

"I'm not surprised. He didn't seem like the social media type."

He'd confirmed my suspicions.

"I know he wasn't an officer for long, but you must have some old picture of him. Either at the police academy, as a cadet, or in the short time he was an officer."

"Sure. We take pictures of all our incoming classes."

"Could you do me the biggest favor and send me over a photo of him?"

"That's a big ask," he said.

I'd heard that a lot lately.

"I know," I said. "I think it's an important part of the story."

"I could probably manage to find the photograph of that class."

He was teetering on the edge. My impression was that part of him wanted to do it - likely to fuck over Graves and Vale - but the other part was weary of getting involved.

"Thank you so much. You have no idea how important this is. Remember, I will never mention your name. Shit, I don't even know what it is."

I hoped that the other dispatcher hadn't told him about our conversation earlier that day. If I was caught in the lie of not knowing his name, Gil Jones might turn on me.

"Do you have a fax machine?" he asked.

He could just as easily text it, but I don't think Gil wanted me to have his number. I couldn't blame him. And a fax actually would likely produce a lousy picture, but what did I care? It's not like there really was some article I was writing.

I gave him the number of the fax at my office. For about the 20th time in the last year, I told myself I needed to get a fax for my apartment as well.

"I go on a fifteen-minute break at five. I'll fax it over then."

"Thanks for all you've done."

"It's for a good cause, right?"

He suddenly didn't sound so sure of his decision.

"If Dean Graves is as bad as you say, then yes, it is."

"Check your fax at five," he said and then abruptly hung up.

I didn't think I'd be talking to Gil Jones again.

I started walking over to my office a few minutes before five.

It was always a debate of whether to drive or walk, being about three-quarters of a mile from my apartment.

Today I felt like I could use the fresh air.

I passed some local businesses and waved at a few people I knew.

The sun beat down on me and it felt good. I was still a bit white from the winter and could use some time in the sun.

I arrived at my office and instantly headed to the fax machine.

There was one sitting there, and considering I didn't get many faxes, it was almost certainly the one I was there to see.

I tossed aside the cover page and turned the fax over.

Another moment of truth.

And just like that, the air was let out of the balloon.

There were sixty people in this picture and everyone's face was so small. It was also over a decade ago. There was no way I'd recognize Timothy Vale from that picture.

I then realized there was a second fax sheet that was sticking to the other.

I slid my finger between the two sheets of paper and they came loose.

I turned the second piece of paper over and stared at the picture in front of me.

I started to get a little light-headed.

Fearful that I was going to pass out, I put my arm down on my desk.

The second fax was a blown-up picture of Timothy Vale's face.

It was undeniable.

My suspicions had been confirmed.

I was staring at the face of the man who tried to kill me.

CHAPTER 29

After some time taking in all I'd learned, I called Tom Butler. I couldn't go to the cops just yet, but maybe I could try this case in the media.

"Hey, Quint."

"Tom, when was the last time I asked you for a favor?"

"Probably that time you asked to use my reporters and then ditched us three days later."

"Nice try. That was your idea."

"Not the 'you leaving us at the altar' part."

"That's fair. I'm not meant to be caged, Tom."

Tom laughed my comment off.

"You were hardly caged, Quint. So what's this favor you want?"

"I've got a whopper of a request."

"I'm listening."

I told him all the evidence I'd gathered on Dean Graves.

"Jeez, Quint. This is a humongous story if you're right."

"I know. That's why I'm trying to be smart and cautious about it. What do you think of the evidence?"

"Sounds pretty convincing," he said.

Last time I'd been laughed out of the room. Tom's opinion had changed drastically.

"Convincing enough to let me write an op-ed for the paper?"

"Why an op-ed? Why not a feature-length article?"

"Because that would take a few days to write. I may have put myself on Graves's radar yesterday and he's not exactly one to stand down. I worry he might try to enact his revenge. If I'm right, he's already tried to kill me once."

"And you think writing an op-ed will prevent him from trying to kill you a second time?"

"If you allow me to write the op-ed and I end up dead, he'd be the number one suspect. I'm hoping he'd realize this and stay away from me."

"That might be wishful thinking."

"That's all I've got to go on," I said.

"Did you know that the "OP" in op-ed doesn't stand for opinion?" Tom said, slightly changing the subject.

"I do. You taught me that years ago. It stands for opposite because op-eds used to be opposite the editorial page."

"Good memory. That's right. However, opinions are what drive op-eds. It's usually someone's opinion on something."

I got the point he was trying to get across.

"My opinion is that Dean Graves is responsible for all these murders."

"That's not what I meant by opinion."

"Then call it whatever you want," I said. "I just need to get it on record that Dean Graves is a suspect in the murders in and around the Berkeley Marina."

"And you can't go to the police?" Tom asked, despite knowing what my answer was going to be.

"That would be akin to me committing suicide."

"You sure that's not what you're doing anyway? You're poking the bear every chance you get."

"I'm doing this for Henry."

Tom didn't respond right away. When he did, his voice was as serious as I'd ever heard it.

"You're putting me in a really tough spot, Quint. If you are somehow wrong, can you imagine the consequences?"

"I'm not wrong."

"I'm going to have to talk to our attorneys. I can't make a decision like this without consulting them. Krissy too."

"I completely understand, but I was hoping to get this into tomorrow's edition."

"This is the best I can do," he said. I could tell he was thinking as he was talking. "Why don't you come into the office early tomorrow morning? I'll have an attorney or two there as well as Krissy. You can tell them what you've told me and if they give me the green light, I'll slot it into tomorrow's afternoon online edition."

Tom was sticking his neck out for me.

"Thank you, Tom. I know how difficult I've made this for you."

"If our paper goes under, you can write the obituary."

"And if Graves kills me in the meantime, you can write mine."

"Don't say that, Quint."

"You're right. I'm sorry."

I shouldn't have said it, but I still viewed it as a real possibility.

"So, shall we say 8:30 a.m. at the office?"

"I'll be there. Thanks again, Tom."

"I haven't said yes yet."

And with that, Tom hung up.

~

"This is crazy, Quint. Haven't enough people told you to let this case be?"

I'd called Sophie to tell her I didn't think we should meet up tonight. I'd run through everything I discovered, but she still wasn't convinced.

"I'm so close, Sophie. I thought you'd want to know I'm going to catch your father's killer."

"And for that, I'm grateful. I'm just worried about you."

"This will all come to a head tomorrow and then we can hang out every night if you'd like."

She wasn't willing to forgive me that easily.

"So, my father was right about everything?"

"It sure seems that way. He mentioned not to talk to the cops and boy was he right about that."

"I know why he didn't mention Dean Graves in his fax; because he didn't know who he was yet. But why didn't he say something about the Chief of Police?"

"I've given that a lot of thought today. I think he figured if I started asking pointed questions about the Chief of Police, people would have become aware almost immediately. That's why he dropped Needles' name and let me work my way through the case."

"You think he thought all that through?"

"Your father was a smart guy. Yes, I do think this was intentional."

"And this asshole Timothy Vale killed him?"

"That's my guess. He's been with Graves since their time in Sacramento."

I couldn't get Vale's face out of my head. Without some luck, it could have easily been the last face I'd ever seen on this earth.

"You know you're on my shit list right now, but you really have done some amazing work, Quint."

"Thanks, Sophie. You can tell me that in person tomorrow night."

"If I'll have you back."

Her playfulness had returned and I was here for it.

"We're going to have a rollicking good time tomorrow night."

"Rollicking?"

"You're damn right."

"I'll wear a nice dress."

"It won't be on for very long."

I heard Sophie laugh, but when her voice returned, it had turned serious, much like Tom Butler's had minutes before.

"So tomorrow you're going straight to *The Walnut Creek Times?*"

"Yes. And then, I have one more crazy idea."

"I'm afraid to ask."

"Once the article is posted, I was considering driving down to the Berkeley Police Department, asking for Dean Graves, and then making a scene."

I was expecting Sophie to hate the idea. I was wrong.

"I think it's smart. Do it in front of twenty cops so they all hear what you have to say. They can't all be under his spell."

"I've got a feeling he's got a small, but extremely loyal, group."

"Then shout your accusations from the rafters and have the other cops decide on their own."

"That's my plan."

"Then go do it. I have faith in you, Quint."

"I'll see you tomorrow. I love you."

If I'd said that a few minutes before, I'm not sure I'd have gotten a response. Now I knew I would. It did come with an addendum, however.

"I love you too, Quint, but please be safe tomorrow."

For my third call in fifteen minutes, I reached out to Paddy Roark and told him everything I'd discovered.

"Are you fucking kidding me?"

"I wish I was."

"You're a crazy man, Quint."

"This will all be out in the open tomorrow."

"You're one hell of a P.I., I'll give you that."

"I'll stop by and see you and Dennis soon. Thanks for all your help."

"Looks like it's been put to good use. This Dean Graves sounds like a bonafide asshole."

"That's putting it too mildly. The guy is a sociopath who won't let anything stand in his way."

"I know I always tell you this, but be careful. If you're right about this Graves guy, he's not going to take this lying down."

I was so sick of being told to be careful. Not that I didn't under-stand why I kept hearing it.

"I'm on full alert. I'll call you tomorrow."

"Goodbye, Quint."

CHAPTER 30

I woke up early the following morning, going over in my head what I planned on saying to Tom, Krissy, and the assorted lawyers.

It got to the point where I'd rehashed it in my head so many times that I was starting to forget parts of it. It was only 7:00 a.m.

I made myself another pot of coffee.

My planned confrontation with Dean Graves gave me greater joy.

I couldn't wait to tell him what I thought of him. I'd yell at him in front of all the Berkeley police officers and see their faces turn ghostly when I accused him of all the Berkeley Marina murders.

And then - as my mind often did - I was brought back to earth.

What if Graves arrests me for being disorderly?

What if I'm put in a cell run by one of his subordinates?

What if they murder me and frame it as a suicide?

I suddenly wasn't as eager to confront Graves.

I'd meet with Tom first and then reconsider that part of the plan.

Maybe I'd ask Tom's lawyers what they thought of that part of the plan, even though I already knew the answer. They'd hate it.

I told myself to calm down a bit.

My mind was moving way too quickly for my liking. Maybe five cups of coffee hadn't been the best idea.

~

A few minutes before eight, I got a text from Sophie.

"Can you do me a favor? I have some important work stuff that I think I left in your car. I've checked everywhere else."

I texted back: *"When? I can't even remember driving you around recently."*

Sophie: *"Not sure when exactly, but I need it for work today. Can you please just go check right now? It's important."*

Me: *"Sure. What exactly am I looking for?"*

Sophie: *"It's about ten pages total. Will be stapled together."*

Me: *"I'll text you back in five minutes."*

~

I put on some sweatpants and a pair of flip-flops and headed down to the parking garage.

I passed by a woman who'd recently moved in. She took the stairs and I chastised myself for being a lazy ass and always riding the elevator. I arrived at the second floor where the parking garage was located, got off the elevator, and started walking toward my car.

Within a few seconds, I knew something was wrong. Someone had stepped out of the shadows. The only entrance was the elevator. Whoever this was, they'd been hanging out in the garage.

I didn't dare turn around and let them know I was on to them.

I felt them getting slightly closer.

If I ever needed to think quickly, now was the time!

About ten feet from me was a fairly high retaining wall that came up to about my shoulders. For about ten to fifteen seconds, he wouldn't know what I was doing, but once he passed the wall, I'd be back in plain sight.

I knew what I had to do. Two things I had to do, actually.

As soon as I started walking behind the retaining wall, I grabbed my phone. I went to Paddy Roark and as quickly as possible, texted: *Getting kidnapped. Follow my GPS.*

I could tell the man was right about to join me on this side of the retaining wall. He'd be directly behind me. I only had a few seconds.

I started to dial 9-1-1. As I finished typing in the numbers and went to press send, someone came out of nowhere and tackled me into the retaining wall. He'd knocked the air out of me and my back slid down the wall. I looked to the ground below and saw my phone. I hadn't pressed send yet and the man picked up my phone off the ground.

"Just in time," he said.

I looked up. He had a gun pointed at me.

The man who had been following me was now towering over me as well.

He was a monster of a man - a true Goliath - easily surpassing three hundred pounds and probably 6'6" or so.

He was also holding a gun.

"If you try to run, we'll shoot you," he said.

His expression told me he meant what he said.

A third man appeared, a Taser in his hand.

"Follow us or we'll tase you."

They led me in the direction of a waiting car.

My only hope was that a fellow tenant walked down into the parking garage at this very second. Then again, these thugs would probably just shoot them.

We arrived at the car. It was a nondescript sedan from the mid-2010s. The perfect car if you're trying to be inconspicuous.

Another man stepped out. There was no mistaking him. It was Timothy Vale, the man who'd tried to kill me, and most likely had killed Henry and the others.

"We meet again," he said.

"If it's not the failed Sacramento cop, Timothy Vale."

He tried to form something akin to a smile, but it just made his face even uglier.

"Put your hands behind your back and don't say another word," he said. "If you utter a peep, I'm going to shoot you in the groin."

It's not like I had many options. I put my hands behind my back and they quickly put a zip tie around my wrists. I wasn't going anywhere.

Goliath pushed me into the back of the car, where there was another huge guy sitting on the other side. Even if my wrists weren't zip-tied behind my back, there would be no escaping.

All my hopes were now pinned on Paddy Roark.

Vale jumped in the passenger seat and the fourth man took the driver's seat.

"Let's get out of here," Vale said.

The driver handed Vale the phone.

"He was trying to call 9-1-1. I tackled him before he could press send."

"That's good work, Hopper. Let's see if he called anyone else," Vale said and started going through my phone.

"Hmmm, looks like you were able to fire off one text before we got to you. Well, it's going to be hard for Paddy, whoever the fuck that is, to follow your GPS with a phone that's turned off."

I watched as Vale powered down my phone.

I was truly screwed.

The driver exited the parking garage and we were now out on the city streets.

Suddenly, a horrific realization came to me.

The only way they could have known I was going to be in the parking garage was if they'd texted me from Sophie's phone.

I was sickened to my core.

◠

The drive to our destination was interminable. At least, it felt that way to me.

My only saving grace was that if they wanted me dead already, they would have killed me in the parking garage. I kept going back to that. It's all I had to hang my hat on. The entire situation was dire.

I tried to avoid thinking about Sophie. It was too painful. She was either dead or had also been kidnapped. Those were the only scenarios that made any sense. This wasn't some amazing coincidence that she'd texted me as they waited in the parking garage. No, they knew I'd be entering that parking garage. And they knew because they'd abducted Sophie and had texted me from her phone.

Fuck!

I should have listened to the myriad of people who'd told me to drop this case. I'd been warned over and over. By Sophie, by my mother, by Detective Mixon, and by Dennis and Paddy, who now happened to be my last hope on this earth.

And what hope did they really give me? Sure, Paddy would receive the text, but what next? My phone was turned off. And how exactly would he have pulled up the find my iPhone anyway? It's not like he knew my password or login information.

I should have dialed 9-1-1 first. I'd fucked everything up and it was probably going to cost me my life.

After what felt like two hours, but was probably more like thirty minutes, we arrived at our destination, pulling into an abandoned warehouse. The two Goliaths got out of the car and shut the monstrous door behind them.

It was a vacated warehouse that would have given me the creeps even under mundane circumstances.

I knew we were somewhere in Berkeley, but I couldn't tell where exactly. It was very rundown and I hadn't seen a person on the street for the last half mile. It was far from the glitz and glamor of the Berkeley Marina. My guess is that we were somewhere down by the docks. In the abandoned part of town.

There were surely more rats than people down where we were.

The driver got out of the car, followed by Timothy Vale. The two monsters were back from shutting the warehouse door and waited on me to exit the car.

"Let's go," Vale yelled.

I was petrified over what I was going to encounter next. I prayed that I was wrong about Sophie.

I was waiting too long to get out of the car. Goliath #1 grabbed me out of the car, needing only one hand. He escorted me down the long, barren warehouse and toward the far corner. The other three from the car followed behind us.

As we approached, I saw two people.

The first person was Dean Graves.

And the second was Sophie.

I wanted to cry.

Hopelessness had kicked in.

CHAPTER 31

"Go ahead, hug your girlfriend," Dean Graves said.

Sophie was sitting in a chair, a zip tie connecting her wrists to the chair. There was a chair opposite her, which I assumed was meant for me.

I had my own zip tie around my wrists. A hug would have been near impossible.

Dean Graves looked at Timothy Vale.

"Cut his zip tie," he said.

Vale gave him a quick stare to which Graves responded, "Don't worry. He's not going anywhere."

Vale took a little pocket knife out of his jeans and did as Graves had instructed.

I walked over to Sophie and gave her a hug.

"I'm so sorry," I said two or three times. I couldn't really tell.

"It's not your fault," Sophie said, but we both knew that wasn't true.

"I'm going to get us out of here," I said and the five other men in the room laughed as if it was the funniest thing they'd ever heard.

"You didn't tell me Quint was a stand-up comedian?" Vale said to Graves.

"He's got a curious outlook on life. I was told he had the same morbid sense of humor after you put him in the hospital."

Sophie glared over at Dean Graves and Timothy Vale.

"Don't say anything," I whispered to her.

This whole situation was beyond fucked up, but I couldn't allow to them start hurting Sophie. I wouldn't be able to take it.

"I have a request, Graves."

"This should be good," he said.

"Let Sophie go."

The room was filled with laughter again.

"Don't make silly requests, Quint. You lessen yourself."

"Then promise me you won't touch her. You can do whatever you want to me, but please, don't lay a finger on her."

Graves walked closer to us. Hugging time was now over. He called one of his goons over, who set me down in a chair opposite Sophie, and reapplied a zip tie to my wrists, which were now also connected to the back of the chair. Theoretically, I could stand up since my feet weren't fastened, but my hands would be attached to the back of the chair. There was very little I could do.

"You're not in a position to negotiate. What you should be asking yourself is why you are still alive."

"Alright, I'll bite. Why?"

"You'll learn soon enough," Graves said, a wicked smile on his face. "And I honestly think you'll be quite impressed. I know I was when I came up with it."

I had no idea what he was talking about. The other people in the room looked a little befuddled as well.

"You've been very well-behaved thus far, Quint, but I'd like to give you a few warnings. While this warehouse is abandoned, and there's not a person within two hundred yards, if you start yelling, I will duct tape your mouth shut quicker than you can say '*Boo.*' And if you try to make a run for it, I will have one of my guys shoot you in the leg and then we will go straight to torturing both you and Sophie. Is that understood?"

"Yes."

"Good. Let's try and handle this like adults."

I wish I could kill Dean Graves then and there. Handle this like adults? Was he fucking kidding me? He'd kidnapped my girlfriend and me, surely with plans on eventually killing the both of us. And yet, he was acting like he was some responsible adult looking after us. He made me sick.

Timothy Vale walked over to Graves and they started whispering to each other. Graves looked gripped by what he was being told.

He walked over to me.

"Paddy called. He's not going to be able to make it," he said and let out a monstrous laugh.

"9-1-1 either," he added.

"Ah, who needs them?" I said. "I'll enjoy this more when I get out of this myself."

Dean Graves managed to smile.

"You've got balls, I'll give you that. Now, let's get down to business. I'm going to ask you a series of questions. If I think that you are lying or misleading me, I will have my friend Timothy inflict a little damage on you. If you lie or mislead me more than once, I will have him inflict a little damage on the beautiful Sophie here."

I looked around, seeing if there was any hope of my escape. The answer was a resounding no. There were five of them. They had weapons. And I had my wrists zip tied to the back of a chair.

My only hope remained Paddy.

And that was a long shot of the highest degree. My phone was off. He had no idea where I was. Even if he called the cops, what the hell would he give as my location?

"I'll answer your questions honestly," I said to Graves.

"Good. I figured you would."

Sophie looked over in my direction. I quickly looked away, ashamed that I'd put her in this situation. Then I became equally ashamed that I'd looked away and returned my eyes back to her.

"I love you," I mouthed.

She could have mouthed pretty much anything at that point and

I would have understood. *'I hate you'* or *'Look at where we've ended up'* or even *'Fuck you.'* All would have been warranted.

"I love you too," she mouthed back.

"I forgot to tell you, boss, but Quint knows who I am. He said something like, *'Failed Sacramento cop'* to me or something similar."

Graves smiled at me.

"Impressive. What more do you know? And remember my warning about telling the truth."

I saw no reason to lie. They had no plans to keep us alive, I knew that for sure. I still had no idea why Graves had kept us alive this long, but was sure we'd find out soon.

Most importantly, the longer I talked, the more time I gave Paddy. Time was the only thing we had on our side. So I would tell Graves what he wanted and try to drag it out as long as I could.

I began to start my story and then realized I'd have to rat out Detective Mixon and the dispatcher from the Sacramento PD. I couldn't do that. Graves may well kill me, but I couldn't put others in harm's way.

I tried to think about what to say. Graves beat me to the punch.

"You're not as good a P.I. as you think, Quint. Do you remember that time you went and asked some cops outside of the Berkeley PD who really ran the department? Did you not think that was going to get back to me?"

Since he already knew about that incident, I decided to use that as my fulcrum for finding out more about Graves. It would help me avoid referencing Mixon.

"Well, one of those cops made the mistake of mentioning your name."

"I know. As I said, I hear everything."

"Once I heard your name, I wanted to find out everything about you. And I'll be honest, I was instantly suspicious. I'd remembered your name from the hospital visit and I started wondering why such a high-up officer would come to my room before I was to be released."

"And what conclusion did you come to?"

"I think part of you was there to mock me as if to say I didn't get you this first time, but just wait. And I think the other part of you was fascinated by me. Who was this P.I. investigating this case and how the hell had he survived being hunted by your right-hand man," I said and looked in Vale's direction.

Vale made no expression back. I'm not sure he was capable of one.

"Not bad, Quint," Graves said. "Not bad. And you're close. But the real reason I went there was to say my goodbyes. My plan was to kill you within a week or two of your release, but then this case just got a little too hot. The news kept talking about the Berkeley Marina murders and I just thought it was better to bide my time. I knew it would come. And here it is…"

He let out a grotesque laugh and his pathetic minions all followed suit.

"What's the opposite of a tough crowd?" I asked. "These clowns will laugh at anything you say."

"You don't want to piss them off, Quint. They'll do just about anything for me."

"It's like you're breeding your own robots. Congrats."

"They know who they answer to," Graves said.

"I'll give you one thing," I said. "You've been able to keep this conspiracy out of the public eye for a long time. It won't last, though."

"That's the problem, Quint. You think everyone in the Berkeley PD is in on it. You're wrong about that. I've limited it to the people in this room. Sure, there are other cops who either admire or despise me, but they don't know what happened down at those docks."

"You mean like trying to get pictures of the Chief of Police in compromising pictures with a younger man?"

Graves smiled, but it resembled Timothy Vale's attempt from earlier. It was more a sadistic smirk than a smile. It told me he didn't like what I'd said.

"Once again, you've proven yourself a worthy adversary."

"There's a lot more where that came from," I said.

I was trying to keep Graves guessing. I knew that at some point his plan was to kill us. I had to extend that for as long as I could. And dropping little breadcrumbs, while not giving away everything was the way to do it.

"How did you find that out?" Graves asked.

"We'll get to that later," I said defiantly. "First, I have a few questions of my own. Do you have to plug the robots back in nightly? How long is their shelf life?"

One of the Goliaths spoke from behind me.

"Can I slap this guy upside the head and prove to him that I ain't no robot."

"Ain't no robot is actually a double negative insinuating that you are, in fact, a robot," I said.

Graves laughed.

"He got you there," he said.

I turned my neck to see Goliath #1 inching closer to me, but Graves put his arm on his chest and he retreated.

"You're talking like a man with nothing to lose, Quint. That man could break your neck in seconds."

I was about to respond when Sophie spoke up.

"Is he the one who killed my father?"

Graves pretended to be hurt by her question.

"Your father was never supposed to die, my dear Sophie," he said.

I despised him for referring to her as '*my dear.*'

It's Graves's neck that I wanted to snap.

"You didn't answer my question," Sophie said.

"No, he did not. He and his twin are more for protection."

The Goliaths weren't just monsters. They were twin monsters.

"What is he for?" I asked, pointing to the man who'd driven the car.

"Hopper is a very valuable asset to my team and he'll be proving his worth later."

The man looked on as if that was news to him, but he didn't dare say a word. Graves's "robots" only seemed to respond when spoken to.

"You still haven't answered my question as to how you knew about the Chief of Police?" Graves asked.

"That's right, I haven't."

"You're brave, Quint, I'll give you that. However, we are getting to the stage where I might start causing you and my dear Sophie some pain. You see, that's the reason I brought you here today. I want to find out who you've told about your suspicions. I'm hoping it's something we can nip in the bud. There's been so much death already, wouldn't you agree?"

"I would. So why don't you let us go? I can promise neither one of us will ever say a word about it."

Graves laughed.

"If only that were true. You've got a big mouth, though. I can't trust you on this one. The only question is whether you two are going to suffer or not. That's literally the only thing left to decide."

I didn't want to give up any of my sources. Nor could I sit aside and watch Sophie get tortured. I was going to be left with a true Sophie's Choice. The irony of her name hit me at that moment.

"So, would you like to tell me how you knew about the Chief of Police?"

A mention of Dexter Lund would surely mean a death sentence for him. The guy was a worm, but I couldn't do that. I had to find a believable way to talk around the truth.

I had an idea.

"Henry laid it out for me."

"Her father?" he asked incredulously. "I doubt that. He was the first to die."

"I'm going to assume that your hitman, Mr. Vale over there, was the one who killed Henry."

Graves didn't answer, ostensibly admitting it was him. Sophie glared at Vale with a fire in her eyes.

"Ask him if he smelled a little fire when he happened onto Henry's boat."

Graves looked at Vale who thought about it and then nodded.

"I didn't know what it was," he said. "But I smelled it."

"What it was, Mr. Shitbag Murderer, was the smell of paper

burning," I said, directing my words at Timothy Vale. "Henry saw your dumb ass coming and brilliantly decided to fax his daughter everything that happened. The problem was that Sophie literally never uses her fax machine and this information didn't come to my attention until several days ago."

It was plausible, which considering I came up with it on the fly, was about the best I could do.

"Is that true, Sophie?" Graves asked.

"Every single word of it."

Graves turned back to me.

"What exactly did it say?"

"It said he was on his dock a few nights before and saw the Chief of Police and a young man hop onto Rupert Shinn's boat. They were having a good time together if you know what I mean. Several minutes later, Henry saw a photographer taking pictures of the unsuspecting pair. Well, at least the Chief was unsuspecting. And that's when Henry knew something was up. He called Needles out on it the next day and that's when Needles went to you, and since you're a sociopath, you decided you had to kill everybody."

Graves took a step back and didn't speak for several seconds.

"You're proving my decision to kidnap you was the right one. You know way too much to be kept alive."

"You already admitted you were going to kill me anyway."

"That's correct, but with this new information, I won't lose any sleep over it. I'll know I made the right decision. It was either you or me."

I almost blurted out that I'd already sent all of this information to Tom Butler. My goal would have been obvious, hoping to prove to Graves that killing me and Sophie wouldn't stop this information from getting out. The problem was that it would have been a likely death sentence for Tom and he was still planning on killing me no matter what. There would be no benefit.

"I have a question for you," I said to Graves.

"This should be good. What would you like to know?"

"Why did you wait to kill Blaine Travers? Henry, Needles, and

Frank Manning all appeared to be killed within twenty-four hours of each other."

"You really don't know?"

"No."

"Yeah, I guess you couldn't know. Oh, this is going to be a doozy. You're going to regret asking."

"Just tell me, Graves."

"It's because of you, Quint."

That was certainly not the answer I was expecting.

"Because of me? What the hell are you talking about?"

Graves looked down at me. I could tell he was going to enjoy telling me.

"Needles was friends with Blaine Travers. I guess Blaine had taken him out on his boat a few times. It sounds like everybody loved Blaine. Sophie's father included. They used to have beers together quite a bit. And yes, I know they were having beers together on the day Henry confronted Needles about his boat and the Chief of Police. But we didn't learn that until later. Originally, Needles didn't tell me that Blaine was there that day and I'm 99% sure it's because they were friends. However, once you started going down to the dock and asking Blaine some pointed questions, we started to reconsider. Maybe Blaine had been there. So I had Mr. Vale over here go and install a few bugs on Mr. Travers's boat. Once we heard him agree to a meeting with you, it was obvious he knew what happened and I decided I had to kill you both. So you see, Quint, it was your investigation that brought Blaine to his bloody demise."

I believed Graves was telling the truth, but I couldn't let him get to me. I could feel terrible about Blaine sometime in the future. For now, I needed all my attention on the moment at hand.

"Which leads me to a question, Quint?"

I didn't answer so he continued.

"Who was the good samaritan who saved your life? That couldn't have just been unbelievable timing. I'm assuming you had someone following you around."

"Seemed like a good idea with everyone ending up dead," I said.

I'd managed to answer the question without bringing up Paddy or Dennis.

Speaking of which, it had probably been over an hour since I'd texted him. I was doing everything I could to postpone the inevitable, but there was no telling when Dean Graves would decide to end this once and for all.

C'mon, Paddy! You're my last hope.

Who was I kidding? He has no idea where I am.

Fuck. I was going to die out here, in the middle of some abandoned warehouse. Even worse, Sophie was going to die along with me. A woman I loved, but had been unable to protect.

"We're nearing the end, Quint."

Dean Graves said the words I'd been dreading.

"You're never going to get away with this," I said. "You may kill me, but you'll be caught, tried, and spend the rest of your worthless life in jail."

"That's the surprise that I couldn't wait to tell you about," he said, grinning from ear to ear.

I still had no idea what he had planned, but I hated the fact he was smiling. He seemed too confident. He couldn't just get away with all these murders, could he? You wouldn't think so, but he'd gotten away with them up to this point.

Graves looked at me, his face still grinning from ear to ear. I was reminded of the Joker, sans the makeup.

He turned his back to me, Sophie, Vale, and his other three co-conspirators. I could see his right arm rotating as if he was tightening a jar or something akin to that.

"Close your eyes, Sophie," I said. "I love you."

"I love you too. This wasn't your fault."

She was wrong. This was all my fault.

Dean Graves turned around, holding a handgun with a long silencer attached. It's what he must have been fastening. He raised the gun.

I was about to yell *'I've sent every newspaper all the information I know.'*

Something made me pause.

Dean Graves was raising his gun toward his friends, not us.

In rapid succession, he shot the two Goliaths twice each in the chest. The getaway driver, Hopper, turned to run but didn't get more than a few feet. Graves shot him in the back twice and he crumpled to the floor.

Sophie let out a scream.

"What the fuck are you doing, Dean?" Vale said. "Those guys were loyal to you."

"I'm sorry, Timothy, but we both know they were all expendable. And now, we're going to be able to pin all those murders on them."

I looked down at the ground. None of the three men were moving. They were all dead.

I'd been through some crazy things as a P.I., but this may have topped them all.

"How the hell are you going to pin the murders on them? This is really fucked up, Dean."

"The cops will think that Hopper was the ringleader and that Mac and Sal were his muscle. They'll trace the emails from Dexter Lund to Hooper and know that he was the one who planned all of this. Plus, this gun's ballistics will match the gunshots of Needles, Travers, and Quint."

Graves inched closer to Timothy Vale as Vale's face turned white.

"But that was an email that I set up. I was the one contacting Dexter Lund."

Graves pretended to look surprised, but it was all an act.

"Oooh, that poses a problem, doesn't it?" he said.

Dean Graves was sick. I now knew why he'd had that huge smile. He was going to pin all these murders on his right-hand man, Timothy Vale. Vale was a murdering thug himself so I had no love lost for him, but this was all sorts of fucked up.

"What are you doing, Dean?" Vale said as Graves inched closer.

"I guess you could say I'm tying up loose ends."

"There has to be another way."

"For me to continue on, this is the only way. Are you willing to make the ultimate sacrifice?"

I'd assumed Graves was going to shoot him, but that wouldn't work. He was trying to make this look like a murder/suicide. Like all of this had been the work of Timothy Vale. The gun would match. The emails to Lund would be connected back to Vale. Jesus.

"This is the only way, Timothy. Are you willing to make the ultimate sacrifice?"

I knew what was going to happen next. Graves was going to give Vale the gun and Vale was going to kill himself with it.

Shouldn't Vale just shoot Graves when handed the gun? Of course, but he was too far under Graves's spell to do anything else. He'd been brainwashed, likely since their time as Sacramento police officers. He truly was a robot.

After Vale killed himself, Graves would grab the gun and kill us. Likely after gloating for a few minutes at his perceived ingenuity. Or, maybe it wasn't just perceived. Against all odds, this sounded like a plan that just might work.

THINK QUINT!

THINK!

Yelling at Vale to disobey Graves wouldn't work. I knew that in my heart.

THINK OF SOMETHING ELSE!

THINK!

THINK!

THINK!

I'd have a split second from the time Vale shot himself to the time when Graves picked the gun up. Maybe I could stand up in my chair and rush at Graves. I didn't have use of my hands, but maybe I could knock him over and use the chair to incapacitate him. It was unlikely, but not impossible. If not, Sophie and I were dead.

I had no other option. I had to act.

I'd rather die trying to save us than be murdered by a crowing

Graves a few minutes later.

I'd made my mind up and turned my attention back to them.

"I'll never forget you, Timothy, but this is the only way."

They were only about ten feet from me. I'd have to jump up at the very instant that Vale shot himself. A second early and Vale would shoot me. A second late and Graves would have picked up the gun and he'd shoot me.

Graves grabbed Vale's hand and set the gun in his hand.

"Dean, please. There has to be some other way," Vale continued to plead, but each plea sounded less convincing. He was becoming resigned to the fact this was how it was going to end.

"You've been the perfect right-hand man. Now it's time for you to save me. That's why you've been with me so long. You're sacrificing yourself so that I can go free. That's the ultimate loyalty, Timothy."

Vale grabbed the gun from Graves's hand.

"Close your eyes, Sophie," I whispered.

I ever so subtly swiveled my chair so that it was a straight shot to bum-rush Graves.

"Goodnight, Timothy," Graves said. "Thank you for what you're about to do."

Vale slowly raised the gun to his head. Graves was looking at him and not at me. I was ready to pounce.

"Goodbye, Dean," Vale said. "Continue with our plan."

He pointed the gun to his head and pulled the trigger. I was running toward Graves a split second later. He looked over at me in shock. He didn't have time to pick up the gun, which had slid about fifteen feet across the floor.

I ran into Graves like a linebacker attacking a quarterback. I hit him perfectly in the chest and sent him backward. I was on him a second later. I raised the legs of the chair up and brought them down on his face. He tried to protect himself with his hands, but one of the legs got through and connected hard with his cheekbone. With the weight of my body on top of it, the strike caused some damage.

He screamed in agony.

I did the same thing again. It connected more flush this time, his hands not able to protect himself.

I brought the chair down again. I knew that I couldn't give him even a second's break. If he escaped, he'd run to the gun and I'd be a dead man.

I brought the chair down again. And again.

Graves was bleeding profusely, but he was still conscious. I needed to incapacitate him.

I went to bring the legs of the chair down on him once again.

This time, he was ready. He slid his face out of the way and the legs of my chair hit the ground at an odd angle.

I careened to the floor, my wrists still tied to the chair, and my butt now dangling from it.

Graves was badly hurt, but now he had his chance. He slowly tried to rise, blood continuing to gush from his face.

With my hands still zip-tied behind my back, it would be near impossible to go and pick up the gun and I certainly couldn't fire it. Maybe I could run and kick the gun under something, making it impossible for Graves to retrieve it. But under what? It was a huge warehouse.

And I'd still be a sitting duck with my body attached to a chair, but I had to try something.

I rolled the chair over and got to my feet at the same time Graves did. We both ran toward the gun. I was a few feet closer which made all the difference.

I arrived first and gave the gun a swift kick down the warehouse. It probably traveled eighty feet on the concrete. I ran toward it a second time, hoping to kick it into a corner or under something.

I didn't make it. Graves sideswiped me and I went to the ground.

This time he would make it to the gun first.

He looked at me, bleeding all over, and yet the blood couldn't hide his disgusting smile. He knew he had won.

He slowly made his way over to the gun.

I'd given it my all, but it was over.

I was a dead man.

CHAPTER 32

E verything that happened next felt like a dream.
Graves turned around, the gun in hand, and started walking toward me.

I'd scampered my way back over to Sophie and was trying to bring the legs of my chair down on her zip tie, hoping by some miracle to jar it loose. I was fighting a losing battle, so instead, I just stood there, shielding Sophie, and telling her I loved her.

When Graves was still a solid forty yards from us, and just as all hope was about to vanish, the massive door to the warehouse sprung open. Three people beelined toward Graves, guns in hand. I was half expecting to see Paddy or Dennis or Lefty, but no, these were Berkeley PD.

"Put the gun down, Dean," one of them yelled.

Graves was in as much shock as I was.

"Who the fuck called you guys in?"

"It doesn't matter," one of the officers yelled back.

"Miller, is that you?"

"Yes."

"This is all one big understanding, Miller."

"We see four bodies, Dean. This is a lot more than that."

"A friend of mine, Timothy Vale, went crazy. Started shooting everybody."

It was time to jump in.

"Graves is lying," I yelled. "He shot and killed all four of them. He was going to kill us next."

I looked over at Graves. He was facing the three officers, meaning he'd have to swivel in order to shoot at us.

"That's the truth!" Sophie screamed.

The men looked over in surprise, not having expected to hear a woman's voice.

"Put the gun down, Dean," another voice yelled.

"Bohanon? You're in on this too?"

"We're not in on anything. We're here to make sure no one else gets killed."

I continued to shield Sophie. If Graves decided to swivel and shoot in our direction, I was going to be between him and Sophie.

"You just have to let me explain!" Graves yelled.

"You can do that without the gun."

We were at a standstill. Graves didn't want to give up his gun, but the cops didn't seem willing to shoot him.

"He shot and killed these four people," I interjected once again. "Make him give up his gun."

"We don't need your help," one of the cops screamed in my direction.

No one said anything for a few seconds.

Finally, one of the officers spoke again.

"Dean, I'm going to approach you. If you decide to open fire, my colleagues are going to kill you. No one here wants to die. Give up your gun now."

Another pause.

"I'll approach you instead," Graves said.

"Are you going to drop your gun first?"

"I'll drop it when I'm halfway there."

"That doesn't make any sense, Dean. Drop it now."

I looked over. Graves was now staring in my direction. His gun was still facing the officers, but it would only take a fraction of a second to whirl it in my direction.

"You're one lucky fucking duck, Quint," he said.

"Give up your gun, Dean."

Graves continued barking in my direction.

"Vale should have killed you outside of Kincade's. I should have killed you twenty minutes ago. You've truly got nine lives, you rotten fuck."

"Give up your gun, Dean! This is your last chance."

"He's going to try and shoot us," I said. "Please don't let him."

"We've got this under control," one of the officers said, although that was clearly not the case.

No one knew what was going to happen next.

"Dean, put your gun down, and let's talk about this like adults," an officer yelled, harkening back to something Graves had said to me earlier.

If I wasn't still petrified, I'd have taken some satisfaction in that phrase coming full circle.

"This is absolutely your last chance, Dean. If you don't give up your gun, I'm going to shoot you in the leg."

"Okay, okay, okay. I'm walking over. And I'll give up my gun," Graves said.

I looked in his direction. I knew enough about this scumbag to realize that he was never going to turn himself in. His plan to frame the Chief of Police and take over the Berkeley PD had failed miserably. He didn't seem the type who'd spend his days rotting away in some jail.

"I'm walking over," he said again.

I looked over and we made eye contact one last time as he started to raise the gun in our direction.

"He's going to shoot us," I yelled.

An instant later, the warehouse erupted in fire and Graves went down in a heap. He'd been shot several times, and even though I was still a good distance from him, I could tell he was down for the count.

"Moving in," one of the officers said.

The three men started approaching Graves.

"We're going to be alright," I said to Sophie.

"Are you sure?" she said, her voice barely above a whisper.

I looked over as they arrived at Graves.

Their reactions told me all I needed to know.

Graves was dead.

"I'm sure," I whispered to Sophie, holding her tight.

A minute later, one of the officers approached us.

He cut off the zip ties and escorted us outside of the warehouse. They had five dead bodies and more than enough work to do. They wanted us as far away from the crime scene as possible.

As soon as we arrived outside, what appeared to be every police car in the Berkeley PD started pulling up to the warehouse.

Meanwhile, I was holding on to Sophie the whole time. Considering the circumstances, she had been stronger than I would have thought possible and probably could have stood on her own. Not that I was going to stop holding her.

The officer who escorted us outside found an arriving officer and quickly rehashed all that had occurred. The second officer approached us and asked if we were ready to answer some questions.

I answered in the affirmative, continuing to hold on to Sophie.

As the officer led us to an awaiting car, I looked back toward the warehouse. The door was ajar and I could see inside.

Dean Graves was still on the ground and he was never getting up.

CHAPTER 33

The next several hours were spent being interviewed by the Berkeley PD, both outside the warehouse and at their main precinct.

They questioned us together and then separately and I asked them several times to please release Sophie and me at the same time.

Finally, after the longest morning of my life, they released me. It was now afternoon and the sun was shining bright. It almost didn't seem possible this was the same day.

Sophie was already waiting as I walked outside.

We hugged each other and then both started crying.

The officer assigned to drive us home just stood there, giving us a minute.

When we were ready, he asked us where we wanted to go.

"To your apartment," Sophie said. "I certainly don't want to be in my big house alone tonight."

I gave the officer my address and we set off to Walnut Creek.

∿

We had several visitors over the next few days.

My mother, my friends, Sophie's friends, and a few more officers who had some follow-up questions.

Sophie never went home. I paid a friend of mine to come over and pick up her key and then go down to Pleasanton to pick up her clothes and bring them back. It's a trip we could have made together, but we seemed content staying in the apartment for those first few days.

At one point, I made the mistake of turning on the T.V., and we saw Dean Graves's photo staring back at us. We both recoiled at the sight of him and vowed that we'd only search the movie channels for the foreseeable future.

We were sleeping a lot each day.

There were tears shed, but Sophie was taking it surprisingly well. She was much stronger than I realized, but I guess I should have known, considering how strong she'd been during my investigation of her father's death.

Which I had finally solved.

~

There really wasn't much more for us to learn.

We learned a few tidbits from the officers who visited us, but I felt like I already had a grasp on the whole conspiracy. Most of this I'd known before being kidnapped and Graves just confirmed my suspicions at the warehouse.

And all for what?

To frame a Chief of Police and try to accrue a little extra power? What a fucking waste.

~

On the fourth day after the murders, Paddy Roark and Dennis McCarthy came and visited.

Sophie said hello but said she was exhausted and wanted to go to bed. We decided to talk in the living room.

"How is she taking this?" Dennis asked.

"Better than I ever could have expected. Sometimes I think it's her who's holding me up."

"We've only met her a few times now, but she's a strong woman. She's going to be okay."

"I think you're right," I said.

"Have you thought about taking some time off, Quint? You could use it," Paddy said.

"Ain't that the truth? Yeah, Sophie and I have been talking about taking a vacation. The weather is getting nicer so we were thinking about a trip somewhere warm. Heard good things about Punta Cana in the Dominican. Or maybe the Bahamas. Maybe even Hawaii."

"Indulge in some ridiculously sugary umbrella drinks that will make you gain ten pounds?"

"That sounds just fine by me," I said.

Neither one responded and there was a bit of an uncomfortable silence. I could feel Dennis staring at me.

"What is it?" I asked.

"This isn't my idea, Quint," Paddy said. "I would have been just fine never bringing it up at all."

"What's going on, guys?"

Dennis took the floor.

"Do you remember texting Paddy on the day of?"

"Of course," I said.

Had they saved the day for me again? I had a feeling that's where this was headed.

"Well, Paddy took things into his own hands," Dennis said, confirming my suspicions. "Usually, he knows to run things through me, but I was out of town with the wife and taking a much-needed weekend off. Kind of like the one you need, Quint."

"What exactly happened?" I asked.

"I'll let Paddy tell you."

Paddy begrudgingly started talking. He'd never been one who liked to accept credit.

"After you texted me that you were getting kidnapped, I immediately called my guy watching Sophie. He went into her house and noticed she was missing, but her car was still there. After our conversation the night before, I figured Graves was in on Sophie's abduction. So, I thought about my options. I considered what you would do in my situation. You and Sophie could be anywhere. I came up with a plan. I called Lefty and told him to find out Dean Graves's wife's address. Cops can always find those things out. Lefty met me in Berkeley and we went to her house. Lefty was in uniform but it was for the SFPD, so we had to incorporate that into our story. Lefty told her that Graves had been abducted in San Francisco, but we couldn't risk calling or texting him and alerting his abductors. We told her we needed to use the search your iPhone app to find out where they'd taken him. She took some convincing, but Lefty played his role perfectly. He said I was a high-ranking lieutenant in the SFPD and we could call the Chief if she didn't believe us, but that didn't prove necessary. She begrudgingly agreed to go online and find out where Graves's phone was. He'd powered off his Berkeley PD-issued phone - probably for fear it could get traced - but he'd left on, whether accidentally or not, his family phone. She gave us the address. As soon as we left her house, we started driving to that address. Meanwhile, I called 9-1-1 and said I'd just witnessed Dean Graves kidnap two people at gunpoint. I gave them the address we'd procured. They asked if I was referring to the Berkeley police officer Dean Graves. I assured them I was. I was hoping that would make the dispatched officers wary of him and he wouldn't be able to talk himself out of anything. We arrived at the warehouse about fifteen minutes later and were ready to go in ourselves, but the Berkeley PD had already arrived. The rest is history."

I had been flabbergasted many times over the course of this case, but none more so than at that moment.

"I have no idea what to say, Paddy. That's some next-level shit. I certainly don't think I would have come up with that."

"Thanks, Quint."

"I'm serious, though. Amazing work."

"That's enough. You know I don't like this type of recognition."

I leaned over and gave him a hug.

"I already owed you guys a lot from the last several weeks. Now, I'll never be able to pay you back."

"Just keep on living, Quint. The world is a more fun place with you in it."

And just like that, Dennis and Paddy got up to go.

I thanked them a final time, but they'd already heard enough.

We vowed to see each other soon.

Sophie came out of the bedroom a few seconds later.

"I thought you were sleeping," I said.

"Nope. I could tell they had something important to say to you."

"So you made up that story of being tired?"

"Yup."

I gave her a quick kiss.

"You continue to amaze me. Do you want to know what they told me?"

"Surprise me. Wait until we're on one of these beaches we've been talking about."

"I say we book it right now."

"For real?" Sophie asked.

"Yes. Which place sounded the best?"

"Let's go with the Bahamas."

"Over Hawaii?"

"I could use a quick break from the U.S."

I laughed.

"I can't blame you for that."

A week later, Sophie and I were sitting on a beach in the Bahamas.

We'd been there for four days already and had never been more at peace in our life. It was the opposite of all that had come before it.

We both had one of those infamous umbrella drinks in our hands. She, a Pina Colada, and me, a Mai Tai. We were finishing up our third drink each and the sun was starting to go down.

"I love you, Quint."

"I love you too, Sophie."

"Is that cheesy?"

"What?"

"Saying I love you while drinking a Pina Colada on a Caribbean beach? Seems like it's a scene out of a movie or something."

"Then it's a movie I want to be in," I said.

"Me too."

I leaned over and kissed her, getting a little of the red/yellow of my Mai Tai on her lip. Not to be outdone, I now had a little of her Pina Colada on mine.

"Do you want to go back to the room and fool around?" Sophie asked.

"You're reading my mind."

We stood up from the beach, wiping down the sand from our bodies.

Everyone at the resort had their own little golf cart that they used to get around. I walked up to the path where our cart was and put our beach towels and little backpacks on the back of it.

Meanwhile, Sophie put our umbrella drinks on the console, I turned the engine on, and we drove off - literally - into the sunset.

THE END!

ALSO BY BRIAN O'SULLIVAN

Thanks for reading PERSONA NON GRATA!

I'd be honored if you left a review.

And I hope you'll check out any or all of my novels below.

THE BARTENDER

THE MASTERMIND

QUINT ADLER NOVELS:

REVENGE AT SEA

THE BAY AREA BUTCHER

HOLLYWOOD MURDER MYSTERY

NINE DAYS IN VEGAS

QUINT ADLER P.I.

A KNIFE THROUGH THE HEART

PERSONA NON GRATA

FRANKIE AND EVIE NOVELS:

THE PUPPETEER

THE PATSY

THANKS FOR THE SUPPORT!

SINCERELY,

BRIAN O'SULLIVAN

Printed in Great Britain
by Amazon

44941838R00155